Praise for
Back in the Saddle

"*Back in the Saddle* is an uplifting and heartwarming story about two wounded people using the power of faith to find the courage to change. A dramatic ranch setting, rich characterization, and a beautiful love story make this a book to savor. This is a strong beginning for what promises to be an exciting trilogy. Ruth Logan Herne is my new favorite author!"

—KAREN WHITE, *New York Times* best-selling author

"Heart and hope combine in Ruth Logan Herne's sweet tale of old wounds and ties that bind. Where faith and forgiveness are present, old scars can be healed and new love can bloom. Sometimes, you really can go home again."

—LISA WINGATE, national best-selling author of *The Story Keeper* and *The Sea Keeper's Daughters*

"Not your average cowboy story, *Back in the Saddle* is the action-packed tale of an emotionally wounded prodigal (from Wall Street, no less!), his family's dysfunctional ranching dynasty, and a unique heroine with a heartbreaking secret and an adorable son. Cowboys and kids, trouble and tragedy, Ruth Logan Herne delivers a tender romance wrapped in a wise, heart-touching blanket of redemption and grace. Highly recommended!"

—LINDA GOODNIGHT, best-selling, award-winning author of *The Memory House* and *The Rain Sparrow*

"From the first pages, readers will be drawn into the community of Gray's Glen, the amazing cast of characters, and the lives of the hero and heroine. Angelina and Colt fill the pages of this book with a romance that will have readers wanting to know their past, their future, and the story that intertwines their lives. With *Back in the Saddle*, Ruth Logan Herne takes us on a journey that we will want to continue!"

   —BRENDA MINTON, author of the Martin's Crossing series

"Wrapped up in Ruth Logan Herne's heart-touching style, *Back in the Saddle* delivers an engaging, romantic tale of a spunky heroine with secrets to keep and a sigh-worthy cowboy hero finding his way back home."

   —GLYNNA KAYE, award-winning author of the Hearts
      of Hunter Ridge series

"As always, Ruth Logan Herne shoots straight to the heart with *Back in the Saddle* . . . the heart of the story and the reader. This is one cowboy love story you'll want to enjoy to the very last page."

   —DEBRA CLOPTON, author of *Kissed by a Cowboy*

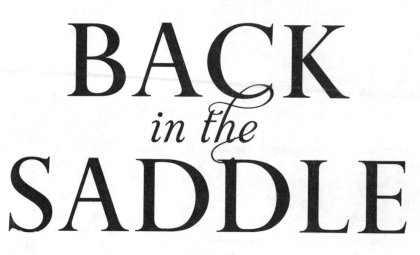

S̶S̶ DOUBLE S RANCH, BOOK 1

BACK
in the
SADDLE

A Novel

RUTH LOGAN HERNE

MULTNOMAH
BOOKS

BACK IN THE SADDLE
PUBLISHED BY MULTNOMAH BOOKS
12265 Oracle Boulevard, Suite 200
Colorado Springs, Colorado 80921

Scripture quotations are taken from the King James Version and the Holy Bible, New International Version®, NIV®. Copyright © 1973, 1978, 1984 by Biblica Inc. ® Used by permission. All rights reserved worldwide.

The characters and events in this book are fictional, and any resemblance to actual persons or events is coincidental.

Trade Paperback ISBN 978-1-60142-776-2
eBook ISBN 978-1-60142-777-9

Cover design and photography by Kelly L. Howard

Published in the United States by WaterBrook Multnomah, an imprint of the Crown Publishing Group, a division of Penguin Random House LLC, New York.

MULTNOMAH® and its mountain colophon are registered trademarks of Penguin Random House LLC.

Library of Congress Cataloging-in-Publication Data
    Names: Herne, Ruth Logan.
    Title: Back in the saddle : a novel / Ruth Logan Herne.
    Description: First edition. | Colorado Springs, Colorado : Multnomah Books, [2016] | Series: Double S ranch
    Identifiers: LCCN 2015036956| ISBN 9781601427762 (softcover) | ISBN 9781601427779 (electronic)
    Subjects: LCSH: Man-woman relationships—Fiction. | Domestic fiction. | BISAC: FICTION / Christian / Western. | FICTION / Contemporary Women. | FICTION / Christian / Romance. | GSAFD: Christian fiction. | Western stories. | Love stories.
    Classification: LCC PS3608.E76875 B33 2016 | DDC 813/.6—dc23
    LC record available at http://lccn.loc.gov/2015036956

Printed in the United States of America
2016—First Edition

10 9 8 7 6 5 4 3 2 1

*This book is dedicated to my wonderful
literary agent, Natasha Kern, for her
constant faith, hope, and love in so
many things . . . including me!*

*And to my son Luke, a financial
wizard and a constant source of love
and encouragement! Luke, your
quiet humor is a marvelous blessing.
So are you. I love you.*

ACKNOWLEDGMENTS
AND SINCERE THANKS

*N*o book is the act of one person, and this one is no exception. Thank you to my son, Luke Blodgett of Angelo Gordon in New York City, for his expertise regarding Colt's life, work, and position in Lower Manhattan. Hedge-fund managers don't often talk about their work, so having raised one gave me an inside look at the workings of big finance. Luke, I appreciate your help, your time, and the coffee! I love you, kid!

To Shannon Marchese of WaterBrook Multnomah for her straightforward humor and the opportunity to give my cowboys—and me!—a chance. This delightful series of books wouldn't have happened without her input and her seal of approval.

To the Washington Cattlemen's Association in Ellensburg, Washington, for their excellent website and referenced websites that helped formulate initial research, and to Mary and Ivan Connealy for their firsthand knowledge of running a solid cattle operation. Thank you for always answering whatever questions I might have. I love coming to visit the cows!

To Cle Elum for being just the kind of town I wanted Gray's Glen to be: close-knit, part of the whole, and welcoming to strangers. We loved stopping in various shops, and the maple bars at the bakery won my heart!

Huge thanks also to Natasha Kern for her candid observations about Central Washington: climate, flora, fauna . . . all the little things a person knows about her place.

And to Lissa Halls Johnson whose candid advice helped shape and define the final product so beautifully.

And a final and righteously sincere knuckle bump to God, the Ever Present, the Most High, who granted me the talent . . . and the time . . . to see this happen. Well played, my Lord!

ONE

The sharp metallic click meant one thing.

Someone had a gun pointed in Colt Stafford's general direction.

He sucked a breath and realized two other things. First, these might be the last two thoughts he'd ever have—and that would be a downright shame, wouldn't it?

Second?

It was clear he'd been away from the Double S too long when he couldn't tell what kind of gun it was by the sound of the mechanism. Was it his father's Ithaca Deerslayer or the vintage Remington short barrel?

He put his hands high, figuring this was about as good a welcome as he could expect after being gone nearly nine years. "I'm unarmed and this is my home. Kind of. Who in the name of all that's good and holy in the West has me at gunpoint?"

An explosive stream of Spanish brought him two more thoughts. The person speaking wasn't his sick father—the man he'd come home to help. It was a woman, and not too tall gauging from the direction of the Hispanic tongue-lashing being laid down.

He turned his head slightly.

Backlit from the foyer light, her features were hard to make out.

Her silhouetted frame said she was petite and most assuredly feminine.

The gun, however, wasn't.

"I'm Colt Stafford, Sam's son, and I told Dad I was coming home to help. Whoever you are, let me turn around, and you can see who I am."

She paused, then issued a command. *"Darse la vuelta."*

Which he would have gladly obeyed if he'd taken Spanish in high school and understood her request. But he hadn't. He'd taken Latin because he thought it sounded cool to say he'd taken Latin. That was only one of many stupid moves he'd made over the years. "I have no idea what that means."

Would his confession earn him a bullet? And where was his father? Why hadn't Sam Stafford stormed down the massive rustic front staircase and welcomed his prodigal son with a nice beef barbecue after all this time? Didn't anyone around here read the Bible anymore?

Dude, your mother was the churchgoing member of the family. Dad? Not so much. The whole prodigal's great return thing might be lost on him.

"Turn around."

That he understood. The thick accent disappeared with the deliberate shift to English, leaving only a hint of Latina. He turned slowly, respecting the size of the weapon and the temerity of the woman holding it.

"Turn on that light behind you. Please."

Please? Did she just add "please" to her direct order, as if she might believe him? He'd hold back on the humor of the situation because either the Remington or the Ithaca would make short work of him at this range, and his pricey wardrobe was about the only accessible tangible he had left after years of hard work and financial ladder climbing. Bullets rarely hit seams, and fixing a hole in the middle of his lapel would be impossible, even for the best Manhattan tailors.

He hit the switch but kept his focus on the woman. When soft light flooded the area, his heart hit pause.

Untraditional beauty.

He wasn't sure what he expected. Maybe some aged *abuela* working to earn money for her family. Streams of Central American immigrants came north to work the vast fruit orchards of Washington. Some stayed, sending money back home to help those still south of the border. His smattering of Spanish came from working alongside some of those laborers as a kid.

But the woman facing him was nobody's grandmother. Angular planes lent a hint of Native American attributes to her exquisite face, perfectly sculpted brows deepened the angles, and eyes the color of dense, dark smoke appraised him.

And in that gaze? She found him lacking.

So what else was new?

In Stafford-speak, you toed the line and lived for the ranch. Sam Stafford was an all-or-nothing guy, and Colt had broken the rules. Now it was time to eat crow, humble pie, and anything else they served prodigals these days since the fatted calf refused to make an appearance. "I'm Colt." He gestured toward the picture on the far wall. "I'm on the right, next to Nick and behind Trey."

"I'm not blind." She stared hard at him and slowly lowered the gun. "You have been away many years and have no use for your father. This I know well."

"Good." A quick chill climbed his back. "That saves us the customary exchange of pleasantries. And you are?"

"Angelina Morales." She said the name with unusual crispness. "I am your father's housekeeper and cook." Her tone softened, but her expression stayed tough. "I help keep things running smooth. And"—she sighed, and her posture said she didn't like admitting this next part—"I am sorry I pointed a gun at you. It's late and I heard a strange noise."

"I tried calling. No one answered."

She flushed. "I was away this evening. The men were off, and your father is having tests in the hospital. I stopped to see him, then ran errands in town."

"Hospital? How bad is he?" Colt moved closer and relieved her of the gun. He unloaded the Ithaca bent barrel, his father's favorite, then set it back above the fireplace, old-style. "He told me he's been losing strength, but my father isn't exactly an old man." He studied Angelina's face. "Is he going to be okay?"

"He's not okay. You know he is a private man and will want to tell you things himself." She motioned toward the stairs of the classic western home, her expression serious. "I haven't dusted your room in two weeks or washed the blankets in a long time. I apologize for this, and I will take care of it in the morning, but for now it will have to do."

"I spent a lot of years riding herd. Sometimes I fell into that bed dog-tired and plenty dirty. A little dust and unwashed blankets are nothing."

Doubt and disparagement filled her eyes as she scanned his designer suit. "Dog-tired is still fine. Sleeping dirty in a clean bed is not."

Bossy. Antagonistic. Well, he wouldn't be in the house enough to have her tough-girl attitude bother him. And if he wanted to fall asleep dirty at the end of a long day riding herd or freeze-branding beef, he'd do it.

He started for the stairs, realized he was reacting more like a five-year-old than a thirty-five-year-old, and turned. "Thank you, Angelina. For not shooting me and for your good care for my father."

Disbelief claimed her features at his lame attempt to man up, and in that one look he knew Angelina Morales wasn't easily impressed by anything, which was probably why she was able to put up with his father.

Like you're the easygoing one of the family? Yeah. Right, cowboy.

Reality hit home as he climbed the stairs with the small carry-on bag he'd brought into the house. He would bring in the meager balance of his possessions tomorrow. For tonight, this was enough.

He'd come back west tired, disillusioned, and filled with self-doubt, but at least he had a place to come back to. A lot of his Wall Street associates were out on the street after this latest market correction and Ponzi-style fiasco. He should be counting his blessings, even though he had an option most guys in New York wouldn't understand. The chance to mount up and man up.

God's timing is eternal and perfect.

His mother would have said that. She'd have been wrong, but

she'd have said it, and he would have believed her because Christine Stafford was honest and kind and exuded warmth like the golden rays of angled sunlight on a late-August afternoon.

He lost her thirty-one years ago. He was four years old, just starting preschool.

He remembered being scared, so scared that first day of school. The building, big and brown. All those windows. People everywhere. Kids running, playing, laughing. He wondered how he could get out of there, but his mother took his hand, led him to a quiet corner, and squatted low. "Trying new things is good for us, Colt. It makes us stronger, like eating spinach when we'd rather have candy."

"I don't like spinach."

"But you tried it and made me so proud." She'd leaned in and kissed his cheek. "And now it's time to try this."

He'd sighed and looked around, and she'd waited for him to make the decision. She'd put it in his hands. That was another thing to miss once she was gone. His father wasn't the make-your-own-decision type. Sam Stafford's motto was "my way or the highway," with the guts and grit that built a multimillion-dollar beef enterprise while others around him failed.

He'd looked up at his mother and whispered, "I'll try it, Mom. I promise."

She kissed his cheek, ruffled his hair, and slipped out.

He never saw her again. A semi carrying an unbalanced load spun out of control on the two-lane. The ensuing crash killed three people—including Christine Stafford.

He'd kept his promise. He'd tried school, and he did well. Over the years he'd tried a lot of things and done well until a few weeks before when the market nosedived and abject failure found him. He'd have been all right if that was all that happened. The hedge funds he governed were designed to withstand market pressures, but when the stock market slide revealed a mammoth Ponzi scheme run by a major Wall Street investment firm—a firm he'd trusted with a massive amount of money—his investment in that fund crashed along with a lot of people's money. Good people, normal folks who trusted his expertise. He'd failed them. He'd failed himself.

And now he was back in the West, humbled by circumstance, not choice. The Manhattan DA had some of his assets in lockdown, some were in critically hit market funds, and some had disappeared in Tomkins's well-shielded pyramid structure.

God's timing, eternal and perfect?

What a joke.

But he'd made that promise to his mother, to try things as needed. Right now he could use a job, and his father needed hands on deck. Colt was a numbers guy, and the mathematics of the situation wasn't lost on him. In the end it all came down to simple equations. One plus one equaled two.

Unless the human factor messed things up. And in Gray's Glen, Washington?

That was entirely possible.

"Slick City Boy Comes Home." Angelina didn't find the imaginary headline amusing as she strode toward her first-floor suite beyond the state-of-the-art kitchen and washing facilities. The extended hallway gave her just enough distance to provide space and privacy to be her own person, even on Stafford land.

She walked into her room and closed the door, trying to sort old memories from current concerns.

You pulled a gun on Colt Stafford.

Holding Sam's son at gunpoint fell neatly into the realm of current concerns. What was she thinking?

Her heart hammered as she crossed the room. She listened to the messages on the house phone, and there it was. "This is Colt. I'm on my way from the airport. They switched my flight, so I'll be there tonight instead of in the morning."

Information that would have been helpful thirty minutes ago.

How could she have been so stupid?

Not stupid, her conscience argued. *Your training kicked in, plain and simple. Launching into Spanish, though? That was a blast from the past, chica.*

Her ability to deepen or lose her accent had worked in her favor on the Seattle police force but was not helpful now. Detective Mary Angela Castiglione could role-play at will, but here at the Double S, Angelina Morales should be unchanging—a simple housekeeper who liked to cook, clean, and sew tiny gowns for grieving parents.

What if Colt's father took offense at her actions? What if he fired her?

Sam loves you. He treats you like a daughter, and he knows the truth. He knows you; he knows your past. He understands. He'd never let you go.

The mental reassurance sounded nice, but then she'd never pulled a gun on one of Sam's sons before.

First time for everything. Being stubborn, Staffords, and male, they probably half expect it.

The truth of that almost made her smile. The cold, hard look on Colt Stafford's face erased the temptation.

She'd dealt with his kind before. Cool, calculating men in designer suits with a head for finance and a heart for gambling. Lust for money and power had taken too much from her already.

Never again.

She'd brought her mother and son inland and nailed her two familial objectives: safety and obscurity. Her mother was discontented but safe, and her precious son was protected. She'd found an incomplete peace in Gray's Glen, a small western town nestled in a broad valley of rolling fields. It was a respite from the dark crimes of city streets.

Managing the ranch house had been the ideal solution to myriad problems, but she may have ruined everything by grabbing that gun.

Anyone who takes offense at a woman defending herself isn't worth the bother, her conscience chided. *The gun is above the fireplace for a reason. This isn't Country Décor 101. It's the Old West, a century removed, but still a place where it's not only okay to own a gun, it's downright smart to know how to use it.*

She'd known how to use a gun long before she moved here. Anyone brought up by Isabo and Martín Castiglione understood the basics of self-defense. Raised in a poverty-stricken village in Ecuador, her parents had come to America and acquired citizenship before she was born. They'd given her the right to be an American, and her policeman father's exemplary service record set the bar high. How proud he'd been at her academy graduation. Eyes moist, he'd hugged her and praised God for a second generation Castiglione cop.

And then he'd been killed because she'd rattled too many racketeer cages as a detective. Her choice to follow in his footsteps became her father's shroud, and she had the rest of her life to deal with that.

She sighed, eyes closed. *Father Almighty, Creator blessed, hear the plea of your daughter. Forgive my stubbornness, my pridefulness. Guide me in the paths of righteousness and humility.*

Guilt stabbed.

She tried to staunch it, but to no avail. If she'd been righteous, she wouldn't be a mother.

If Ethan had been honest, you'd be a wife as well as a mother.

Angelina shook her head. She refused to make excuses for herself. Yes, it was more acceptable to be an unmarried woman bearing a child these days, but she'd promised to do things the right way. Then she broke that word by believing a tall, good-looking Ivy League financial investor. For a short while, she thought the rich blue blood meant to marry her. Cinderella to the max.

Wrong. Ethan Harding intended no such thing, which made her somewhat stupid for a smart girl. His selfish goals for their relationship had never included a happily-ever-after, and he didn't care that a small child bearing his DNA came into being.

Angelina did care. She'd refused Ethan's proposed payoff. She didn't need anyone else in order to raise her son God's way. And when Noah Martín Castiglione was born, he gripped her finger and didn't let go. It had been that way ever since. A tiny boy, wise beyond his years, trusting her to do what was right.

With so much more to lose if things went awry, she'd do whatever it took to protect those she loved. Living a secretive life had become imperative after they buried her beloved father. She hoped, no *prayed,* that she hadn't just lost her tucked-in-the-hills job.

The scent of grilled steak and fried eggs woke Colt bright and early.

His belly growled a welcome. His gut clenched in anticipation. His mouth watered, imagining the taste as he scrambled into blue jeans and a designer sweater—not exactly everyday ranch-hand attire.

Would racing to the kitchen look too desperate?

Yes.

Plates clattered and silverware clanged as someone set the table. He made himself stroll when he longed to run. He hadn't had more than a nibble of real food in two days. He was way beyond hungry, heading straight toward famished. He rounded the corner from the front stairs into the kitchen and came face to face with Irwin Hobbs, a longtime Double S cowboy.

"Colt. Good to see you! Welcome home!" Hobbs grabbed hold of his upper arm. The old boy's iron grip said he'd stayed in shape as the years rolled on. He squeezed lightly but kept any opinions about Colt's lack of muscle to himself. "It's good you're back. We've got over a thousand calves due in the next few weeks, and you're sorely needed." Hobbs waved a hand toward the long kitchen table where a couple of men Colt had never met sat drinking coffee, waiting for breakfast to be served. "Colt Stafford, this is Dylan McGee and Brock Stiles, a couple of local yahoos who hired on last year. These days we don't take on any but our own locals," Hobbs added. "Too many people usin' this, that, and the other thing to mess up their brains. Your father don't take kindly to the way drugs are comin' to the Northwest."

Brock stuck out a bronzed hand. "Nice to meet you, Colt."

"You too." He shook Brock's hand, then leaned across the table to repeat the gesture. "Dylan."

"Did you really work on Wall Street?" The young cowboy seemed amazed, almost star-struck.

Hobbs fought a grin.

Colt grasped the younger man's hand in a quick shake. "For nine years."

"Wearing a suit?" The kid uttered the phrase as if wearing a suit was either the worst punishment ever or a crowning glory.

"Every day."

"I see them New Yorkers in the mornin' sometimes when I dial up them news shows," Hobbs said. "Sittin' there in front of their glass windows, the people and weather goin' straight on by behind 'em." Hobbs shook his head. "Settin' inside, while life passes on. Can't get my head 'round that, no how."

"You'd rather be caught in a blizzard, old man?" Brock stared at Hobbs as if the older man might have a screw loose.

"Well, not exactly a blizzard, but a snowstorm?" He shrugged, unimpressed. "They ain't that bad. Just regular. Though I hear that global warmin' stuff means we'll probably be tropical by the time Nick's girls are growed. We'll be raisin' flowers for them lay-ee things they hand out in Hawaii instead of fattenin' cattle."

"Old man, you might be pushing up flowers by then anyway, so it don't much matter."

Hobbs's grin showed the gap in his lower front teeth. "The good Lord will call me when it's my time, not a minute before."

"Sit," Angelina said, removing a sheet of biscuits from the oven.

"Shouldn't I go see Dad first? And where's Nick?"

"Right here," his younger brother said as he strode in through the back door, looking every inch the rugged cattle rancher he always wanted to be. At least someone's dreams came true in the whole convoluted reality-TV-style mess of three brothers with five different parents. "You ready to jump in?"

"You got work clothes for me?"

"They'll be loose." Nick cast an amused glance at the other two men. "You're not as bulked up as you used to be."

"I've been using my brain instead of my brawn," Colt replied. A part of him wanted to go toe-to-toe with Nick for five minutes just to get it out of their systems. He hadn't pounded on anyone since his last visit ended badly, but the enticing odor of lean grilled steak and farm-fresh eggs took precedence. For now.

"Brain instead of brawn." Nick jabbed Colt's right shoulder. "How far'd that get you?"

Colt paused. Began counting to ten. Made it to five before he lunged forward aiming a fist at his brother's laughing face.

Nick's quick block made it a glancing blow, but Colt pulled up tight, ready to do whatever his little brother thought necessary to get this over with now.

A rolling pin smacked hard on the counter, inches from them.

They swung about, and Colt found himself staring into those same smoke-filled eyes he'd met the night before. It seemed Angelina was adept at finding weaponry in every room of the house, making her one of the most versatile women he'd met in a while. "One drop of stupid Stafford blood gets spilled in my clean kitchen, and I'll take the hide off both of you."

Nick straightened but looked somewhat reluctant to back off—which was kind of how they'd both been since Nick was born. "Sorry, Angelina. I—"

"You!" She waved the pin at Nick, and he stepped back, hands up. "You are upset by many things these days, here and at your home with the girls, but is this"—she stretched out the word as she pointed toward Colt—"the example a loving father sets? Picking fights with others? Or do you want your beautiful daughters to see a man who rises above, who goes the distance for his family? You are their only model of behavior now." She set the rolling pin down, and Colt was pretty sure he heard a collective sigh as the three men began to breathe easier. "I believe you should make it a good one. Seeing you fight with your brother will show your daughters more division. They've already seen enough of that, haven't they?"

Nick surrendered without an argument, a rare moment in Stafford-land. "You're right, Ange. Like usual."

"And you." She shifted her attention to Colt and indicated the platter on the table next to him. "Would you rather fight? Or eat?"

Colt pulled out the chair in front of the plate and sat in it.

"I thought as much." She reached over and poured Colt a steaming mug of fresh hot coffee, the kind he wished he could find in New York City. No one roasted and brewed coffee like they did in the Pacific Northwest.

"Thank you."

She paused, said nothing, then went back to the cooking area.

The guys exchanged quick looks. Despite their size and number, it was clear who ran things at the Double S—the inside things anyway. He hadn't expected this, but he'd steered clear of the Double S for a lot of years, leaving him with no idea how things had changed. Any good cowhand knows that keeping the cook happy keeps everyone happy.

Silence reigned as the men ate an astonishing amount of food for this time of the morning. Colt plowed through a strip steak, fried potatoes and onions, three eggs, and a hunk of Texas-style toast. He knew the rigors of calving would burn this away well before supper. On range days, the guys went out with a lunch in hand, knowing a hot supper would be waiting when they returned at night. A long day, a hard saddle, and tough, tugging work awaited him.

Since the coffee she set before him beat anything New York had to offer, maybe his trade-off would be okay.

About two-thirds of the way through his breakfast, he turned toward Nick. "Over a thousand calves, still? Aren't we a little late this year?"

Nick shrugged. "Last year's tough spring messed up some

timing. This year's crop started dropping yesterday. Meat calves. The seed calves for propagation are due later. It'll be like popcorn—the first few here and there, then the explosion of dozens a day, then back to a few here and there."

Colt understood bad timing real well. He met Nick's gaze. "About those clothes."

"I brought you a bag of 'em."

Angelina appeared at his side to refill his mug. She moved his empty plate to the counter, set a bag of clothes on the table, then bent to pour the coffee. Her proximity put him in instant sensory overload. Long dark hair, held back with a clip at the nape of her neck, tumbled over her shoulder. Sugar and spice wafted his way, a mix of cinnamon and vanilla—a scent that was pure woman and way nicer than the high-priced perfumes popular in Lower Manhattan. He reached out to take the freshened mug. "Thank you."

She paused. Turned slightly. She didn't speak, but the dip of her chin acknowledged his gratitude.

"There are extra coats and boots in the closet," Nick said. "Gloves, hats, whatever you need. We brought the herd down a notch last week, but if we get hit with this storm coming, we could be in trouble. We're talking a lot of rangeland to cover. I figured on hooking you up with Newsie."

Yesterday's News, *his* horse, still here, working and waiting. Would the big chestnut remember him? Not likely, but there was something earnestly right about pairing with his old friend again.

"Having the cows down a level is easier on your dad," Hobbs noted.

"Is someone going to fill me in on Dad, or do I have to play twenty questions?"

"He's sick." Hobbs offered up the info in a style Colt remembered like it was yesterday. "He got one of them hepatitis things last year that messed with his liver. He's weak but he's doing better. Some days. But then he went and got tossed around by a protective cow who weren't takin' none too kindly to your daddy's attention to her baby. A rookie mistake, so we knew somethin' weren't right from the get-go." He turned a no-nonsense look to the two younger cowboys on the far side of the table. "Never turn your back on an angry woman, boys. Words to live by."

"Whereas I would prefer 'Do unto others as you would have done unto you,'" remarked Angelina, but she slanted a look of amusement and affection toward Hobbs.

"Does he need a new liver?" Colt looked from Angelina to Nick to Hobbs.

"We don't know." Eyes down, Nick gripped his mug. "We don't know all that much right now."

"So you're not bein' left out, you're bein' included on the same lack of knowledge we're all sharin'," Hobbs said.

"Until they know if Dad's body will recover on its own, it's a waiting game." Strain tightened Nick's observation.

"I hate waitin'," Hobbs grumbled.

A chorus of agreement circled the table.

Angelina made a low sound, and Colt noticed all the men sat straighter, shoulders back, chins up. "Look at you sitting here, all fed and round and good, whining about waiting for a little information while hundreds of cows that have been carrying calves for nine months are about to deliver babies in the snow and wind. Bunch of whiners. Your mothers should take a switch to your behinds."

"When she's right, she's right." Hobbs stood. "I'll take the four-wheeler 'round the back way and meet you guys." He pointed to Colt. "Boy, you gonna hold that bag of clothes all day or get 'em on? Time's wastin'."

Colt took the bag upstairs, dumped the contents on the bed, and dressed as fast as he could. Nick was a touch broader and an inch taller, but not a big enough difference to matter. As he applied the layers, he caught sight of his Armani suit draped across the easy chair on the opposite side of the room. The irony of the situation caught him.

When he'd stormed off the Double S years ago, he was determined to never come back—at least not to work. And he'd kept that promise a long time.

Now he pulled on jeans and a dark green turtleneck and grabbed the Carharrt rancher coat he'd taken from the downstairs closet. He put it on and glanced in the mirror.

What he saw surprised him.

Looking back at him was Colt Stafford—the real Colt Stafford—a guy who played square, shot straight, and never messed anybody over, no matter how bad things got. He gave the reflection a long, slow look, then grabbed the hat and gloves from the bed. The guy in the mirror had a job to do and needed to get on with it. As he left the room, he glanced back.

The mirror showed nothing now but a messed-up bedroom, tousled and strewn. But he knew what he saw. He saw the man he'd been, before Manhattan got hold of him. And seeing that man made him realize it had been way too long since that guy had put in an appearance anywhere.

*A*ngelina." Sam Stafford tried to cover the gratitude in his voice with a dour look, but he couldn't fool her. He breathed in, deep and slow, and tried to sit more upright. That triggered a coughing fit that refused to stop. *Note to self: broken ribs and bronchitis are not a good match. Next time? Keep a sharp eye over your shoulder.*

She moved forward, raised the head of the bed by pressing a button, then helped ease him into a more upright position by posting a pillow behind him. She stepped back, swept the new angle with a glance, and asked, "Better?"

He breathed slowly, without coughing. "Much."

"Coughing hurts, I expect."

He grimaced. "I've had busted ribs before. I'll have 'em again, good Lord willing."

"Not if you stay out of the way of an angry cow mama." She shook her finger at him. "A new mama with her first baby, and you turned your back on her."

"Tricked into a false sense of security by years of having easy-going cows. That one's a she-devil. She'll be off to market once that baby's weaned."

"And then you'll lose the opportunity to have her become an experienced mother. Aren't most first-time mothers a little whacked?"

"You tell me."

"Nothing we should speak of now."

He changed the subject. "The guys doing okay at home?"

"We avoided a brawl at the breakfast table, so that was good."

"A brawl?" He paused, then eased against the pillow. A standoff at daybreak could mean only one thing. "Colt's home."

"For a guy who turns his back on a cow fresh out of calving, you're a smart man."

"Did he and Nick go at it?"

"Stopped by the presence of a rolling pin. Hardheads, just like their father." She pulled up a chair next to him, withdrew a bit of fancy work from her bag, and started making tiny stitches on a doll-sized garment. "But they also suited up and headed out, knowing snow's coming and wanting to get the first-years in as close as possible."

"How'd he look?" Sam knew his voice sounded a little desperate. How odd was it that the only person he could let down his guard with was a housekeeper with a shadowed past? "Is he all right?"

"He will be." She poked the tiny needle in and out with quick, unwasted motion. "He was hungry."

Hungry? Colt?

Regret stabbed deep.

He'd ordered him out of the house a long time ago. He told Colt if he wasn't interested enough in the family business to help with it, he wasn't needed.

Regret blossomed to remorse.

So much to fix. And maybe not enough time. "Like he hadn't eaten, hungry?"

She raised her eyes. Met his.

Sam swallowed hard. That's exactly what she meant. Colt had been on top of the world. He might have been on the opposite side of the country, but Sam had kept tabs on him. His rise to power, his ability to assess and appraise the business climate and invest appropriately. He'd built a name for himself in an acclaimed investments firm and was managing multimillion-dollar wealth when Wall Street faced a major hiccup. The jolt showed irregularities. Bernie Tomkins got busted for fraud and money laundering. The online client list named Colton Stafford of Goldstein & Greenbaum as one of the innocent but major hedge-fund investors.

And now he was home and hungry, with empty pockets.

You wanted him to come crawling back. He's done it.

Sam clenched his teeth. He'd wanted that because he was a surly, full-of-himself jerk, and that's the only side Colt ever knew. Remorse escalated to self-ascribed guilt.

"Beating yourself up gets you nothing but beat up."

"A true sage." He growled the words, but Angelina seemed unfazed by his tone. "I've got a lot to make up for. I alienated Colt after his mother died. Instead of being the father I should have been, I married Rita, thinking she'd fill a gap. Except for having a beautiful boy together, our marriage was a major mistake. She didn't want me or a ranch or a couple of wild little boys running around."

"I still fail to see how that was all *your* fault." Angelina's tiny needle flashed with each miniature stitch.

"I married her, didn't I?"

"You did. But she could have stayed, Sam." Angelina paused her sewing to lean closer and catch his eye. "She had a little boy. A son. A gift from God. Rita didn't just leave you, she left Colt and Nick because they weren't important enough to keep her here. That's a harsh reckoning for little kids."

"A smart man would have seen that money meant more to her than family from the beginning. That still makes it my mistake."

"A smart man would have taken the time he needed to grieve the loss of his beloved wife," she said softly.

And there it was, the simple truth that haunted him for decades. He'd lost the love of his life on a bright September day thirty-one years before, and he'd spent all this time—*decades*—angry. That meant his two biological sons and his adopted son all got short-changed. "I don't know how much time I've got left, but I know I've got things to fix." He frowned, agitated by variables out of his control. Angelina's usual "let go and let God" spiel was like a burr under his saddle. Sam Stafford hated handing over the reins to anyone else. Right now he had no choice, and that just aggravated him further.

"And God willing, you can fix them. If not all, then most. But if you come home with that scowl embedded on your face," Angelina warned, "it will take you much longer."

"I ain't one of them happy-go-lucky types, Angelina. I believe you know that."

She stopped sewing and leaned forward, eyes sharp. "Then learn."

He sat back with a grumpy snarl and pointed at the tiny garment in her hands. "Doll clothes. Who's got use for more doll clothes at the Double S? Don't the girls have enough with what you made them for Christmas?"

She smoothed the tiny dress in her hands with gentle fingers. "This is not for a doll. I am making these for the hospital here. They are for babies. The tiniest babies." She lifted her gaze back to his. "I will donate these for when tiny souls are called home to heaven. Something precious for a precious loss."

Once again he'd spoken too soon and too gruff. Would he never learn to just be quiet?

"And might I remind you that an entire community exists outside the Double S? It would behoove you to become further acquainted with the people who share your community."

"Apple-pickin', grape-growin' clowns."

She sighed loudly on purpose.

"You know they'd love to see us out of the valley." He'd told her this all before, but Sam was determined to have his say. "All that talk about cow burps and gas and e-friendly nonsense. When God made the animals, the necessity to pass gas came along with them, just like you and me. But now a bunch of tree-huggers want to picket outside the slaughterhouse upstate and protest calves-to-market days. Where did these know-nothings come from? And what business is it of theirs how we make our money?"

"Are you done?"

He wasn't, but her expression stopped him.

"First, focus on getting well. Work with the doctors to increase your mobility, which will help your injury heal. Then they can zone

in on your other issues. They can't do anything if you're not coop-
erating. Second, if you'd lived more peaceably with your neighbors
in the past, you'd be in a better position to deal with this now. They'd
like you more and would cut you some slack."

"Those tree-huggers wouldn't. Bunch of fresh-faced folks coming north, driving prices up, wanting to break up farms and build
mini-estates. In the end, where do they think food comes from?"

"Your medieval-baron treatment of the area peasantry has earned
you some enemies. You might want to tone it down, don't you
think?"

"But I'm not a jerk now," he protested.

She sighed again, set down the garment, and met his eye. "It
takes more than a few months to cleanse the egocentric work of
decades."

"It was for the ranch! Not for myself," Sam said.

Sam's protestations didn't even cause her to pause. "More impor-
tantly, your sons have had their own share of suffering. Colt's been
thrashed mentally, Nick's trying to be father of the year to those two
little girls—and failing miserably—and Trey's buried himself in his
music since his wife died. Healing takes time, Sam. And effort." Her
needle began to move in and out on the small gown again. "Has
Reverend Cowell been in to see you?"

"Earlier, yes. I was sedated. I might have made a more generous
contribution to the church than previously planned."

"Buying God's love doesn't work."

"Wasn't doing anything of the kind. I was making up for past
lapses."

"In that case, good." This time she smiled at him and patted his hand. "I know you have recommitted your life to God. To faith. This is a marvelous thing. But while God is a God of second chances, I believe he appreciates atonement for our sins."

"Man up and put up."

"Yes."

Sam sat silent a minute before he raised the question of the hour. "You think I've got time, Ange?"

"I pray you do. But if not?" She rested her hand on his. "You've given yourself back to God, you've started a new path, and no matter how long that path may be, paradise waits at the end."

She was right. He'd been the miserable land baron Angelina noted, with over three decades of shameful behavior. Thirty-one years of messed-up priorities. He knew he'd come late to this change of heart. Amazing how a man's sensibilities shifted when given the possibility of a shortened timeline. Short path or long, he'd realigned his beliefs back to where they'd been before he lost Christine and let work, money, and the ranch take over his life. Now he needed to make things right. Not because he thought he needed to score points for heaven but because Christine would have wanted him to make amends.

Angelina pressed her hand to his, stood, then bent to kiss his cheek. "You have much to think about and time to do just that. Your son has returned, there is work to be done, and now there are extra hands to do it. Rest and heal, my friend."

He gripped her hand. "I thank God for you every day, Angelina."

She laughed, a soft, musical, deep-toned laugh. "You and I know we have much in common. We both have old mistakes and welcome new chances. God bless you. And stop giving the nurses a hard time," she said as a robust nurse strolled into the room.

The nurse winked at Angelina as Sam offered his other arm for vitals. "As far as I'm concerned, Mr. Stafford is one of the nicest patients I've had in a while." She beamed his way. "And that's appreciated by all of us."

Sincerity laced her words. That made Sam feel like maybe he wasn't the worst cur on the planet, that there might be hope yet.

"Of course the big box of chocolates wins us over every time," the nurse added.

Surprised, Sam turned toward Angelina.

Eyes soft and knowing, she squeezed his hand lightly before she left.

Angelina had sent candy in his name. She'd taken care of his son when he couldn't. She'd come to see him, even though there was plenty of work at the ranch. He was blessed by her thoughtfulness, truth, and integrity.

She'd scoff at that. She'd made mistakes. Regret dogged her days, much like it did his. But Sam knew what he knew. Angelina's quality went deep. He understood that more fully now. When he was married to Christine, he hadn't appreciated his wife the way he should have. He hadn't given his all to her. Then she was gone, and nothing could bring her back.

He'd suffered. Colt suffered. And then his other sons, Nick and Trey, because he wasn't man enough to put them first. Had God sent the Latina beauty to help him see the error of his ways? Sam believed he had.

Two years ago he'd been in grave need at the ranch. He'd fired the third housekeeper in less than a month. When ranch hands were more worried about empty bellies than cattle, little got done.

Juan Morales said he had a cousin of a cousin looking for work. Angelina showed up for her late afternoon interview as scheduled, with more interest in cooking than talking. In ninety minutes she had a meal ready to be served in hearty, man-sized portions—a meal that won the men's respect and Angelina a job.

Sam had built an empire making gut decisions. He'd done the same thing then. He hired her on intuition because, despite the delicious meal and her skillful fielding of his interview questions, Sam was pretty sure Angelina Morales had never been anyone's cook or housekeeper. He gave her the job anyway, instinct telling him he was doing the right thing. Time bore him out. He helped her and she helped him in return, leading him back to a faith he'd abandoned. She'd led him to this second chance, a concept he would have scoffed at as a younger man, and Sam didn't take that lightly. She'd brought him to reckoning and then to faith. He owed her everything.

So, yeah. Whatever Angelina needed, he'd see she got, because without her his life would be shaping up differently right now.

Colt had forgotten what ice cold felt like.

The memory came rushing back as he scoured midlevel sagebrush late morning. He wasn't about to run home to add layers

he should have had the sense to put on hours before. Words of recrimination flooded his half-frozen brain, but he brought Yesterday's News
around the far side of a thick stand of brush, scouring the landscape
for newborns.

A wretched-looking red calf blinked up at him, her little face
pleading for help. He turned slightly. Mama was uphill, looking
tired and worn. Although it was ice cold, it was not as wicked as it
could get when the north winds picked up. So was the cow sick? Or
just tired?

He eyed her and hoped for the latter. Either way, she allowed
him to approach her baby. He dismounted, gathered the calf into his
arms, and laid her over the horse, then climbed back on. With a click
of his tongue, he moved the horse into an easy motion, hoping the
cow would follow.

She didn't. He looped around again, knowing time was of the
essence. This baby needed to be warmed up and fed. If mama wasn't
up to the task, he had to help things along. He brought the horse
close to the reluctant cow, nudged her out of the brush, and let her
approach in her own time, despite the cold. She sidled up to the
horse, then inhaled deeply. The smell of her calf made her more cooperative. He prodded the horse into a slow walk, and this time the
cow followed along.

Nick rode by as they headed down the slope. "That's the cow I
was looking for. She delivered?"

Colt looked down at the calf. "Let's hope it's hers."

"Get it warm and fed." Nick issued the order, then urged his
horse into high gear toward the outer range perimeter.

As if Colt didn't know that. He wanted to bark words back but stopped himself. He wasn't in charge here. He couldn't take the lead like he had for years in New York. At the Double S, he was nothing more than a common laborer, and the sooner he got used to that idea, the better off they'd all be. He focused on the cold calf as he shut his mouth and rode to the ranch below.

"There's a calf in our basement." Angelina watched him from the doorway of the sublevel workroom. Beyond her comment, she seemed at a loss for words—which surprised him. Hadn't she been at the Double S long enough to see calves warming in the lowest level? That seemed at odds with her take-charge attitude.

"Warming her and dredging her. Mama was a little distracted by her own needs and most likely figured her baby would be okay on her own for a while. But baby was fading fast."

"Heifers." Angelina's expression disparaged first-time mothers as she moved closer. "And this playpen?"

He looked up, confused. "What about it?"

"Did you bring it with you from New York? Because that had to be an interesting flight."

"Of course not. It was behind the workbench where it's always been," he said, gesturing to the corner before glancing back up at her. "We keep it there for this sort of thing. That way the newest babies are warm and fed and monitored by whoever is in the house."

She started to say something, then stopped. "I'd be glad to keep an eye on her. She's a pretty little thing."

"You don't mind?"

Her lips twitched as if amused, but her eyes stayed steady. "Not at all. Stew's on for supper, the bread is baking, and bathrooms are cleaned. She'll be good company."

"Thank you, Angelina." He moved toward the stairs. "I'm heading back out, but I'm grabbing a couple extra layers first."

She scanned his jeans, turtleneck, and Carharrt ranch jacket, then winced. "No thermals."

"Yup."

"Didn't Nick have some in the bag of clothes?"

"Possibly." He paused. "Probably," he amended. "I grabbed from the top. My bad."

"You must have frozen out there."

"Let's just say my office here is less climate controlled than what I've grown accustomed to. A rookie mistake I shouldn't have made."

"Ouch."

He appreciated the sympathy in her voice, then indicated the calf. "She should be all right now that she's eaten. I'll let her warm up, then I'll take her out to mama in the lower barn later. The bread smells amazing, by the way."

This time she smiled. "The first loaves are cooling on the counter. And there's soft butter. Grab a piece before you go out. Nothing like fresh bread to warm you from the inside out."

Fresh bread. Soft butter. A beautiful woman watching him from across the subterranean level of the massive Stafford home. Something inside him eased up. For just a moment, meeting her gaze, he didn't feel like a total loser.

He hurried upstairs, re-layered, and stopped by the kitchen on his way out. Angelina was there ahead of him. She held out a paper sack. "Your bread. You don't want to keep that horse waiting."

He took the sack and inhaled, grateful. "Thank you. My PB&J from this morning will be pretty cold about now."

"This will help." She laid her palms on the counter. "I saw your father a little while ago."

His ailing father had been on his mind all morning. He hated not knowing what was going on. Not being in charge. "How is he?" *Did he ask about me? Does he want me to visit? Has he missed me at all?*

"Comforted that you've come home."

His presence had never comforted Sam Stafford. Not once that he could remember. Old bitterness rose up from somewhere deep within. He swallowed hard, determined to be polite. "That would be a first, Angelina." He held up the sack. "Thanks for the bread."

Stubborn, like his father.

Rigid, like his father.

Square-shouldered, chin raised, and in your face, just like Sam Stafford. What woman in her right mind would find that kind of stiff-necked bullheadedness attractive?

You. You forgot to mention to-die-for handsome when his blue eyes met yours.

Angelina swallowed a sigh. When those same eyes went wide with appreciation after smelling the rich, yeasty aroma of freshly sliced bread, her heart hammered. She'd fought a smile, keeping her face placid on purpose. The last thing she needed was for her boss's son to think she was flirting with him. Which she wasn't. She'd been duped by one high-profile investment banker already. Once was more than enough to convince her to flee from men who put more stock in what they earned than in helping others. She'd learned the hard way, but she'd learned.

The house phone rang. Lucy Carlton's name and number flashed on the display. Angelina answered it as she turned off the flame under the simmering stockpot. "Lucy, hey. How are you?"

"I've been better," the young mother admitted. "Belle has spiked a fever, the van won't start, and I need to get her seen at Quick Care. Can you—"

"I'll be right over," Angelina said.

Lucy, their nearest neighbor, was a widow with three small children, scraping an existence from the only thing she owned—a small plot of farmland just east of the Double S. She minded her own business, sang in the church choir, grew plants and Christmas trees, and rarely asked for help. For Lucy to place this call was a big deal.

"Thanks, Ange."

Angelina checked the bread in the oven. Just right.

She tumbled the loaves onto cooling racks, rubbed them with a stick of fresh, cold butter, covered the stew, and headed out the door.

Sam had used his water rights to punish the owners of the neighboring farm years before the Carltons bought the land. If Sam was ready to right old wrongs, he could start with the struggling family next door who had inherited the damage he'd inflicted on the previous owners.

Her cell phone rang as she approached the big SUV. The name that flashed in the display came straight from her old squad on the Seattle police force. "Tony, hey! How are you? How's the family?"

"Jody misses you, the kids miss you, and it's time to hang up your oven mitts and come home to Seattle," Tony Giambrino told her. "The boss says we've got a place for you on the squad. I'd like nothing better than to have you come back to narcotics and fill it, Mary."

She hadn't been called Mary in over two years. In the beautiful hills of central Washington, she'd been Angelina to everyone she'd met. Hearing Tony's voice, his offer, and her real name instigated a yearning she couldn't give in to. She climbed into the SUV and started the engine. "Tony, you know why I left."

"Because you lost something wonderful and needed to protect your own. I get it, Mary. But it's been long enough. It's time to come home."

Funny, she didn't think of Seattle as home anymore. Not with her father gone and her mother and Noah here. "Hey, I—"

Tony cut her off. "Let me remind you that as horrible as your dad's death was, that was the first retribution slaying we've had in a decade. And the first one of a family member in over two decades. So while I understand your concern, what I really want is to have one of the best and most versatile Seattle detectives back on the job. No pressure of course."

Going back would solve the ongoing problem of her mother's discontent. Isabo Castiglione would dance for joy to be back in Seattle, but there was no way Angelina could leave Sam in his current condition. He'd helped her, cared for her family, and given her a job while she tried to regain balance in her life. In the meantime, she'd fallen head over heels in love with the rolling hills, fertile fields, and towering trees of central Washington.

She didn't want to leave Gray's Glen. But she didn't want to be a housekeeper forever either, even though she worked for a generous man. At some point, she needed to make choices, but not with Sam sick and not at the start of calving season, no matter how much her mother missed her old home and her old friends. "Tony, I've got to hang up. I'm picking up a sick child at the neighbor's. Your offer is totally impossible now, but . . ."

"But it might not be impossible soon?" he pressed. "Leave me hope, chica."

This was a compliment of the highest order. The Seattle Police Department didn't make a habit of calling former employees to see if they'd come back. Although the possibility of leaving Sam and the Double S wasn't something she could currently entertain, who knew what six months might bring? "This would make my mother happy. Being sequestered in the country with a little kid didn't make her bucket list, so she's chomping at the bit."

"Our ears to the ground say there's no apparent danger now that your father's killer has been put away. Barnham called him a rogue assassin, and we've got nothing that disputes his assessment."

Hearing the original evaluation reaffirmed was a relief. She wasn't big on having her family become anyone's target practice again. A return to Seattle would benefit her mother, but leaving the Double S, Sam, and the adopted extended family she'd come to love would be hard. She was happy in Gray's Glen, but her mother wasn't, and she owed her mother a chance at happiness. However, with her father gone and all her mother had sacrificed for Angelina, it wouldn't be right to send Isabo back to Seattle alone, either. A conundrum, either way. "I'll let you know when things lighten up here. Okay?"

Tony sighed loud and long. "Flipping pancakes and making beds aren't as important as you make it seem, Mary, but I understand. I'll call back if you don't contact me. Good talking to you."

"And you." She hung up the phone as she pulled into Lucy's drive. Tony's offer added another level of conflict to an already layered situation, but she couldn't weigh those choices now. That was something to discuss with her mother. They'd both lost something of irreplaceable value on the streets of Seattle—a husband and father, retired police captain, a man renowned for fairness and integrity, executed on the street because she'd collared a racketeer with a network of fierce friends. She'd been so proud of that takedown. Her whole squad had celebrated that group of arrests. And when they'd put the convicted racketeer and killer behind bars for a life sentence, one of his minions had done a drive-by on Angelina's father. It tore her apart to know that this man of substance, valor, faith, and worth had died alone, bleeding out on a cold, wet Seattle street, with his trusty black Lab beside him.

She hauled in a breath, unlocked the SUV doors, and mentally shoved the offer and the memories aside.

"You have what in the basement?" Nick stared at Colt as if he'd just grown another head. "A cow?"

"The calf." Colt put his saddle aside, hung the blanket to dry, and grabbed the horse brush. "She's in the playpen with a warming light. Angelina said she'd keep an eye on her."

"She did, huh?"

"Yes." Colt drew out the word. "I'm not getting what's funny about any of this."

"Did you notice any other calves in the basement?"

He hadn't, but he figured it was early in the day. A niggle of awareness caused him to push his hat back. "No."

"And did you think yours was the only one we needed to keep an eye on with weather conditions growing worse?"

Put that way, Nick's question made sense. "Like I said, I figured it was early."

"And you missed the space-age-looking igloos by the back barn?"

He'd seen them, kind of, from the side, but he had no idea what they were used for. "I might have noticed them."

Nick burst out laughing. Colt had to think really hard before deciding whether to deck him or laugh with him, but since his brother had faced his own share of rough moments the past few years, he let it slide. For now. "They're for calves, I take it?"

"That's exactly what they're for."

"And my little gal in the basement?"

"Needs to go join her mother and her friends."

He wanted to swear, but he held back. Nick wasn't being a total jerk, and if he'd made the same mistake, Colt would be treating him in kind, which meant maybe they weren't the two worst brothers in the world.

Realization hit. He groaned. The red calf needed to be lugged over to the far barn, and he'd just put his horse up.

"I'll help you."

Ten hours back, pride would have kept him from accepting his brother's help, but a day in and out of the saddle, tracking cows, and herding stubborn due-to-calf cows and heifers made him bone weary. "I'd appreciate it."

By the time the calf was resettled with her mother, the other men had gathered to eat. "Got your little girl put up for the night?" Hobbs asked, verifying that one thing hadn't changed in Colt's years away—cowboys gossiped worse than a clutch of old women.

"She's back with her ma, and the basement's cleaned up. And yes, I'm stupid, but I'm too hungry to argue the point. So you boys have all the fun you want at my expense while I eat some of this stew. The smell alone is enough to warm up a long, cold day. And Angelina?" He waited until she looked his way. "Thank you for not laughing at me this morning. That was real nice of you."

"Your efforts were commendable, and the sincerity was downright sweet." Her smile widened as she worked pie crust across a well-floured board. "And a little funny."

"Deserving of a hearty laugh is what I'd say," Nick teased, "but then you turned around and did okay this afternoon. It just doesn't seem right to make light of that."

"Unpracticed but not forgotten," Colt said as he helped himself to more stew. "I'm sure I'll be feeling every misstep and rabbit hole come morning."

"There's muscle cream and pain meds upstairs in the main bath," Angelina said. She finished crimping the pie and set it aside before starting a second. "Nick, are you having the girls catch the bus here in the morning? Or are you taking them to school yourself?"

"I think I'll have them catch the bus at home, then have them dropped off here in the afternoon. If we lose power on the ranch, we've got backup. I don't want to risk having them cold and miserable at home with their afternoon sitter." Nick shifted around to Hobbs and Colt. "Can you guys start at first light? That storm's due in by nightfall tomorrow, and the more mothers we've brought down, the better chance we have of getting through this unscathed."

"How many heifers did you cover for market beef?" Colt asked.

"Nearly two-hundred first-years and roughly the same in second-time mamas. Then we have a ten-day break before the older cows come due."

"That your idea or the old man's?"

Nick frowned at Colt's reference to their father but didn't fault him, and that was a first. "Mine. But he saw the sensibility of it. Gives us first look at the new mothers and the inexperienced second-years. That way they get the TLC they need and we have fewer casualties."

Numbers.

Good business always came down to numbers. In that way,

ranching wasn't much different from hedge funds on Wall Street. Except Wall Street had the advantage of central heating and cooling.

"You look done in, Colt," Hobbs observed, but he seemed approving too. "It's okay to call it a night. Light don't come early in February, but when it comes, we'd best be ready to ride."

"I'll be ready." Realizing how tired he was, he stood. "See you guys tomorrow. And Angelina?"

She glanced up as if she didn't think much of his presence, which didn't seem one bit fair because she'd been on his mind all day. "Yes?"

"Thanks for dinner. It was great."

"My job." She shrugged off the compliment as if it was no big deal, but he sensed appreciation for his words. And something else. Something he couldn't put his finger on. Weariness hit like the north wind that had battered him throughout the day. He waved to the guys and headed upstairs, too tired to think straight. But when he could? He was going to figure out what was bothering him about Angelina.

THREE

*A*ngelina drove back roads, took two purposeful wrong turns, then steered the ranch SUV up the gravel drive overlooking the more distant eastern meadows of the Double S. She rolled into the thickly forested nook for the turnaround, grabbed the plastic bag of necessities, and hurried into the small cabin that most had forgotten. The cabin's obscurity had become her blessing when she came to Gray's Glen.

"Finally, you are here." Frustration put an unaccustomed edge on her mother's tone. "Come in. That wind is sharp and will bring more snow tonight."

"Deep snow, from the sound of things." Angelina took off her coat and scarf, then turned as a three-year-old spitfire raced her way.

"Mama!"

"Noah, my darlingest of all darlings, how is my handsome boy?"

"I'm sick," he announced and pushed out his lower lip. "*Abuela* is making me take medicine, and I don't like it." He folded his arms across his chest in wounded indignation. "I want chocolate milk and colorful cereal—not icky grape stuff."

"Colorful cereal?" Angelina asked, surprised. Her mother held up a box of Froot Loops. "Ah," Angelina said.

"This he has made known to me no small number of times," her mother observed wryly. "To which I say . . ." She redirected her attention to her grandson. "When a grownup tells you what to do—"

The small boy didn't look happy, but he muttered the expected reply. "—you do it."

"Exactly." Angelina smothered him with kisses and hugs until he wriggled free. "We must always respect our elders and one another."

"'Cept I don't have another." Noah motioned to the television sitting atop a table on the far wall. "I only have TV and 'Buela."

Regret tightened Angelina's throat. "This will not always be the case, Noah. But for now you have Abuela and me, and we love you very much."

"If I'm good, can I go see some cowboys?" He ran to the west-facing window and pointed out. "I saw them a really long time ago."

Noah didn't have a real grasp of time, so a really long time ago might mean last month or yesterday afternoon. "Were they working hard?"

"Yes!" His voice ramped up with respect. "They looked so teeny, teeny, but 'Buela said th-they weren't really that way. It's because th-they are so far away from us." Excitement over his news made him stumble over some of the words. "There were cows too. I could maybe help the cowboys catch the cows and stay with you. Can I?"

His eyes, so round. His voice, filled with hope. His tiny stutter, endearing. His gaze, locked on hers, begging quietly.

She swallowed hard and pretended to think it over. "There is a big snow coming later, but as winter winds down, we can talk of this. Right now my boss is coming home from the hospital."

"Is he sick?"

"Very." She kept her face and tone serious. "He could be sick for a while, and that might make things difficult. Even the quietest of little boys make some noise, and sick people need rest."

"My cars make a lot of noise when they crash," he admitted. He drew his brows together, then asked, "Will your boss get better?"

A question with no answer, so Angelina bent low and gave her son the simple truth. "We don't know yet. He will come home, and I will be very busy caring for him and for the men who are delivering many calves these next few weeks. But then Abuela and I will talk about what is best."

"A return to civilization would be my vote," her mother muttered. "For over three decades I walked the city streets unafraid. Should I live the rest of my days buried in the hills, surrounded by trees and snow? May sweet Mary, Mother of God, hear my plea, because my own Mary listens to no one." She smacked a washcloth to the counter as she wiped it down.

"I know, *Mami*. We probably should have made a change last fall, and I didn't. I'm sorry about that."

Her mother kept wiping, eyes on her work, her mouth set in a firm, thin line.

Angelina moved closer. "I meant what I said to Noah. We'll figure out what's best and make changes as soon as we can. I promise."

Noah pointed out the window. "I would be best with the cowboys." He spoke firmly, as if trying to convince his mother—if only she had the sense to listen. "I could have my own cowboy hat and some boots, and I could help your boss all the time. And th-then he would feel better because he'd have more help."

"This is truly something I must consider." She kissed his forehead, then indicated the table just inside the door. "If you look inside the bag, you might find something special."

"A present?"

Angelina tousled his hair, smiling. "Look and see."

Noah opened the bag, handed her a bottle of cough syrup and children's pain reliever, then shrieked. "A puzzle! With cowboys! How did you know I wanted a puzzle with cowboys?"

"Mothers are wise creatures," Isabo Castiglione said. "Most of the time. Even old mothers." She moved to the small kitchen on the back side of the three-room cabin. "I have a large pan of cinnamon rolls rising for you to take with you."

"Bless you." Angelina hugged her mother. "I went to visit Sam this morning, then came straight here, so my baking time is cut short. Mami, I really—"

"I used a double recipe to make sure there would be plenty," her mother interrupted. "That way you can relax while you are here with us."

A good reminder that Noah needed her, a fact her mother pressed regularly. Angelina had brought them here, opting for safety. She'd taken herself off the radar intentionally, but Noah was no longer a baby, and living in seclusion wasn't healthy. She needed to bring them into the open. For her mother, that meant back to friends and the life she loved in Seattle. But could Angelina let her go back there alone, with no family around? No.

"Tony called me." She kept her voice soft as Noah worked the puzzle packaging open.

"He wants you back on the force," her mother guessed. "This is good, because you are your father's daughter, an officer of acclaim."

"He reminded me how well we worked together and that good police work should rule the day." Angelina watched as Noah concentrated on a particularly tough corner of the puzzle box. When he got it open, he screeched success.

"I did it!"

"So you did, clever boy. Dump them out, and I'll be right there to build it with you."

"Okay!"

Isabo kept her voice soft. "They have space on their squad?"

"He suggested there would always be a space for me."

"You miss it." Her mother slipped plastic wrap over the tray of sweet rolls. "As your father did before you."

She missed parts of it. She'd loved her job. But shouldn't sacrificial love always take precedence? "I miss being on the force. But I'm the reason we're here. Perhaps more diligence after the conviction would have saved my father's life. So now we have different choices, Mami."

"You have no guilt." The rise of Isabo's voice drew Noah's quick interest. She breathed deep and softened her tone. "Guilt lies with the coward who pulled the trigger. Not with the daughter who served her city so well, who filled her parents with such pride. We are family, Mary Angela. But I do not like being alone all the time, even with my precious grandson so near. Too much cold, too much snow, too much darkness. I think sometimes I am to go crazy here."

"I will change things soon, I promise you."

Tears brightened her mother's eyes. The solitude and the long darkness of winter were taking their toll. "I know you want to go back." Angelina sighed, watching Noah spill the forty-eight piece puzzle onto the floor. "Although I have come to love it here."

"A trained detective, working as a domestic."

"Well, it's a little more than your typical housekeeper's job," Angelina replied. "I don't mind the work and I love the people. I feel as though I am a member of this family. And I love this part of the country. So open, so free." She handed her mother a clutch of tissues. "But I want you and Noah happy, so we must look at that."

"We pray for guidance," Isabo declared as she swabbed her eyes with the tissue. "Do not mind me. The long hours of darkness wear me down. I will be fine, and Noah will be fine. In the meantime, there is a small child who waits."

"His wait is now over," Angelina announced as she crossed the small room with a fresh cup of coffee in hand. "I've come to do puzzles with my boy."

"How many? A lot?" Noah's emphasis meant he was concerned about how much time she had.

She set her coffee down and sat beside her son on the floor. "I have an hour. How many do you think we can do in an hour?"

He made a face. "How long is an hour?"

"It is the length of two *Dora* episodes. Plus a little bit more."

Noah scrubbed his runny nose with some tissues, his forehead wrinkled with intensity. "Th-that is a long time. I think it is at weast four puzzles."

"L-l-least," she taught him, stressing the *l*. "Then we shall test your theory and see, my son."

Five puzzles later, Noah glanced up. Always at the end of her visits, he would study the clock as if wondering why the small machine had so much power over his mother. And despite their reclusive life, Noah already sensed differences in their existence. He saw families on TV living together. Moms who came home from work and had supper with their children. One day soon he would ask why they were different, and how would she answer? Besides, was he really any safer here, on the far side of the ranch, than he would be in the ranch house with her?

Having a degree of separation had made sense when she first moved here, her father's murder fresh in their hearts and heads. But it didn't make sense to keep hiding her mother and son any longer. And Tony's phone call opened a new door of possibility.

"Will you come tomorrow?" Noah looked up, hopeful.

She shook her head as they boxed up the fifth puzzle. "There's a snowstorm coming."

"How can you tell?"

"There are scientists who study the air over the ocean, and they watch what is happening in Canada, the land north of us. They see that a great wind and a big push of cold air are going to mix together, and that will bring a lot of snow."

"Like when I help 'Buela mix things?"

"Yes, but bigger. This will bring much snow for many miles. The roads will have to be cleared. After that I will come."

"If you lived here, I wouldn't have to miss you so much." Head down, he whispered the words, not daring to look at her.

Her heart shattered into a thousand tiny sharp-edged pieces, and it took great effort to keep her face placid. "I know. And one day soon that will be the case. But right now we are so blessed to have a warm home for you here with your grandmother who loves you as much as I do."

Her mother placed the large wrapped pan of cinnamon rolls next to Angelina's purse.

It was time to go. Past time, actually. She stood, grabbed her coat, and bent to kiss her son's soft head. "I will be back soon, little man."

He nodded, still looking at the puzzle.

She didn't push him to give her a long hug good-bye because she knew his tender nature. He'd do it if she asked, but his sympathetic heart was better equipped to handle the moment of separation if she quietly went out the door. A hug of longing would make them both weep. In the end, staying unemotional was the better way to go.

She climbed into the car, started the engine, and cried all the way home.

Colt stared, rubbed his eyes, then peered through the first sifting snowflakes, precursors to the impending storm.

His father's SUV, the one Angelina took to the city that

morning, was traveling down the old gravel road that led up to the rustic cabin his father and uncle had used for hunting long years back. The forest on that slope had thickened over the last decade. He couldn't see the cabin from where he stood. Nor could he see any smoke that would be coming from the wood-burning stove if someone was staying there.

Why would anyone—he corrected himself—why would *Angelina* drive up to the old cabin?

The SUV slid as it turned onto the curving two-lane below. The car swerved, skidded, then straightened, but not before his heart did the very same thing.

The dark green SUV disappeared from view. If it actually was Angelina, that should put her home in about fifteen minutes. Maybe twenty with back roads already growing slick.

He turned the red gelding and scanned the thick woods again. Nothing.

But he couldn't let it go.

Working hedge funds was a lot like playing poker. A skilled player keyed in on more than the cards, and Colt was a skilled player on Wall Street. He'd developed a keen instinct for subterfuge that usually served him well in the financial markets—especially his skills in assessment of people.

Concerns about Angelina had been eating at him.

She brushed off compliments, but liked them.

She maintained a quiet profile, even when happy.

She kept an almost solemn affect, an even keel in every situation.

He'd seen guys with the same MO in downtown Manhattan. A little too careful, a touch overcautious, trying too hard to blend. But what did a Latina American housekeeper in Gray's Glen have in common with some of the more successful financiers on Wall Street?

A secret.

Why else would the beautiful housekeeper venture up the eastern slope if not to go to the empty cabin? Was she hiding something there? Someone?

Probably a boyfriend, he reasoned. *She gets to have a life, doesn't she?*

The bawl of a calf brought him back on task, but as he spurred the horse over to help Hobbs, he decided a trip to the old cabin would become a priority once the storm passed. If there was something shady going on without Sam Stafford knowing, it was up to him and Nick to check it out.

He pulled up alongside the old cowpoke, helped direct three young cows through a gate to the lower pasture, then backed up the horse to give a calf room to follow. The calf sidestepped through the gate as if dancing; unfazed by the combination of wind and cold.

Hobbs's offhand remark from the night before came back to Colt as he headed back up to lead more pregnant heifers to the accessible lower pasture. *"Too many people usin' this, that, and the other thing to mess up their brains."* Could someone be using the out-of-the-way cabin for illegal purposes? Could Angelina be involved in something like that?

The flood of drugs hadn't seemed as problematic when he was

growing up. Or maybe it was because his father kept them too busy and too tired to have much time for messing up their lives. When Trey's wife died of a drug overdose four years back, they'd faced a new reality.

Could the beautiful house manager be part of a culture that brought so many to dire straits? Surely not. And why did he hate the idea that Angelina might be involved in something clandestine? He barely knew her. But if he was honest, he'd have to admit a part of him would like to change that, maybe get to know her better—with no weaponry involved. He'd become adept at short-term relationships back east. No harm, no foul. Around here, that kind of thing wasn't the norm. Too many folks knowing too many other folks' business, with a nod toward the straight and narrow.

Colt liked his freedom, liked it just fine, thank you.

Marriage hadn't boded well for the Stafford men. Trey lost his wife to drugs, and Nick's wife ran off to be with another man. Recalling the grief of his father's two marriages, he realized the so-called sacred institution was anything but sacred in his family, and that was reason enough to avoid the state of matrimony.

<hr>

Nick needs a wife.

It took about three-point-four seconds for that news flash to smack Colt upside the head a few hours later, so his earlier conclusions bit the dust.

The sight of his two young nieces spilling into the kitchen while arguing over who should sit in the front seat of Daddy's big Ford truck spelled the solution right quick. If Nick had a wife, she'd be riding up front and the girls would be sitting peaceably in the second seat of the extended cab. End of quarrel.

"I get to sit up front on the way home." Dakota hung her jacket on one of the lower hooks inside the kitchen door and moved toward the chair next to her father's. "Daddy said I could sometimes, as long as I use my booster. So I will."

"No, you're not, Dakota. I'm older; I get first pick."

"That's not a rule!"

Cheyenne hung her jacket on the back of the chair to her father's right with a proprietary look and slid into the seat. "It should be." She picked up her napkin, snapped it with just enough vigor to make her sister unhappy, then smiled across the room at Angelina. "Supper smells divine, Angelina."

Colt watched, waiting for Angelina's smackdown. No way was she going to let the girls' snippy behavior go unchecked, not after the rolling-pin incident the previous morning. And where does an eight-year-old learn phrases like "supper smells divine"? Not in Gray's Glen, that's for sure.

"Thank you, Cheyenne. How were your dance lessons today?"

No smackdown, no warning, no . . . nothin'. Obviously snippy little girls were held to a lower standard than grown men.

Like that's a surprise? They're little kids. Cut them some slack.

The slap of conscience felt wrong and right. Colt didn't remember ever being allowed slack except with Hobbs and McMurty—the other long-established backbone of the Double S. "Murt" had retired and gotten himself married the year before, possibly not in that order, and he hadn't come around as yet. Colt would have to call him. See what was up.

Considering the girls, he wondered if maybe kids should be given some rope. Not enough to hang themselves, but enough to feel their way.

Cheyenne looked like she wanted to bark out something she might regret later, but then she paused and drew a deep breath. "Lovely, thank you."

Colt read her face about the same time she noticed him in the doorway. And when she did, she didn't look the least bit snippy or snarly. At that moment she looked like a happy-faced little girl. "Uncle Colt?"

"That's me."

"Our Uncle Colt is here?" The younger girl spun and looked at him, then her father. "This is Uncle Colt? For real?"

"The one and only," Nick told them as the other men took their places around the solid planked table. "We needed his help because Grandpa's sick. So he came all the way here from New York."

"New York." Cheyenne gazed up at him, mouth open. "Have you been to Broadway?"

"I sure have." He moved across the slate-tile floor. "I've been to Broadway and to Fifth Avenue, and I've spent a lot of time in Battery Park visiting Zelda the wild turkey."

"You what?" Her expression made him feel cut down to size, a feeling he should have grown used to on the ranch. "You visit a turkey?" She said it in a way that meant he was a few cards short of a full deck.

"We have lots of turkeys here, but I bet your turkey is the nicest." Dakota's innocent approval made Colt feel tall again.

He squatted low. "She was special because she was the only one. I liked going to visit her because it reminded me of being back here. In the hills." He smiled into a pair of innocent blue eyes. "Big cities don't have animals like you do in the country, and to have a wild turkey living in the park is a wonderful thing."

"Can you shoot 'er?" Hobbs stayed to the practical side of birds and food.

"No, Hobbs." Colt shared a look with Dakota that made her laugh. "She's like . . . a pet."

The old guy snorted as he helped himself to a plateful of food. "We're up to six weeks of spring hunting on wild birds now. They're everywhere. Just the toms, of course, but that's some mighty good eats right there."

"I don't want you to shoot your turkey, Uncle Colt." Dakota whispered the words and put a soft hand against his cheek. "It's okay to love her so much."

His heart pressed hard against his ribs. Her face, her tone, the baby-soft look of understanding she shared with him made him feel like everything could be okay.

Would it?

Time would tell.

Dakota's tiny smile of belief made him realize it could, and that was half the battle. "Would you like to sit next to me, Dakota?"

"Yes, please!"

Cheyenne pouted like she'd been bested. Colt followed

Angelina's lead and ignored the behavior, but when Cheyenne's ill-placed foot hit his shin and not her sister's, his dark look put an end to her not-so-subtle kicks.

Clearly Nick needed a wife to ride herd on these girls. Then, as the girls squabbled, he decided every kid should be an only child. He'd make note of that if the marriage bug ever hit him square in the jaw. No siblings meant less fighting at dinner. Digestion was tough enough without constant squabbles rounding the table.

For now, he settled in next to a tiny feminine person and found his dinner companion to be one of the most inviting creatures he'd shared a meal with in years, realizing that might say something about his personal choices.

As Dakota chattered on about why certain fairies turned bad, he glanced toward the kitchen and caught Angelina looking at him with approval. Without trying or wanting to, he'd scored points with the Hispanic beauty.

He had no idea what she was up to, and despite his careless handling of family matters in the recent past, protecting the Stafford legacy meant a great deal to all of them. And yet—he liked her approval. An enigma.

A slight smile quirked her cheek, and when her eyes crinkled in sweet appreciation of his easy regard for his six-year-old niece, he felt good inside. That wasn't a bad deal, as long as it didn't compromise his intentions. He'd like to figure out what was going on behind Angelina's careful facade and what Angelina was doing in the upland cabin. Once the storm was a thing of the past, he'd do just that.

chool's cancelled for at least a day," Nick announced as he came down the back steps of the sprawling house a few hours later. "Maybe two days depending on how long the cleanup takes once the storm's over."

"The girls must be thrilled." Colt withdrew his handgun and shotgun from the gun safe in his father's office and settled in to clean both. "Remember how we loved snow days? We could beat up Trey, go sledding, eat lots of food, and beat up Trey again."

"Someone had to establish pecking order," said Nick reasonably. "And they weren't real smackdowns. Were they?"

"I think they qualified."

"Well, he wouldn't take kindly to that now," Nick replied as he settled into the wide leather recliner opposite Colt. "And the girls don't care about snow days. They like school."

Shock stopped Colt's wiping. "What's wrong with them?"

"They're girls, Colt. They're different."

That made no sense, but Colt didn't have kids, so what did he know? "They're beautiful kids."

"Yep."

"And I bet they're smart."

"Real smart."

"Do they ride?"

Nick hesitated too long. "No."

Colt wiped down the gun one last time, then addressed Nick's response. "Why not?"

When Nick faltered again, Colt understood. "Whitney didn't want them to."

"She preferred to have them dance."

"So you teach them things they'll never use and avoid the useful western stuff? Even now?"

Nick's gaze went hard. "What's that mean?"

"Well . . ." Colt spoke slowly, but with conviction. "Whitney's gone. What would be wrong with the girls learning how to rope and ride now?"

"You think it's that easy? You don't understand anything."

"Which part? The wife leaving? Or raising two girls who might want to learn about the ranch but their father won't teach them?"

"You know nothing." Nick stood up, quick and hard. "You don't have kids, you've never had a wife, you've probably barely had a girl-friend for longer than a month—"

Nick was wrong. There had actually been a couple of six-month relationships in Colt's past, but he could tell by Nick's expression that he'd better back down. He did, but only because his brother had been handed a raw deal by any guy's standards. Wives walking out on husbands, children, and sprawling ranches didn't make Colt's short list. "Hey, don't be mad at me. I'm not the one who left you."

"Actually, you did," Nick retorted. "You walked away from

everything Dad built and went off to the big city to make it on your own. How's that working out for you, by the way?"

Anger claimed Colt. His neck muscles tightened. He had started to rise out of his chair when Angelina appeared behind Nick in the doorway, about the same time a wind gust announced the storm's arrival. "If you two can stop posturing long enough to be of some help, I could use the fires stoked at both ends of the house. If we lose electricity, the generator will kick in, but you both know it's better to make use of the wood stoves when we get hit hard."

Colt stood the rest of the way. "I'll take this one."

"And I'll get the north end."

"There's gas in all the generators?" Angelina looked at Nick, and he nodded.

"Checked them this afternoon. You think the hospital will be okay?" Nick asked, sounding a little worried.

That Nick would be concerned with their father's fate kind of surprised Colt. Nick and Sam worked together, but they'd always been miles apart on most everything. Maybe Nick had done some growing up in the past nine years too.

"They're secure. If the roads are cleared tomorrow, we can bring him home tomorrow night. As long as he doesn't spike a fever or anything."

"How does he look?" Colt asked.

Nick and Angelina turned toward Colt in unison. "You'd know the answer to that if you would have bothered coming home once in a while," Nick said, sounding exasperated.

Angelina seemed to consider her words carefully. "Being ill has aged him. He's a little frail now. Hopefully that will change as he heals. But there is a light in his eyes that didn't used to be there."

"A light?" Colt paused, confused. "Like . . . what, exactly?"

"Faith," Nick said. "Hard to believe, I know. He's like those field workers who showed up late and got a full day's wages. He seems sincere enough. He's even planning to go to church with us on Sundays."

"Our father?" Talk about an unexpected bend in the road. "Sam Stafford's going to church of his own accord? Will wonders never cease? Better yet, will the church survive?"

"And how often did you grace the churches of Lower Manhattan with your presence?" Angelina asked smoothly, but with enough bite to make Colt take notice. "There are churches of all kinds there, I believe?"

"Yup."

"And you went to . . . ?"

"Not a one." He half smirked because taking time out of his busy week for church had never occurred to him. Despite his mother's sweet assurances about God when he was a child, Colt had figured things out pretty quick and pretty early. You got one chance at life, one go around the big wheel of fortune, and whatever you did, you did.

Nick's expression should have warned him off, but it was too late. Angelina moved toward him, and when she narrowed her eyes, he was amazed and not a little scared at how quickly the transformation took place. "You brag about this?" She took another menacing step, encroaching on his space. He looked to Nick for help, but Nick seemed to be enjoying the turning tide. "As if turning your back on the One, the Only, the Most High is something of note, a source of pride?" She uttered something quick and sharp under her breath in Spanish, then stopped suddenly. Held up her hands. Dusted them together as if he wasn't worth the bother it took to ream him out. She looked up, met him eye to eye. Her cool, hard stare made it clear that any gains he'd made since their first face-to-shotgun meeting were now long gone. She shook her head, and her voice took on a different, flat tone. "If for any reason the generator does not kick in when we lose electricity, there are candles in your room and bath."

He started to say thank you, but her swift retreat showed no interest in his gratitude. He watched her leave, heard the firm click of her door, and turned toward Nick. "Is she always like that?"

"Tough, strong, kind, antagonistic, and brutally honest? Yes. And every time I think I'm right about something, it turns out I'm wrong. I've learned to shut up and let her take charge."

Colt wasn't any too happy as he tended the stove. It was an odd state of affairs when an outsider—and a woman at that—was taking charge around the Double S.

"And don't make the mistake of thinking you can best her just because you're a man."

Colt swung back toward Nick. "This is our ranch. Our house. Our home. I might have been gone a long while, but I'm still a Stafford. And Staffords don't take guff from the hired help."

Nick clapped him on the back. "You're in for a rude awakening, Colt. But then you never did want to learn things the easy way. I'm going to bed for a few hours. Hobbs is covering the barns right now. I'll take next shift. You take the predawn one. And yes, there's a towline rigged up in case the storm's bad. It leads to the middle barn. Set your clock for four. Will you be okay on five hours of sleep?"

He'd worked days on end and barely caught naps on his office sofa when things were hopping in the financial district, so five hours of sleep would be fine. "Which room are the girls in?"

"The first-floor wing, just below your room."

"I'll be sure not to disturb them." As he walked up the stairs, his butt ached, his back hurt, and every muscle in his body screamed rude words at being suddenly reawakened to ranch work. When he crested the stairs, he faced the big, broad lead-paned window overlooking the eastern exposure of the Double S.

Snowflakes swirled from angled dormers, mixing and mingling with wind-driven flakes. The storm careened on a wicked slant, the wind howling, the snow forming sloping drifts along the porch below him. The outdoor lights barely broke the whiteness, so there was little to see other than the storm raging beyond the layered, tempered glass.

He stared out anyway, envisioning the sprawl of land, the cowering cattle hunkered down in the back hills. He hoped they'd be all right. He knew the score; he was ranch hand enough to know animals generally did okay, but every now and again a bad storm laid claim on too many cows or pigs or horses. They'd know once the storm blew itself out. The ruggedness of the upper terrain meant they might suffer some casualties in the hills, but the animals there were the more mature, wiser cows. Most of them had been through storms before, giving them a greater chance of survival.

Despite the cool distance Sam Stafford maintained from humans, his father wouldn't wish the destruction of cattle on anyone. Each one saved was a plus that had nothing to do with money and everything to do with respecting life. On that one thing they agreed. Life should be cherished.

———— ⌇ ————

At 5:00 a.m. Colt spotted the laboring heifer's angst and grabbed his phone. He hadn't pulled a calf on his own in a lot of years, and if they had some new apparatus lying around, he didn't want to look stupid again. He hit Nick's number and was surprised when Angelina answered the phone. "I was calling Nick."

She probably knows that because you called Nick's phone, Einstein. But why was Angelina anywhere near Nick's phone? Nick had gone inside to catch a little more sleep almost an hour ago. And why does the image of Angelina with Nick unnerve you?

"His phone is with me in the kitchen."

Instant relief swept him, a ridiculous physiological response he'd examine later. He stowed the surprising emotion as Angelina continued, "Do you need help?"

"Gotta pull a calf. I know how, old style. Just wanted to make sure I was on the right track."

"I'm coming over."

Great. Now the kitchen help would boss him around in the

barn. Why had he bothered to call? Why hadn't he just gone ahead and directed the cow into the area with the pulley and helped her move this baby?

"Oh, it's Caramel."

Colt turned at the warm sound of Angelina's voice. Anticipation stirred something inside him. He carefully shut the reaction down to maintain his cool, calm facade. "You know a thousand cows?"

"I know the two hundred young ones. They've all been born since I've been here, and I've done a turn or two in the barn."

"Because?"

She moved to the sink, turned on the hot water, and lathered her hands and arms while he got some feed to coax the cow to the farthest stanchion. "I like to learn. The more helpful I can be, the better off we all are. No one needs me in the kitchen 24/7."

Colt could still taste the goodness of her soup and homemade bread, so he wasn't sure he'd agree. Kitchen talents were few and far between these days, but maybe that was a New York City thing. In any case, being at Angelina's table wasn't exactly a hardship, especially considering the rough two weeks he'd put in prior to catching that flight. A table laden with great food became a wonderful welcome home.

She moved to his side after he had the cow in place. As the cow strained mightily, he used the opportunity to lock on to the single visible foot with the obstetrical chain.

"Have you checked to make sure the head's not back?"

He tried to not take offense because the cook was questioning him as though he were a novice. "Nose forward. I think mama's overwhelmed. Baby's a little big, but positioning seems okay."

"Good."

She kept her voice soft, and Colt followed suit. She spoke words of comfort to the young cow, and when the second foot appeared, Colt looped the chain around it, well above the hock. "I'll get the puller."

"All right."

He put the apparatus in place and was able to provide gentle traction with each push from the cow.

"Caramel, he's beautiful," Angelina crooned. "You're doing so well, little mama! I am so very proud of you. Giving birth is not an easy process, and men have no idea about the truth of such words, my pretty girl."

"Says the woman with no experience," Colt grunted as he leveraged the sizable calf forward. "And how do you know it's a bull? We haven't gotten that far yet."

"The stubborn look in the eye," she whispered softly. "I could be wrong, of course. But not usually."

Her cocky attitude almost made him smile. He liked self-confidence in a person, but bossy, know-it-all women didn't appeal to him. They were growing in numbers on Wall Street, and it made for a different dynamic, not one he liked all that much. Coming home to find a similar situation in what had been a male-dominated domain seemed weird.

He returned his focus to the calf. Once he had its shoulders free, the heifer finished the job herself with one last push.

"Oh, well done, little mama, well done!" Angelina said. "He's beautiful! He's got your eyes and a red-toned coat that will most likely turn to black as he matures. Quite a beauty, I must say."

"You're talking to a cow." Colt tickled the calf's nose with a piece of straw. The calf gave a mighty sneeze, then shook his head and bawled. Colt pulled him to the far side of the birthing pen so that mama—*Caramel*—wouldn't step on him when she backed out of the head gate. He started to offer his help as Angelina unhooked the belly strap, a clever winch device that kept the cow from sitting or flopping down during a rough birth. The upright position was better for the cow and the calf when assistance was needed. But Angelina didn't need help. Murmuring soothing congratulations, she had the cow released quickly, then stepped aside, allowing the mother to acquaint herself with her newborn. She moved outside the area and watched the pair as Colt sterilized the OB chain. He finished the cleanup, then moved to her side. "Nice calf."

"Beautiful." She breathed deep as if she didn't mind the smell of cow and dung and hay and straw. "This whole thing—the flow of life and raising good food. It's marvelous. I wouldn't have thought it would be like this, but it's wonderful."

"A lot of folks would disagree these days."

She laughed. "I used to be one of them."

He turned, surprised. "A vegetarian?"

"Vegan. But in any case, I am now a total omnivore who loves to barbecue or wood-fire a steak when the weather's not foul. I look back at that twenty-two-year-old with so many goofy ideas, and I can't believe it was me."

"We all go through goofy stages growing up."

"And make our share of mistakes." Regret briefly deepened her features.

Colt had a laundry list of those himself, some more serious than others. Being on the ranch, reconnecting with old faces and friends, made him feel as if something had changed. It hadn't, of course. He was still back in Gray's Glen, a town pretty much owned and operated by Sam Stafford. But standing in the snug barn with the storm howling outside and a doe-eyed calf rooting for his first drink of life-giving milk softened something inside him.

Angelina gave the cow one last pat on her shaggy head. "Well done, my friend. Well done." She straightened and moved toward the door. "Breakfast at eight. No use feeding everyone early so they can sit around and watch the snow. And Colt?"

"Yes?"

"You didn't need help. You did fine."

He had, but as she crossed toward the door adjacent to the towline, he said, "But it was nice having you here, Angelina."

Would his words pause her?

She hesitated at the door as if she wanted to reply, and Colt marked that a victory. She thought he was a shallow, money-grubbing New York investor. Right now he felt the need to be something else. Someone else. He wasn't sure who or what, but watching Caramel give her baby a warm welcome to the planet made him feel more content than he'd been in a long time.

"I want out," Sam growled when Angelina picked up his call on the house phone midday.

Angelina tucked the phone beneath her left ear while she scraped cake batter into two nine-inch pans. "That's not the way one begins a phone call, Sam. Try this instead. 'Good morning, Angelina. It appears the snow has stopped falling. When will the roads be clear enough to pick me up and bring me home?' And in answer to that unasked question, it's not safe for people to be out right now. The snow just stopped. Perhaps by early evening."

"Too long," he retorted. "There will be chores to do around the barn and cattle to check up north. I need to be there. Not here."

"You couldn't do either even if you were home, so what's the hurry?" she asked, hoping her crusty boss would get her point. He did, but not because he wanted to.

"I miss everyone."

"Now that's an honest answer. I checked with the town highway department, and their timeline puts clear roads around four."

"What's their timeline for mostly clear roads? I want to come home, Ange."

Her heart sympathized. She'd watched Sam Stafford's transformation the past six months, and while long overdue, it seemed sincere. She hoped and prayed it stayed that way.

"How's everything on your end?" he asked.

He meant her mother and Noah. It had been Sam's idea to tuck them in the cabin across from the sprawling ranch. "Restless. Like you. And ready for winter to end so we can move on with our lives."

He grunted. "We'll have to figure something out."

"We will, Sam. It's time. We can talk about it once we have you home."

"Understood. I'll see you later. And tell the boys to drive fast."

"Promise." She hung up the phone, turned to put the cakes in the oven, and saw Colt watching her.

"My father?"

"Yes." She opened the oven door and slid the pans onto the center rack.

"How's he doing?"

Was it remorse, anger, or guilt coloring Colt's question? Probably all three, she decided. "Chomping at the bit and wishing the roads were clear so you guys could get him right now. The doctor has signed his release."

"He said that?" Nick had entered the kitchen from the other side.

"He's ready, but the roads won't be clear for four or five hours. I'll make his favorite supper, and you guys can go get him then, okay?"

Nick looked at Colt. Colt jumped into action without a word. They grabbed winter gear from the hooks by the back door and began layering up.

"What are you two clowns doing?"

"Hospital breakout."

"Rescuing the old man."

"You can't find something constructive to do for the next four hours and let the road crews do their work? What is the matter with you two?"

Colt grinned the first sincere smile she'd seen since pointing a gun at him a few days before. "Gotta cowboy up."

"I'll stow shovels in the back," Nick said.

"I'll—"

"Has either one of you thought of blankets or pillows? This is a sick man with broken ribs you're about to transport over snow-filled roads and drifts."

"A few rough patches of road might even up some of the score of forgetting he had kids for a decade or two," Colt told her as he checked his phone, then slid it back into the leather pouch on his belt. "At least he'll be home where he wants to be."

She saw nothing but honesty on his face. She thought of Noah, the light of hope and grace shining in his gaze.

She went to the downstairs linen closet and withdrew two pillows and blankets. She put them in a large plastic bag and thrust them into Colt's midsection with well-practiced force. He grunted. Good. She hadn't lost her touch. "There's time for recriminations later. You go easy and bring him back here pain free. Or at least as pain free as possible. Got it?"

Oh, Colt got it, all right. He got it enough that he was rightly tempted to toss the blankets and pillows to the floor and either argue with her about her bossiness or take her in his arms, but he had enough crazy on his plate, so he settled his best cool look her way. "Got it, boss."

She flushed.

Good.

A part of him longed to get to know her better, while another part brushed off her tough-girl ways. He must have imagined the softer side he'd glimpsed in the shadowed recesses of the calving barn. Blame it on lighting or baby cow sentiment, this woman was hobnail tough and proud of it, and that was plain irritating regardless of venue. "I'll text Hobbs. He and the guys can keep an eye on the maternity ward."

"And I'll get the SUV."

"Daddy! Where are you going?" Dakota came sliding across the long hallway floor in socks, shrieking with delight when her feet lost their grip and she had to grab the breakfast bar to keep her balance. "See? I'm ice-skating inside!"

"We can skate outside later," Colt promised. He refused to look at his brother for approval. Like it or not they had the perfect pond for skating, and everyone should learn how to skate. "Do you have skates?"

"We have a box of various sizes." Angelina said. "Some that will fit both girls, I'm sure."

"It's a date." Colt fist-bumped the little girl, then grabbed the stuffed bag and his hat. "Call us if you need anything," he said to Angelina." And we'll call you if we get stuck."

"And I'll remind you that you should have waited for the plows." She said the words simply, but Colt thought he saw a glimmer of humor in her eye. Did she approve of their rescue operation?

Maybe.

"Can I help get Grandpa's room ready?" Cheyenne asked. "And can we make him some welcome-home cards for his walls?"

"That's a lovely idea." Angelina pointed down the hall. "Gather art supplies from the closet, and you girls can decorate Grandpa's room for him. He'll love it."

Colt was almost to the door when she added that last sentence. He paused, thought about turning, then decided against it. The past was best left to molder. If his miserable, money-hungry father had turned over a new leaf and actually took time with these delightful little granddaughters, then good for them. They got something he'd never had: time with Sam Stafford.

And while he was glad for the sake of his nieces, he wasn't about to be fooled into thinking it made a difference between him and his father. They'd been at odds for as long as he could remember. For the moment they needed to form a peace bond and work together, but if Colt had his way, it wouldn't be for long. Once Sam was better and Colt was financially sound again, he'd grab the first flight east. He may have crashed and burned with the Tomkins Investments fallout, but a good fund manager diversified. Once the markets rebounded, so would his other funds, and he'd be back in the driver's seat, in Lower Manhattan, doing what he did best. Making big money.

loof, skinny, and mad.

Sam studied his firstborn son as Colt followed Nick into the hospital room. Nick had seen Sam regularly since his health problems began. Colt hadn't seen Sam in years. While he assessed Colt, he knew his oldest would return the favor and find him diminished. Would Colt feel sorry for him? Probably not, and that realization deepened Sam's regret.

"Hey." Nick strode forward and laid a gentle grip along his father's left shoulder. "You're getting sprung, huh?"

"And glad of it." He started to stand, heard the nurse grunt a warning, and sat back down. "I don't need a wheelchair, Stacey."

"You need to follow the rules, same as everyone else, Mr. Stafford. Even if your name is on the front of the new wing."

He turned back toward Colt. He wanted to stand and embrace his son, but Colt turned his attention to the nurse, nodded, and procured a wheelchair from the hall outside Sam's door. He wheeled it alongside Sam's bed. "Here you go."

He reached down as if to help Sam up. The thought of his boys having to help him into the chair made him bark. "I'm fine. Leave it."

Colt's face didn't change. His eyes stayed placid, his jaw remained easy, as though nothing Sam did affected him. It was a look

Colt perfected a long time ago. Maybe one that would never change because Sam had taken too long to realize he was a poor father and his sons deserved more. So much more. He lowered himself into the chair, breathed deep, and looked up. "I'm glad you're home."

He spoke carefully because he wasn't just glad to have Colton home; he was thrilled. Ecstatic. Proud. But if he spewed all that on his oldest boy, Colt would most likely sign the commitment papers before nightfall and have him tucked away. Sam never gushed, he rarely approved, and in the past, compliments had been nonexistent. Colt had no reason to believe that had changed. It was up to Sam to show him the difference. He reached out to touch Colt's arm, but Colt sidestepped at the exact moment. Did he do it on purpose? Sam couldn't tell.

Between Nick and Colt they had him fairly comfortable in the middle seat of the big SUV within a few minutes. Nick started the engine and hit the Bluetooth connection. He tried the ranch phone but no one answered. He left a quick message for Angelina saying they were leaving the hospital.

"Strange that she's not answering," Nick said as he put the car into gear. Colt said something softly, and Nick laughed. For just a minute, seeing them side by side, Sam went back in time to two boys, different and yet in some ways the same. Motherless waifs given to a father who took too long to understand the value of a child.

Would God give him time now?

He didn't know, but if he did have time, he had a lot of fence mending to do. He could fix fence as quickly as any hand in the fields, but he needed more practice to carry that success into his home. "They cleared the roads that fast?" he asked as they eased out of the hospital parking lot and turned left toward the highway.

"Not exactly," Nick replied. "The ambulance route was cleared, but once we're back on the two-lane, it might get a little bumpy. I'll take it easy."

"I've broken horses and raised cattle on rough terrain," Sam said. "I can take it. I'm just grateful someone came to get me. I wouldn't have been all that surprised to have been put off a while more. There's been times when our house was a sight more comfortable without me in it. I intend to change that."

Colt said nothing but seemed to ponder Sam's words. "Colt," Sam continued, determined, "I meant what I said. I'm real pleased to have you here. We need you."

Nick glanced Colt's way.

Colt didn't meet the look. He kept his eyes trained straight ahead at the snowy roads and said, "Well, good. It worked both ways."

Sam stared at the back of his son's head. He wanted to press in, explain to Colt how happy he was, how important it was to have him back, but he remembered Angelina's caution and closed his mouth. Colt needed time. He prayed he had it to give, and if he didn't, that was his fault. Before he died, he wanted his sons' forgiveness. From the stiff-necked silhouette of Colt's head, that was going to take some doing.

If Christine had lived, things would have been different. If she'd been watching him mess up from heaven, she'd be mighty ticked off.

He'd turned everything she'd believed in upside down. He'd disappointed her and God and all three of his boys, and his heart ached at the thought of all that time wasted.

"We're home. Dad?" A hand touched his shoulder, Colt's hand. "We're home."

Sam struggled upright. He must have dozed off. Confused, he looked straight into Colt's grown-up face, but in his dream Colt was a little boy, wrapped in Christine's arms as she taught him how to ride through the original front paddock. His young face, eyes wide, with a bright smile for the horse, then his mother—so proud of his accomplishments.

The grown-up version looked so different. Sad. Worn. Taciturn. Like him. It broke Sam's heart. "I was dreaming about you."

"Were you?" Colt asked smoothly, his face and tone flat, uncaring. That was Sam's fault. "Good dreams, I hope."

"Very good." Sam grasped Colt's arm and pulled himself up and out of the SUV with a short, explosive breath, then stood still until he felt steady on his feet. Colt didn't rush him. That was a gift passed on from his mother. Sam rushed everything. "You were always calm and patient with horses, like your mother."

Colt's arm stiffened. His jaw did too.

"She had you on a horse from the time you could walk, leading you, riding with you, showing you how to handle all kinds of things on all kinds of mounts."

"I don't remember anything like that."

They started forward while Nick parked the SUV. Sam continued, "Well, you were little. She rode effortlessly, as if made to ride. You get that ease in the saddle from her."

"Why the sudden change in rules?"

Sam stopped moving. "I don't understand."

Colt replied in a calm, calculated voice—a chip off the old block. "We aren't allowed to talk about my mother. You made that pretty plain when I was a kid and all her pictures disappeared. We didn't want to offend the new wife by keeping pictures of the old wife around."

So much heartache caused by a foolish man's choices. He'd remarried for all the wrong reasons, then left Rita to manage pretty much on her own while he and the men worked for total beef market domination on the ranch, then the state, and finally the country. In the end, what excuse could he make? "I was wrong, Colt. Forgive me."

"Oh. Yeah. Sure. We'll wipe out thirty years of bad feelings because you're sorry all of a sudden. Perfect."

An offhand remark like that would normally make him spit and react, but he spotted Angelina in the doorway. Her words of wisdom came back to him. *It won't be easy. He's hurt, and you hurt him. But with God's help and a hefty dose of unfamiliar humility, it can be done. He'll need patience, Sam. Which means you'll need patience as well.*

He swallowed his pride and said softly, "I'll try harder, Colton. If you give me the chance."

Colt's grip went unchanged. So did his face. Sam had no clue if his words affected his son. While Colt got his talent for working horses straight from his mother, he got his take-no-prisoners attitude from his deal-wrangling father. Climbing the mountain of anger he'd built would take work, faith, and, yeah, Angelina's advice on humility and patience.

And in the end, it might not work at all.

* * *

"Grandpa looks real tired." Dakota crawled onto Colt's lap and stared straight into his eyes after supper. "He said he's going to sleep. Is he dying?"

"Grandpa dying? Of course not," Colt sputtered. Did she know something he didn't? Had she overheard careless adults talking? And was she right? "People get sick all the time. Why would you jump straight to death?"

Her little-kid answer made perfect sense. "Well, when Stripey got sick and Daddy had her put to sleep, that meant dead," she explained in a matter-of-fact voice. "I thought if Grandpa had to be put to sleep, he might die. That's all."

"It's different with people, honey." Nick crossed the room and squatted by the foot of Colt's chair. "The kitty was old."

"Grandpa's not exactly young, Daddy." Cheyenne's eye roll called him out.

"People don't get put to sleep. That would make God sad," Angelina offered as she sat in a chair, a clutch of sewing in her hand.

"So God was happy that we put Stripey to sleep?" Dakota

looked from her to Nick, astounded. "Because I wasn't one bit happy, Daddy."

"Your grandfather is ill right now, but expected to recover." The girls both turned toward Angelina's smooth voice. "People get sick all the time, and usually the doctors can help make them better. Even though Grandpa is getting older"—she stressed the *er* ending on the adjective—"he's not old by any means. And with God, all is possible, little ones. Haven't we talked of that?"

"The doctor didn't save Stripey," declared Dakota. "And I miss my kitty."

"Me too," agreed Cheyenne.

Nick flinched. "I know. And I know I promised another kitty. I keep running out of time."

Colt started humming the chorus from "Cat's in the Cradle," the seventies ballad that chastised a man for never spending time with his son. He sang just enough of the chorus to make Nick twitch.

Angelina saved the day again as she settled into her chair. "Fortunately Callie should be delivering kittens soon, and I expect your father will give you girls pick of the litter."

"Oh, Daddy, that's so perfect! I think we should get two, don't you, Cheyenne? One for you, one for me."

"I get first pick! I'm older!"

"That's not fair, Cheyenne!" Dakota slid off Colt's lap and stood nose to nose with her sister. "I shouldn't have to always go second just because I was born second."

"It's fair."

"Is not!"

"Is—"

"Enough." Nick stood and pointed down the hall. "Bed, both of you. There'll be no more bickering about a nonexistent kitten. If you keep it up, there will be no kitten at all. And tiptoe down that hall. Your grandfather's trying to rest."

Cheyenne glared at her sister. Dakota returned the favor, but as they started down the hall, she paused, raced back, and grabbed Colt in a big kiss and hug. "G'night, Uncle Colt. Thanks for letting me sit with you."

His heart did that weird stutter step again. He returned the hug, and the feel of her little arms and soft curls made him feel like there might be sweetness and light in the world somewhere still. She was living proof, wasn't she? "Good night, honey."

"I'll see you in the morning," she whispered, "And we can talk about kittens and stuff, okay?"

He glanced at the clock and whispered back. "I'll most likely be working by the time you get up. They haven't cancelled school for tomorrow, have they?"

She looked hopefully at the wide window overlooking the broad front yard. "Maybe they will."

Colt remembered yearning for snow days. If one snow day was good, two were certain to be better, no matter how much Nick argued the opposite.

"Dakota?" Her father pointed north. "Bed."

"G'night." Head down, she trudged down the hall, not nearly as quiet as her sister. Once she'd disappeared from sight, Nick turned toward Angelina. "You set me up."

"Helped you out is what I did," she retorted. "You promised them a cat last August. It's winter, and by the time Callie's kittens are big enough to find them homes, it will be spring. Perfect timing."

Nick didn't seem all that appreciative of Angelina's so-called help. "Why is it that people with no children seem to think they have insider knowledge on how to raise children?" His frustrated look swept Colt and Angelina. "Between the two of you, it's become epidemic."

Colt started to turn but paused when he saw a shadow of regret, or maybe pain, touch Angelina's features. She blinked once, then lifted calm, cool eyes to Nick, and Colt wasn't sure he'd seen anything at all. "Are you going to refuse them a kitten?"

He sighed. "Of course not."

"Then stop complaining and go tuck them in. They are a gift from God, those two beautiful children. And to think you're standing here, all mad and cranky over a kitten when you work on a ranch — it's ridiculous."

Colt cleared his throat. He agreed completely. Then he stopped because that meant he was aligning himself with the kitchen manager's edicts. Since when did the men of the Double S need a woman to boss them around?

Hobbs whistled lightly from the back door. "Colt. I need a hand."

Colt sprang up. He wasn't used to sitting. If he had been in Manhattan right now, he'd have just finished his always-elongated work day and he'd be choosing which restaurant would get his money while he monitored markets on his phone. Here, he'd eaten over an hour ago.

Too much talk of family usually made him restless. But sitting in the big front room, talking with the girls, watching the flames of the soapstone stove flicker and swell while Angelina hummed over her fancy work, made him feel strangely peaceful.

He moved toward the door, grabbed his barn clothes, and tugged them into place. He hadn't felt peaceful in decades, and if he didn't watch his step, he'd start to reconnect to ranch hours, ranch life, and ranch people. No way was he about to let that happen.

He hustled out the door, headed for the barn, and spent the next three hours caring for young cows, one after another, as they delivered their babies. Tomorrow he and the other men would ride north into the hill country and gather all the new calves they could find. Hopefully most would be fine, but Colt knew the score when it came to bad-weather birthings. A small percentage was always lost, but by bringing the inexperienced mamas closer to the ranch, maybe they'd curtailed the damage.

And despite the fact that he wasn't at the Double S by choice and had no intention of staying, he sure hoped they had.

―――⌒⊙

"Murt!" Angelina laughed when Murt McMurty showed up at the back door the next morning. "How'd you get out of the house? I thought Annie locked up your boots and threw away the key." She hurried across the broad kitchen and hugged the former ranch manager. "Good to see you. And you're dressed for work."

"His fault." He pointed and Angelina turned to see Colt's quick smile as he entered the room. MacNaughton plaid layered over a thick black turtleneck had never looked so good before. And the thought of chaps over those stonewashed jeans made her see Colt in a whole different light all of a sudden: saddle-up ready. And smokin' hot.

Colt strode toward the smaller man and grabbed him in a hug. If Angelina hadn't sidestepped at the last moment, she'd have been included. The happiness factor between the old man and Colt added poignancy to the gesture. She hadn't glimpsed anything like this when Colt accompanied his father into the grand house the previous day, but joy and respect brightened Colt Stafford's face when he embraced Murt. "You came."

"'Course I did. As if I'd ignore a request from you, kid." Murt jabbed Colt in the ribs, and Colt pretended to wince. "We're ridin' into the hills, I expect."

"Think your heart can take it?" Humor took the sting out of Colt's barb.

"This ticker's handled bein' a married man for near eighteen months now. I suppose it's got spunk enough to hunt up a few cows in the snow."

"Murt." Nick came into the kitchen from one direction as Hobbs and Brock entered through the back door. "You joining us?"

"Appears so."

"Perfect." Nick turned Colt's way and didn't look nearly as happy. "I've been trying to get him back here for months. Must be the power of the prodigal."

Colt didn't rise to the challenge in Nick's voice. He wrapped an arm around the older man's shoulders in an easy gesture of love and respect. "He just wants to see me land my duff in a fair share of snow drifts. Too much city sittin'—Murt's looking for a laugh."

"You betcha," the old man said as he took his place at the table. "Brought my camera phone 'long so's I could record the show. Nick, how're them girls doin'? You ready for me to start their ridin' and ropin' lessons? I got time this spring. Nothin' but time, good Lord willin'."

Nick glanced from Colt to Murt, then back, but Colt was busy filling his plate with fried potatoes, fresh-cooked sausage, and scrambled eggs. "They're pretty busy, Murt."

Angelina made a noise of disagreement in the kitchen, just loud enough for the men to hear.

Nick ignored her and kept his attention trained on Murt. "Riding and roping and jumping are dangerous sports. Dancing is a more controlled environment."

"Do they get a say in this matter?" Colt asked.

Angelina kept her hand near the rolling pin, just in case.

Nick's posture went tighter. Straighter. "I'm their father, so no. They don't. Once you have kids, you realize you bear a great responsibility for their safety and well-being. Which means what I say goes."

"Knowledge is the best safety harness in the world," returned Murt as he filled his plate. "You take a greenie and let them try their hand without learnin', well, then, you're askin' for trouble. But you teach someone the lay of the land and the tricks of the trade so they know exactly how to do it right, then you've not only kept 'em safe but you've given 'em a skill besides."

Hobbs broke in. "At some point you're gonna need to transfer the business or sell, and right now, your girls are the only young'uns you got. Sellin' this place to outsiders means a whole lot of somethin', don't it? Not that I'll most likely be around to see it, but it took a long time and a lot of doin' to build a place like this. Takes a bit of fore-sight to manage it into the future, I expect."

"We've got a few years to figure it out." Nick smacked his plate onto the table loud enough to wake the dead, which meant the two little girls and his sick father down the hall might have been roused for the day. "This is Dad's place. Not mine. That means I've got no say in the matter anyway."

" 'Cept with those girls," Murt repeated in an easy, reasonable tone. "No need to fuss on it now. We've got a heck of a workload ahead of us, and I'm anxious to get some leather under my seat for a change. We can talk again once the weather goes soft."

Nick didn't reply, but Angelina saw Colt's quick look of approval from behind Nick's shoulder as Colt settled in to eat his breakfast. She wondered if he'd called the old guy in purposely to wear Nick down and let those girls grow up like proper ranch daughters. Colt began to eat, eyes down, allowing the conversation of others to make his point.

Clever. Smart. She'd heard he had foresight that served him well in finance and equities and all the things money movers did in Lower Manhattan. But she hadn't realized how intuitive he'd be, which meant she'd need to be especially careful around this oldest Stafford son. She'd let her guard down in Seattle, but part of that was her fault. She'd let the glitz of dating a power-loving, wealthy man tempt her. The consequences of her actions, and his, matured her.

Colt reached out, gripped his stoneware mug with two strong hands, and raised his coffee at the same time he lifted his eyes to hers. Instant attraction flared again. She held his gaze, saw one eyebrow twitch in recognition, and waited to let him break the look.

He didn't, so she had to, which meant he won that round. While that was infuriating, it was intriguing too. Except she couldn't let Colt Stafford intrigue her. Given a chance, he'd be out of here quickly. And after Tony's phone call, who knew where she'd be in a few months' time? Her mother was anxious to return to Seattle, and while Angelina's heart yearned for the wide open spaces and sweet peace of central Washington, her head missed the challenge of police work. The uniform called to her. Like father, like daughter.

She chanced a glance toward Colt.

He was studying her, questions lurking behind the intensity of his look. She had questions too. She'd run out of easy answers when her child's father abandoned her and her own father was gunned down while walking the dog on a rain-soaked afternoon.

Once the men were out the door, she placed a quick call to her mother. "How is everything over there? Are you both all right? You're warm enough?" Sam had installed a heating system so they wouldn't have to use the wood stove with its telltale smoke rising in the air. She bet a strong west wind made the thought of a cozy fire tempting. Fortunately, her mother wore self-discipline like a coat of armor.

Isabo's yawn echoed through the phone. "We are tired. Noah did not sleep well with the storm and his congestion. If one did not wake him, the other did."

"I'm sorry, Mami. Is he all right, though? Is it just a cold or should he be seen?"

"A cold," she replied. "He is fine, just stuffy and a little whiny. If the wind dies down, I will take him to sled on the back hill. At least that will get us out of this small house."

"I hear you, Mami. We'll change things soon. Winter can't last forever." She heard the chatter of little girl voices from down the hall. "I have to go. I'll call back once Sam is up and settled. And I'll try to visit later. If not today, then tomorrow for sure."

"We will wait for your company, then. Go with God, my daughter."

She was trying, but God's directives seemed pretty confusing of late. "You too."

Dakota was first down the hall, no surprise there. "Is Uncle Colt gone already? I wanted to kiss him good morning!"

"When calves are dropping you've got to get up earlier than this to wish the men a good day. They've got to go uphill at first light. Before that they have to check the cows in the barn, saddle the horses, and warm up the four-wheelers."

"I want to do that someday." Cheyenne came into the kitchen in a more sedate fashion, which made her observation more ironic. "I think I'd be good with cows and calves when I'm older. Don't you, Angelina?"

Angelina looked directly at her. "You can be wonderful at everything you do, Cheyenne—which should include schoolwork."

Cheyenne flushed because they both knew she'd been ignoring her teacher's directives.

"As far as the ranch goes, you have the easygoing temperament that works well around animals."

"I practice sometimes."

Angelina listened carefully but kept her face matter-of-fact. "Oh?"

"When Dad doesn't know. I go out to the barn and pretend to know how to handle the cows and the feed and the babies."

"The barn can be a dangerous place." Angelina set a plate of sausage links down in front of the girls next to one of freshly scrambled eggs. She kept her voice nonconfrontational to encourage Cheyenne's confession. "And children should never go inside on their own."

"Well, if I wait for my father to take me, I'll never get to go, so I don't see an answer there," the girl replied sensibly in a more adult tone than most kids twice her age used. "Half of my friends ride. The other half are townies, and they don't know a thing about ranching. When I get invited to the other ranches, I make up an excuse why I can't go, because if they want to ride around a paddock or go on a trail ride, they'll know I'm a greenhorn. That's so embarrassing when you're almost nine years old."

Angelina appreciated the carefulness of Cheyenne's confession. The girl was right. At her age she was years behind the other kids in ranch skills. Ranchers' kids rode herd. They worked crops. They learned the basics early on, often in the arms of their parents.

"Daddy said you should never go into the barn without him," Dakota said.

"You're six. Things are different when you're six." Cheyenne used her haughty big-sister voice that set Dakota off on a regular basis.

"I'm almost seven and at least I listen to Daddy!"

Cheyenne's quiet shrug added a calm measure of insult. Dakota's eyes went wide, and before the first-grader went into a complete histrionic meltdown, Angelina tapped the breakfast bar in front of them. "Hush, both of you. Grandpa needs his rest, and there's no reason for sisters to be so quarrelsome. You should respect one another."

Cheyenne said nothing. Eyes on her plate, she picked at her food.

Dakota frowned, then brightened. "Maybe Uncle Colt will teach us to ride."

Cheyenne perked up instantly. "You think he would?"

"Maybe. He thinks we should learn to ride," Dakota reasoned in her more singsong fashion. "So why wouldn't he teach us?"

"Because your father must first say it's all right." Angelina leaned down and trained a firm look on each girl in turn. "Don't go getting your uncle into trouble with your father. They've got enough to sort out."

"Let me get better enough, and I'll run you gals through the paces," Sam announced in a take-charge voice as he stood in the doorway.

"Oh, *madre mia!* That's all we need. The grandfather with broken ribs and failing organs to give riding lessons to two little girls who need to brush their teeth and get their coats on so I can take them down to the bus. Hustle, ladies."

Dakota slid off the high stool, hugged her grandfather's legs, then hurried off to the nearby bathroom to brush her teeth. Cheyenne hung back, looking up at her grandfather. "Would you really teach me? So I know how to ride and take care of a horse?"

Angelina cleared her throat in warning, but Sam was a Stafford, so warnings didn't mean all that much. "I sure will. I'll talk to your father. He'll be fine with it. Just let me get better, okay?"

Cheyenne released her breath in a rush, then hugged him tight. Too tight, from the grimace of pain that crossed his face, but he remained stoic as he returned the embrace. "I love you, Grandpa!"

His face transformed. His eyes glistened.

"Cheyenne?" Angelina tapped her watch. "Bus."

"Okay!" She hurried down the hall to get ready.

Angelina looked at Sam. "Nick's going to kill you."

"I'll appeal to his common sense."

"He has none when it comes to this."

"Time he learned, I expect."

"I thought you weren't going to start trouble anymore. I believe you promised to respect your sons' wishes and choices."

"When they make sense. This doesn't. He let Whitney decide that the girls should take on more feminine activities. Well, look where that got us."

"Sam."

He ignored her tone, lowered himself onto a chair, then gingerly felt his chest. "I think it's easing up some."

"You better be sure of it before you take on Nick and those riding lessons."

He acquiesced. "Good point. Did I hear Murt out here?"

"Colt's doing."

"That's Colt in a nutshell. A step ahead of a game he's not sup-posed to be playing. When the girls get on the bus, we should talk about the situation in the cabin."

"You're right. I've been putting it off and that seems weak."

"There's nothing weak about you and nothing wrong with a woman protecting her family." Sam hushed when the girls came back down the hall to grab their jackets from the lower hooks.

"Thank you, Sam." Angelina pulled on her fleece-lined coat and hat, then grabbed the car keys. "Let me get the girls to the bus and we'll talk. First, take your pills. Doctor's orders."

"An annoying bunch of know-it-alls." Sam scowled but downed the pills with a glass of water. As the girls hurried through the door, Angelina slid a mug of fresh coffee his way. He smiled, sniffed, and smiled again. "I missed this, Angelina. Nothing like this at Slater Memorial."

"I'll get you breakfast when I come back in. Rest."

"I've been resting," he retorted as he stood carefully. "Doc says I need to move, so that's an order I can work with. Putting eggs on a plate isn't all that taxing."

She touched his hand. "Good point. And I'll try not to baby you too much, but it's important that we take care of you."

"Thank you." Gratitude laced his words, a much-needed new step for the Stafford patriarch. "We're lucky to have you."

"Blessed," she corrected him lightly. "Luck had nothing to do with my arrival, and no matter what happens now, I'm putting it in God's hands. He's served us well so far."

Sam didn't argue. "I'll see you in a few minutes."

"Will do."

By the time she got back up the driveway, Sam was dressed. He poured himself a second cup of coffee and indicated the chair next to him. "Fill me in."

"I've gotten a roundabout offer from Seattle."

"It's either an offer or it isn't," Sam grumbled. "And why you think going back there is a good idea is beyond me."

"It's not the place." She covered his hand with hers, and the feel of his thinning skin was cause for concern. "I love it here. And the thought of raising Noah here is so very tempting, but I have my mother to consider. My son and I are all she has. I have to consider not only my wishes, but hers."

"You're not just a housekeeper here, you know." Sam pronounced the edict as if increasing her job responsibilities made everything better, and in his world, it probably did. "You're like a house manager. And maybe Isabo could learn to like Gray's Glen if she wasn't stuck in the woods like a hermit."

She laughed. "Semantics, my friend. And don't get me wrong, running this place isn't a cakewalk. We both know that. But I miss being on the force. Being part of a team, combining forces for truth, justice, and the American way. And my mother is missing her friends and her life in the city. Being where she and my father lived a good life. I have to be fair to her."

"I hear what you're saying." His thoughtful tone was quite

removed from his normal hard-core demeanor. "I wish I'd put family first long ago. I didn't, and there's the devil's own to pay for it now. But there's no place like these hills to raise kids, Angelina." He hesitated, glancing at his mug, then back up at her. "And I don't want you to go."

"Well, it's only an idea at the moment. You opened your home and your heart to me when I showed up here, and I won't ever forget that." She smiled when he covered her hand with his. "When I left the force, I wasn't seeing clearly. I had a baby and a widowed mother, two game changers. There were too many things going on, too many emotions. All I could see were images of my father, bleeding in the street, with no one around to hold him or care for him. A man who took care of so many died alone. How could I risk a similar end for my mother or my son? I didn't know how to deal with that, so I ran scared."

Sam gave her hand one last squeeze and stood. "Scared? Or smart? There's a reason God gave us fear and intuition, and it's not stupid to pay attention." He set his mug on the breakfast bar as the kitchen phone rang. "I'm going to rest a bit. And pray that you stay here. Selfish or not, that's what I'm aiming for."

His honesty was touching but did nothing to ease her choices. "I'm glad you're willing to rest. It's about time." She saw the neighbor's name on the phone display and said, "I need to get this."

He nodded and shuffled in the direction of his room. She took a calming breath before answering the phone. "Lucy, how's Belle? Is she doing better?"

"She is. I wanted to thank you again for your help."

"It was nothing. I was glad to do it. How's the van?"

"In the shop. Sal's working on it, then dropping it off here later today. It's got issues, some major, some less than major. I'm hoping a few Band-Aids and duct tape will keep it on the road for another year."

"Ouch." The comparison between the ranch and their neighbors hit Angelina square. The ranch had a fleet of vehicles while Lucy scraped by trying to keep one old rust-bucket van on the road. "Lucy, I was just about to go to town. Do you need anything?"

"I hate to ask, but yes."

"Give me a list," Angelina told her. "I'll grab whatever you need."

"Thank you, Angelina. I'm so glad you're nearby."

"Me too."

She jotted down the few items Lucy named and figured if a few extra things found their way into Lucy's bags, that wouldn't be a bad thing.

She ignored the kitchen mess and scribbled Sam a note to let him know where she was going. Helping Lucy was the kind of thing neighbors were supposed to do. She loved that about Kittitas County. When she got back she'd clean the kitchen, make beds, scrub toilets, and see to the laundry while cooking and baking.

Tomorrow you can do it all again. And again the next day. And the next . . .

She clamped down on the pity party, recognizing the source of her unrest. She loved Sam, she loved the ranch, but she missed the challenge of putting her hard-won skills to work. Her mother's unhappiness added guilt to the increasing load. She needed to fix things, but what should she do? What choice should she make?

"I will say of the LORD, He is my refuge and my fortress: my God; in him will I trust."

The psalm offered lyrical cadence of sweet belief, but lately she had a hard time taking her own oft-given advice: let go and let God prevail. Did that make her a phony? Or just confused?

Confused and impatient she decided as she swung by Wandy Schirtz's free library to donate a stack of books. Determined to contain her negative emotions, she picked up tractor parts from the farm-supply store close to I-90, Sam's new prescriptions from the drugstore, and the groceries for Lucy from Super 1 Foods. When each stop took longer than expected, she realized she wouldn't have time to see Noah today, but tomorrow she would put ranch things on hold and spend time with her son. She held back aching tears. Each day she didn't see her son was a day lost. There were so few days of childhood, and she was missing so many.

Right now tomorrow seemed like a long time away.

olt's cell phone vibrated as he reached for his thermos midday. He ducked behind a thick swell of Scotch broom, checked the display, and answered. "Hey, Jake. What's up? Did you find anything?" He'd sent a Manhattan detective friend info on Angelina from his father's files. He hoped the search hadn't turned up anything bad. Despite the animosities between him and his father, protecting Sam—and the Double S—were important.

"You secure?"

Colt glanced around the snow-filled hillside. "About as secure as a body could ever be."

"Your housekeeper is a Seattle detective."

Colt was about to sip coffee. He didn't. "Go on."

"Mary Angela Castiglione was a decorated, highly respected Seattle cop who became a detective. They used her as a hostage negotiator when they needed a woman's touch. She helped bring down some major players in the PNW drug networks. She went off the radar after her father was gunned down while walking the family dog. Father was a retired SPD captain, on the force for nearly thirty years."

"She left the force of her own accord?"

"After his funeral, yes."

"Was the killing retaliatory? Did they kill him to get to her?" It sounded like a TV crime drama put that way, but anyone working Wall Street understood the possible fallout of high-stakes games. Money and power acted as destabilizers on both sides of the law. He also understood the sudden, instant loss of someone you loved. Never far from his memory was that one last kiss and promise to his beautiful mother, a pledge that he'd try new things. And then she was gone.

"I don't have those details, but the killer was caught and sentenced to life in prison. Still, enough to shake someone up. Hey, listen, I've gotta go. I'll send the info to your e-mail."

"Thanks, man. I owe you."

"I'll collect as needed. Bye."

Colt slipped the phone into the leather pouch attached to his belt, gulped his coffee, and tightened the lid to his thermos. He climbed back on the horse and moved through the invasive brush. As he scouted for calves, his mind circled the information. Angelina was a cop, and not just any cop. She was a decorated detective. So why had she been washing dishes at the Double S for two years?

He thrust aside old animosities toward his father. Sam wasn't elderly, but he was compromised with his health conditions. If Angelina was here to take advantage of that, Colt would find out why. Unless she was here to investigate Sam and the Double S? But that didn't make sense for the length of time she'd been there.

He skipped dinner that night and grabbed a sandwich instead, which he ate in the barn. He didn't want to sit in the kitchen watching Angelina—or Mary or whoever she was—play her part with

Tony Award–winning skills. It was better to keep a low profile while he assessed the information.

He guided two calves into the world, and when he finally trudged back to the house at eight thirty, the only person still moving around was Angelina. She sat upright at the kitchen table, scribbling things into a small notebook, which she flipped shut when he came into the room. "A long day," she said.

It had been, so he might as well admit it. "My brain is used to it. My body? Not so much. But it's getting there."

"Ranching is certainly more physical than what you're used to." She tapped her pen against the cardboard cover of the notebook. "Nick said you found as many calves as he did and only two less than Murt."

"The old guy's still got the touch."

Her smile made him long to sink into the chair next to her and ask for an explanation, but he'd been privy to good acting in New York. Angelina's housekeeping gig seemed natural and unscripted, which meant she was good at improvisation. But Colt was in no mood to be played after falling victim to Tomkins Investments' well-orchestrated scheme. "Nick took the girls home," he said, grasping at something to talk about.

"Yes, but not before Dakota left you this." She pointed to the countertop. A construction paper card had his name scrawled on the front, along with a really bad image of a cowboy. He flipped the card open and sighed. "I love you, Uncle Colt!"

Just that, a sweet, simple message. As far as he knew, no one made her write it. The kid had done it of her own accord, and that sent another spiral of warmth through him. If no other good came out of his forced homecoming, getting to know his nieces was a—

He paused before he thought the word *blessing.* He studied Angelina. She was living a lie while tossing out little God phrases like a parochial school teacher. He studied her for long seconds, wondering what parts were real and which were staged, but when she lifted her eyes to his, the direction of his thoughts veered sharply.

Soulful eyes, deep gray brown. Black lashes, thick and long. Sculpted brows, quick to arch. Her bronze-and-cream skin tone set off her features. Even though she wore loose-fitting pants and sweaters around the ranch, the way she moved in them was pure woman.

She watched him watching her, then calmly picked up her notebook and stood. "I think I'll sew for a little bit before bed. Goodnight, Colt."

Sewing. Cooking. Cleaning. Teaching grown men and little girls to mind their manners. She played the part to the hilt, and Colt wished she wasn't so believable. No one could live a lie this well and not be well practiced. The truth in that disappointed him.

The silence of the great house surrounded him as he walked down the hall. He didn't move through these rooms with any sweet nostalgia. He didn't glance at an extra-wide chair and remember warm nights by the fire, listening to stories, or being tucked into bed by anyone, ever. But as he passed by the great room, the heat of the soapstone stove made him envision what this house could have been, if only his mother had lived.

But she hadn't. The empty years that followed her death left him hollow hearted. He went up the stairs, wishing life was easy, wondering what kind of folk lived greeting-card lives. When he looked deep into Angelina's eyes, a longing for that kind of existence rose within him. But the cards were as fake as Angelina's facade, and Colt had lived reality for as long as he could remember. He didn't like it much then. He liked it less now.

In the privacy of his room, he opened his laptop, entered the password, and brought up his e-mail account. There it was, as Jake promised. Not much more than what the Manhattan detective had already revealed, but one new sentence jumped out at Colt. "Nearest relations, mother, Isabo Castiglione, age 55, son, Noah Martín Castiglione, infant."

A child.

Angelina had a child.

Suddenly her cryptic comments about pregnancy and her empathy with calving cows became clear. And so did something else. She hadn't come inland because she was hiding *something*. She was hiding *someone*—her child—following her father's murder. And for whatever reason, Colt suspected, the boy must be living in the cabin on the far side of the ranch.

Colt closed down the computer as a surge of western values reclaimed him. No matter who Angelina was, she and her kid deserved at least a chance at normalcy. And Colt Stafford was going to make sure they got it.

Angelina called Sam from the car once she'd picked up supplies the next morning. "I've got one more stop to make, then I'll be home. How's everything there? You're feeling all right?"

"I'm fine, just annoyed at what I can't do, and that's my own fault."

"No argument there. I should be back in ninety minutes or so. Can you turn the oven down to 250 degrees in about thirty minutes? I want the pork to simmer all day."

"I will. You got a call from someone named Lucy."

"She's your neighbor, Sam. It would behoove you to know this."

"I'm new at this stuff."

"Then practice harder. What did Lucy want?"

"I didn't answer it."

She sighed out loud on purpose. "Why not?"

"Because I only answer my phone. The house phone is your domain."

"*¡Es el colmo!* There's no reason for you to not answer the phone. It's your house and your phone, I believe. I'm but a hired hand. If you truly want to be nicer to people, you need to come off your high horse and meet them at their level."

His burst of laughter said he was messing with her. "This Carlton woman is dropping off a cake to say thank you for helping her."

"Perfect. Dessert tonight. Answer the door when she comes, don't scare her, and say thank you."

"Fine," he said in a teasing tone.

She set her phone on the console next to her. The thought that Sam was feeling better and joking around eased one concern. For

Sam Stafford to repair the damage he'd done to his sons, he needed to live awhile longer. Brokenhearted little boys needed tender loving care, and it was up to Sam to make sure they got it, even if they were full-grown men now.

She parked the car beneath the shelter of tall, broad evergreens outside the cabin. She climbed out and stood straight and still, letting her ears and eyes work the area. All seemed calm.

She withdrew two sacks of groceries and walked up to the cabin door. She knocked lightly, and her mother opened the door almost instantly. "I am glad you've come! My beloved grandson has been missing his mother even more this day than usual!"

"Then it's good I'm here." Angelina flashed a bright smile as Noah raced toward her. She dropped the sacks of food and went down on one knee to scoop him up.

"I missed you so much!" Noah clung to her neck in a grip that said he never wanted to let go. "I kept watching the snow and the clock and the snow and the clock and it took so much time. And 'Buela kept saying, 'She will be here, I promise you!'"

"And 'Buela was correct, it seems," Isabo said as she lifted the bags of food. "'Buelas are very smart. This is good to remember at all times."

Noah nodded earnestly. "I am glad you are smart, 'Buela."

Angelina carried him into the warm, small living room and curled into the corner of the comfortable couch. "Did you like the storm?"

He shook his head vigorously.

"You didn't like it?" Angelina pressed. "But it was so pretty and wild and fun, the snow flying every which way and the trees bending and swaying."

"I would have liked it if we were together." He whispered the words against her neck. Realization swept her. Noah experienced few of life's changing moments with his mother. While he loved his grandmother, he was old enough to lament how things could be.

"We'll do many things together. I promise."

He lifted his face away from her neck, his expression one of innocent resignation. She'd made that pledge before, but he didn't call her on it, and that made it worse.

"Did you make pictures of the snow? Did you go sledding with 'Buela?"

That brightened his face. "I did!" He scrambled down from her lap, started to race across the floor, then stopped cold when a sharp knock sounded at the cabin door.

Angelina's heart froze, but her body had no such luxury. Waving her mother to grab Noah, she withdrew her gun from her back waistband, dropped low, and crept toward the window.

Noah started to speak. She turned and put a quick finger to her mouth to hush him.

His bright expression had turned to fear. Eyes wide, he obeyed, then buried his head against Isabo's shoulder.

Compromised.

As a cop and a hostage negotiator, she understood the gravity of a mother and child in a dangerous situation. The most devastating way to hurt a parent was to threaten her child—which was exactly why she'd moved inland and tucked Noah and her mother away. If her father's killers wanted further revenge, she wanted the defensive edge. She breathed deep, crept to the side of the window, gun raised, and peeked around the corner of the curtain.

Colt Stafford's sharp-eyed gaze met hers. She'd seen pictures of ornery bears that looked friendlier than Sam Stafford's son at this instant. She went to the door and pulled it open.

"Mama?" Noah said.

Noah's voice caught Colt's attention. He studied the cabin, then her, then back behind her again. He strode through the door, pushed it shut against the cold wind, turned, folded his arms, and took a deep breath. "Pack your things."

Angelina wanted to yell. She wanted to rant and rave and tell him he had no cause to throw his weight around like this. But if the situation were reversed and some stranger seemed to be taking advantage of her mother, she'd do the exact same thing. But where would they go? What would they do?

Her brain scrambled for answers, then got even more confused when Colt shucked off his jacket, kicked off his boots, and dropped to the braided rug on the worn cabin floor. "Are these your cars?" He held up an ATV-styled model car and a muscled GTO to Noah. "I used to have races all around the house when I was a kid. Do you race these?"

Noah peeked down from Isabo's embrace. He stared at Colt, mute.

"He's not used to strangers," Angelina began, but stopped when Colt raised those blue eyes up to her.

"Which is why we're moving him and your mother." He looked

at Isabo, raising a hand in greeting. "Mrs. Castiglione, I'm Colt Stafford. Sam's oldest son."

"You know?" Angelina realized she was still holding her weapon. She double-checked the safety and tucked the Glock into the back of her waistband, where it would come in useful if she needed to murder a certain Stafford male. "How?"

"You've got connections. So do I. But we can talk about all that later, because right now we need to get this boy and his grandma—"

"Abuela," Noah whispered.

Colt smiled broadly at the boy's contribution to the conversation. "Abuela," Colt corrected himself. "What's your name, little guy?"

"Noah." The three-year-old breathed the word as if testing new waters.

"Well, Noah, how would you like to come live in the big house with your mom?"

Noah's eyes widened and the volume of his voice increased. "I can?"

"Yup."

"Colt, I—"

He turned toward her, a mix of emotions on his face. She'd surprised him. Well, he surprised her too, so the feeling was mutual.

But then he furthered the surprise and the softening of her heart when he said, "A boy should never have to live without his mother. Not if there's another choice, Angelina."

In his expression and his words, she glimpsed the real Colt Stafford. She saw the scarred child within the grown man. Didn't anyone see Colt that way after he lost his mother? Who had held the little boy who missed his mother? Who rocked him and cried with him at the gravesite in Grace of God Community Cemetery?

She was sure no one had.

She could tell by the lift of his chin that he was determined to get his way on this, and, given time, maybe on other things too. The thought of that warmed her from within, a tiny flame, ignited by Colt's strong demeanor and wounded soul—a precarious combination. She recognized the mix of emotions and appreciated them. "Mami?" Angelina turned toward her mother.

"Yes?" Isabo moved forward, and while her attention was trained on Angelina, her posture said she was keeping a firm eye on the man who had just offered hope out of their shadowed existence.

"Let's pack."

Excitement brightened her mother's face for the first time in two long years.

Colt chugged a team of SUVs over the carpet at a snail's pace. Noah slipped down from his grandmother's arms and took a place on the floor, opposite Colt. He looked at Colt with disbelief and scoffed his lame efforts. "I th-think when I work on the ranch some-day, my four-wheelers will go much faster. Like th-this!" He screeched a four-wheeler along the nubbed rolls of the carpet weave. As his vehicle banked a sharp turn around a couch leg, Colt looked up at the women. "We'll be fine."

Looking down at him, Angelina believed the words for the first time in years. And it felt wonderful.

As the SUV bearing Angelina's family and their necessities pulled away, Colt mounted his horse and called Nick on his cell phone. "We've got a new situation at home. I mean at the house."

Nick sighed. "You might not like to admit it, but it's still home. Get to the point."

"Two new occupants. I'll explain when we're done moving them in. Then I'll rejoin you shortly."

"No need. It'll be too dark soon. But if you can take barn duty later, that's a help. You gonna tell me who's moving in?"

"Angelina's mother and son."

Nick paused. "Well, then. I'll see you at the barns."

"I'm on it."

He directed the horse down the hill and through the fields. Angelina would have to take the long way around, so his beeline riding Yesterday's News got him into the ranch yard ahead of her. He finished taking care of the big, red horse as the SUV circled around to the kitchen entrance. He crossed the broad, stony yard to the house. Just as he reached for the door, it opened from within. His father met his eyes, then saw Angelina, her mother, and the boy climbing out of the SUV. Sam's lack of surprise said a lot. He stepped aside. As Angelina's mother and son moved toward the door, Sam smiled down at the boy, and a quick memory took Colt by surprise.

"Daddy, look! Do you see what I can do?" He was seated on the front of a horse, calling to his father from the other side of a paddock. Firm, gentle hands snugged him from behind.

"I'll be right there, Son."

"Now, Sam." He remembered his mother's voice as she spoke

clearly behind him, a memory that had been muted decades ago. *"Life only gives so many moments. Come see what our son can do."*

Colt waited outside the house, conflicted. What had spurred the memory? Had his father's words about his mother brought it back to life? By Sam openly talking about her, was Colt allowing himself to remember? Or was it being back at the ranch, surrounded by the good and bad of time gone by?

"You are Angelina's mother," Sam said.

Colt watched as his father grasped the woman's hand. She met Sam's look with quiet dignity. "I am."

"Welcome to the Double S."

"We thank you for your long-term hospitality," she said. She started to set down a stack of items, but Sam motioned her toward the stairs.

"Turn left at the top of the stairs. There are two spare rooms there and an extra room over the garage. Make yourself at home. Please." He added the last as if unpracticed, and Colt knew the truth in that.

"This is a very big house," Noah whispered. He squeezed against his mother's leg. "I don't think I've ever been in a very big house before."

Colt bent and held out his arms. "Come here. Your mom and I can show you around."

Colt wasn't sure Noah would accept the invitation, but he did. He allowed Colt to pick him up, and the child relaxed against him. Angelina raised her eyebrows in surprise.

Noah glanced around from his new, higher vantage point and said, "Come on, Mommy!"

Angelina wavered at the entrance to the house. "I must get things from the car."

"I'll see to it in a minute." Colt tilted his head toward the inside. "Let's give him a few minutes to tour, then I'll bring things in before I head to the barn."

Her eyes questioned his. While he had no answers, he knew they'd done the right thing. Whatever was going on, nothing should keep a boy from his mother's arms.

He led the way as they explored the house room by room. Noah's eyes grew wide, then wider. His nose started running, and when Angelina leaned forward with a wad of tissues, the scent of her long dark hair wafted through the thin space between them.

Cinnamon and vanilla again, maybe amaretto too. A sweet aroma, enticing. But Colt couldn't afford to be enticed or coerced or tempted. Too many questions surrounded this circumstance, and once the boy was safely tucked in bed that night?

He was determined to have answers.

Angelina knew the sudden appearance of her mother and an unmentioned preschooler would raise questions.

What would the men think when they came down from the hills? They had always treated her with respect, but that was when they thought she was honest and straightforward. Things had changed. While she didn't want to be concerned, she was. The respect of her fellow officers in Seattle had meant a lot to her. It was the same here. Would her hard-earned trust vanish? How would they see her now as a mother of a child out of wedlock?

"You are worried," her mother noted while Noah took his first nap in the big bed upstairs.

Angelina finished coating the chicken. She didn't look up as Isabo moved to peel a sink full of potatoes. "Worried? No. Concerned? Yes."

Angelina knew by Isabo's grunt that she didn't buy it. "You've kept secrets and you're wondering what others will think. I will tell you what they will think—that you are a brave woman unafraid to put your family ahead of career."

"Or that I ran, afraid."

"God warned us to fear evil. He also promised his protection. So perhaps this oldest son came home for more than one reason."

"Having a major hedge fund fall apart and a significant Wall Street collapse aren't enough?"

Her mother's expression stayed calm. "I see what I see. I am glad he noticed and glad he made a move, for he is right. An abuela is a wonderful thing, but no child should live without his mother. Colt knows this."

"And now you're on a first-name basis?" Angelina sent her mother a wry look, then went back to the original, much safer topic. "I'm still trying to adjust to this new normal. A little numb with disbelief that you're both here."

"I am not numb; I am overjoyed!" Isabo plunked some of the potatoes into the water with zeal. "To have space to move, people to see. Who knew what a luxury it is to live in freedom until it is taken away?" The peeler flew in practiced speed over the next handful. "I'll cook the potatoes and start the salad."

"I could get used to having help in this kitchen."

"This kitchen, this house, this land are pure amazement," Isabo declared. "So much to see. The barns, the stock, the hills and trees. God's bounty has blessed this place, Angelina. But I have a kitchen of my own, of course, back in the city. One we must not forget."

"Can we let the dust of this move settle before we plan the next?" Angelina asked. "You've seen Sam and you understand how busy we are here for the next several months. I can't leave him in a lurch."

To her relief, Isabo agreed. "You are right. And it is not as if my life in Seattle would ever be the same, on my own." She swept the wide kitchen window a look of appreciation. "It is not exactly a hardship to live surrounded by such beauty." Her mother peeled with newfound vigor. "And such a larder of food, a cook's dream! This is like cooking for the mission in West Seattle." She peeled another potato before getting back to Colt. "This oldest son. The one who has just come back?"

Watch yourself. Your mother is keen on detail, a trait she passed on to you. "Yes?"

"He sees much."

"Yes."

"He figured out in days what others have not seen in years."

Angelina had realized that too. "He's intuitive."

"It is not intuition that stirs the look in his eyes."

"I'm not foolish, mother. Nor young. I know what you're saying. I will keep my distance."

Isabo plunked the last potatoes into the pot with a mild splash. "There are times when keeping one's distance is the last thing on God's mind." She set the large kettle on the stove and washed her hands. "I will check on our boy. He fell asleep quickly, but I do not want him to wake in a strange place and be afraid."

"Thank you, Mami."

Isabo sent a knowing look over her shoulder, a look that intensified as the back door swung open and Colt Stafford stepped inside the covered porch. He kicked off his boots, came through the inner door, and glanced from woman to woman. "You were talking about me?"

"No."

His expression said he wasn't buying Angelina's denial.

Isabo raised her shoulders. "Mother to daughter. We speak of our gratitude to you, for seeing a lack of accord and changing it. You are a man of action."

"Or maybe gut reaction," Colt countered, then looked surprised and vaguely uncomfortable when Isabo moved close and seized his hands.

"You have read C. S. Lewis, perhaps?"

"Yes. Well. Some. A long time ago," Colt admitted.

"Mr. Lewis once said how it is funny that day by day nothing changes." Isabo swept the room a quick glance. "But when we look back, everything is different. This is, I think, our juncture. A time of looking back and moving forward. For some reason we are here, at this place, in these moments. God provides and we partake. Or we mess up," she added practically. She released his hands.

Colt didn't step back to create distance. He didn't clench and unclench his hands, a typical reaction to a stressful grasp. Instead, he gazed into Isabo's eyes, then nodded, slowly. "Your daughter takes after you in many ways."

"And her father, God rest his soul," Isabo said. "He would be very proud of her."

"It takes courage to turn your back on something you love to do the right thing," Colt said softly. "I'm sure he would appreciate that."

His words gave praise Angelina didn't think she deserved. Had she done the right thing or reacted in cowardice? Or both?

"Ach!" Isabo flapped her apron, suddenly distressed.

"What is it? What's wrong?" Colt looked at her, dismayed, but then Colt wasn't accustomed to the occasional theatrics that accompanied life as a Castiglione. Nick came through the side porch door as her mother explained. He looked surprised and amused, probably more by Colt's worried expression than anything else.

"I have been talking and enjoying it and forgot I was to go and check on my grandson! It is so good to be among people again!"

Nick watched her retreat, then redirected his attention to Colt and Angelina. "Colt said your mother has come to visit," he said to Angelina. "That"—he thrust his thumb toward the hallway— "must be Mom."

"Isabo," Angelina said.

"Great name. And you have a little boy. Imagine that. Our Ange has got herself a past." She took his amused tone to mean he was teasing. If that was the worst reaction Angelina got, she'd do all right.

"Not exactly visiting," Colt said. "Staying." He changed the subject by opening a box of doughnuts from the café in Cle Elum. He helped himself to a maple bar and sighed, happy. "There's nothing like this in New York."

"Um, hello. Cronuts? Manhattan's latest fried and filled confection?" Angelina followed the change in subject gratefully. "I've heard they're the current rage."

Colt pulled out a stool at the breakfast bar. "No time to waste standing in line for hours. I bet you didn't have to get in line at 7:00 a.m. to buy these, did you, Ange?"

"No." She laughed at the very idea of waiting hours for a pastry.

"Didn't you have assistants who would do that for you?" Nick grabbed a pair of cinnamon crunch donuts, ignored Angelina's pointed look at the clock, and sat down next to his brother. They were a sight, the pair of them. Dirty and mussed, red-cheeked from the biting wind, and messed up from delivering and transporting baby cows. In more hospitable weather she'd have ordered them out of her kitchen to get cleaned up, but the rugged day's work needed its reward.

"I *was* my people. And if you ask an office assistant to get you doughnuts in New York City, you're likely to get sued. Besides, there are no doughnuts like these." He bit into the maple-topped pastry and sighed. "I haven't had anything this good in years. Or pie. I miss apple pie," he said, chewing one maple bar while reaching for another.

"You had more money than God," Nick said.

Angelina growled, and Nick changed his words with a quick apologetic glance her way. "You had plenty of cash. Why didn't you just get pie if you wanted some?"

"You don't just find pie in New York. And if you do, it isn't the same. It's not like here, where you can go to Hammerstein's or Cle Elum and get pies made with local apples. Let me correct myself. On Thanksgiving, you can find pie in New York. But there's no comparison to *real* apple pie."

"Wall Street versus Main Street," Angelina observed as Sam stepped into the room.

Colt swung her way. "Exactly. Small towns have their share of restaurants and shops, and nothing is repeated. But in parts of Manhattan, blocks are simply repeats of other blocks. Not all. But a lot."

"Give me God's country, any time," Sam said. He withdrew a coffee pod, made a quick cup, added cream, then moved toward the elongated breakfast bar. If he recognized the quick silence that greeted his presence, he ignored it. "Although I could find great spots to get a good meal at a decent price in Union Square and the West Village."

"You came to New York?" Colt asked. "While I was there?"

"Twice."

"And didn't let me know?"

"You made it clear you didn't want to see me." Sam shrugged. "I had business there, and I wanted to make sure you were doing all right."

Angelina moved closer to the rolling pin, just in case.

Colt stared at Sam. Sam stared right back. Then Colt took another bite of his maple bar, breaking the standoff. "You could have called. I would have seen you."

"Drowned me in the river, most likely," Sam replied as he pulled up a chair to the table.

"I've got no intention of spending my life in prison over your demise, despite my proximity to both rivers." Colt's rejoinder was mild, possibly sweetened by his intake of maple frosted pastries.

Nick was about to take another bite of his doughnut when Noah raced into the kitchen. "I woke up!"

"You did!" Colt smiled at him.

Instead of running to Angelina's side for a hug and a kiss and a cookie, Noah launched himself into Colt's arms. Colt lifted him comfortably and set him on his lap as if he'd been doing it for years. The little guy hugged Colt's neck, sat back, and took a deep breath. "You smell funny."

A light-bulb realization hit Angelina when the men laughed.

These three men rarely laughed. She'd teased Sam about it often enough. Nick had his own share of trouble the past few years. Broken homes and disheartened children sucked the humor out of many situations. And Colt was a tough-hearted, analytical jerk with the most beautiful blue eyes she'd ever seen, who had little to laugh about since arriving.

But now, in the presence of a child, they laughed together. Talked together. Broke bread in the form of doughnuts together, and for that moment, she glimpsed a family, bound by the common bond of a child.

"And a little child shall lead them . . ." Isaiah's words of peace alive in the Stafford kitchen. Hope infused her as she introduced Noah to Sam's second son.

"Noah, this is Mr. Stafford's other son Nick. Nick, this is my son, Noah."

Nick smiled. "Noah. Nice to meet you. Glad you can stay with us, kid."

"He said I could." Noah burrowed a little closer into Colt's shoulder as he patted Colt's cheek. "He said I can l-live in the big house and l-l-learn . . ." He stuttered slightly as he pushed for the proper letter sound, trying hard in front of his new friends, ". . . about cows and horses and riding four-wheelers and all that."

"Odd that I don't recall three-quarters of that conversation." Colt gave Noah a hug that went straight to Angelina's heart. Noah had never known the affection or example of a man. From the look on his face and the way he gravitated to Colt, she realized he'd bonded instantly with the New York hedge-fund manager.

Great. She'd been there, done that, and it absolutely, positively wasn't going to happen again.

"When the weather softens, we'll have a few lessons," Colt promised. "You, me, and Nick's girls."

His comment hit like a cold breeze through an ill-fitting door. Sam looked approving, but he ducked his head to maintain neutrality. Nick slid off the stool and didn't appear to care when it thumped the ground with his speed. When he spoke, he wasn't any too happy. "My girls are busy enough."

"They keep telling me they want to learn." Colt kept his arm wrapped around Noah and his voice easy. "If we're teaching one"—he dropped his attention to the boy—"might as well teach three."

"Murt's got a nice hand with teaching youngsters," Sam added. "It would keep the old guy in the game and out of trouble with the Missus."

Nick started to sputter, took note of Noah's innocent presence, and strode toward the door. "Discussion over. I've got work."

"Is he mad?" Noah peered into Colt's face. The look of trust he offered the big, rugged cowboy made Angelina's heart choke.

"He'll get over it." Colt broke off half of his second doughnut and handed it to the boy.

"Thank you!" Noah shot a quick, happy look toward Colt, then his mother. "I l-love these things so much!"

"Me too." Colt took a bite and grinned when her son copied him.

Sam watched, the pain in his eyes betraying deeper emotions. Did he see more than Colt holding someone else's child? Was it the past that made him look wistful? Or the uncertain future?

Angelina didn't know, but when she shifted her attention back to Noah, Colt's eyes met hers. Angelina wasn't anyone's fool. He could talk sweet and play western, but in the end, movers and shakers cared only about themselves and assets. Colt might have been born to the saddle, but he'd shunned it before and he would again.

SEVEN

*C*olt waited until Hobbs took over barn duty that evening, then cornered his father in Sam's walnut-paneled office. "I thought we were done with secrets."

Sam set down his phone and frowned. "I don't understand."

"You had people sequestered in a cabin for two years. That doesn't equate as secretive with you?"

"I helped a friend," his father corrected him in an easier voice than Colt was accustomed to. "I expect you'd do the same."

"Why did your friend need help?"

Sam shook his head. "Not my story to tell. Talk to Angelina."

"How did Nick not notice?"

Sam shrugged. "Your brother's had a lot on his plate. And we've kept him very busy."

"Chin tucked, eyes down." His brother tended to focus on what was in front of him. That much hadn't changed. "You raised three boys without a mother. What were you thinking, keeping that little kid over there?"

"He had his grandmother," Sam began, but Colt's look of astonishment paused his words.

"It's not the same. It's never the same as having your own mother. How can three decades go by and you still don't get it? A kid needs parents, and if for some reason he can't have two, he deserves at least one."

Sam paled. He knew what Colt was saying. He may have surrounded them with the opulence of his hard work, but he abandoned them emotionally.

"I'd have given anything to have a parent who loved me," Colt went on. "Who looked at me and thought I was special just because I was theirs. I can't believe you thought it was all right to tuck that little boy away, no matter what his mother said. Don't you ever learn?"

He walked out before he could say any more and passed Angelina as he strode through the kitchen.

She looked at him, then beyond, toward his father's office. Concern drew her brows together, but he didn't need her concern. Right now he needed manual labor, mindless and back breaking, something to help him forget that his career had capsized and he was scraping a living working for his selfish, self-absorbed father—again.

He slammed through the door and stomped across the yard. Hobbs took one look at him when he banged into the barn, and the old cowboy stopped and sighed. "I was hopin' for a peaceful night, but if you go crashin' 'round like a madman, these gals are gonna be droppin' young'uns every which way."

Colt marched straight through the barn, flung open the far door, and stood, breathing in cold, fresh air while his nerves settled. And when the cold bit deep into his cheeks and ears, he closed the door, turned, and faced Hobbs. "I'm fine. I've got this. Go get some sleep."

Hobbs faltered, then shrugged. "You know where I am if need be. We've got two that look mighty antsy and two that might surprise us." He pointed to the near end of the barn. "I think the others have a few days, but I've been proved wrong before."

"Yeah. Me too."

Hobbs turned, then swung back. "I knew they was in that cabin."

That wasn't a big surprise. Age had done nothing but sharpen the older man's vision and wisdom.

Hobbs gripped the rail in front of him, watching the cows he'd separated from the herd. "I weren't sure who or what, but I knew Sam was keepin' someone safe there. And while that's a secretive kind of thing, it ain't necessarily bad, Colt."

Maybe it was, maybe it wasn't, and maybe it was just that glimpse in a really old mirror that upset him. A little boy lost, wishing for his mother to come see him. Tuck him in. Say his prayers with him and read him a story.

This wasn't his fight. Once he got back on his feet he'd catch the first red-eye back to his life at One Financial Center and reclaim his place among the gilded. While here—and while around Angelina, especially—he meant to keep his distance, because every time she turned those smoke-brown eyes his way, the last thing on his mind was distance.

———

Colt Stafford had been carefully aloof—polite but distant—for the past two weeks since bringing Noah and her mother to the house.

It's better that way, Angelina decided as she parked the SUV in a rare empty spot in front of Hammerstein's Mercantile. Ham sat tall behind the seasonal counter of a store that offered just about anything a body could want or need, according to the change in weather. He glanced up and gave her a little wave, friendly, like always. She waved back, kept walking, and ran smack into Colt at the junction of bulk dried foods and Hammerstein's Deli.

"Sorry, ma'am." Firm hands grabbed hold of her as she stumbled, and the smell of roughed leather, horse, and coffee made her take a quick breath of appreciation. "I wasn't paying attention, I—" He stopped when he realized it was her inside the coat and hat, but he didn't let go. Instead, he held her tighter, drinking her in with those big blue eyes. She'd respected his distance for those two weeks, but now . . .

Oh, now . . .

Her heart sped up. So did her breathing. She averted her eyes, refusing to explore the question of what it would be like to kiss Colt Stafford. But for these short seconds, she wondered what it would be like to step closer to Colt instead of away . . .

He dropped his hands, and she shoved her foolish thoughts aside. "No harm," she told him, as if nothing had happened to shatter her carefully constructed safe zone. "Hard to see your way forward when you've got your eyes trained behind you, and I see Ham's got some mighty good-looking help here today." She flashed a teasing smile toward Ham's daughter Gretchen.

Total cowboy, Colt turned toward Gretchen and touched the brim of his hat. "True words."

"Aw, thanks, guys. You've come for your order, Angelina?" Gretchen opened the sliding glass door on the display cooler and lifted out a good-sized bag. "I've got it all sliced, the rolls are fresh, and Dad has your veggie bags in the produce cooler—along with the secret dressing, of course."

"Gretchen, thank you. Having this ready is a real timesaver. This way I won't have to be away too long."

"Calf dropping's a busy time. Glad to help."

Angelina indicated Colt's sandwich bag with a glance. "You got your own lunch?"

"Seemed sensible." He drawled the words while giving her a more intent look. "More peaceful that way."

"'Peace begins with a smile,' Colt." She locked eyes with his. "Mother Teresa liked to say that. You might want to give it a try. It couldn't hurt, and it might knock part of that chip off your shoulder. But there's no one to smile at if you spend every single day alone."

"It's been working so far." He turned and touched his finger to the brim of his hat again. "Gretchen. Have a good one."

"You too, Colt."

"See you later, Angelina."

"Right." She shifted her attention back to Gretchen as Colt headed toward the mercantile's front door.

"Um? Totally smokin'," Gretchen said. She indicated the far door with an admiring look. "My older sister always called him the hot one, as if Nick and Trey barely made the cut. I thought she was crazy." She leaned forward and sighed, purposely over the top. "Now I have to apologize to her because she was spot on. How long is he staying?"

Wasn't that the question of the hour? "I don't know, but he's been a huge help to Nick in light of Sam's illness."

"Angelina, you are so PC," Gretchen teased as she swiped Angelina's credit card and waited for the machine's flash of approval. "I'm sure Hobbs and Brock and Murt are big helps too, but the three of them together don't sport the eye candy of the number one son."

"Colt's good looking?" Angelina made a doubtful face, playing along. "I hadn't noticed."

"Really?" A deep voice sounded right behind her.

Gretchen's change of expression confirmed it—Colt hadn't left the store. Angelina started to move away, embarrassed, but Colt just grabbed the bag of food in one smooth gesture. "Maybe my looks will improve if I help carry things to the car. Ham gave me the produce bags, so I figured I'd come back this way and give you a hand."

Gretchen made a little face of contrition, handed off the receipt, and waved. "Um . . . see you guys later."

"Thanks, Gretchen."

Gretchen started to nod, but then Colt turned back her way. "So your sister thinks Nick and Trey pale in comparison, hmm?"

Gretchen flushed.

Colt winked at her. "Tell her I said hey."

"I will."

Angelina pulled the heavy glass door open, then held it for Colt as he came through. Once the door swung shut behind them, she stopped. She was about to read him the riot act for a number of reasons, including, but not limited to, flirting with girls barely out of college, sneaking up on folks when they were talking about him, and eavesdropping on private conversations held in a public place.

And then he set down the bag of fresh produce, raised his hand, and laid it ever so gently against her cheek. Her skin warmed to his palm. His eyes met hers and held for long, slow, sweet seconds. And then he grazed her cheek lightly and sighed. "We could be in big trouble here, Ange."

Angelina stiffened. A good cop was supposed to be skilled at avoiding trouble, but right here, right now, trouble in the form of Colt Stafford looked mighty nice. Worse, she was pretty sure Colt understood his appeal to women and probably used it to his advantage. She didn't need or want to put herself in that situation again. Ever.

"I think about you all the time." His eyes traced her face, her eyes, her lips . . . lingered there . . . and then he lightened the moment with a teasing smile. "It actually borders on annoying."

"Then stop," she told him, wishing the attraction away. "Stop thinking about me."

"But what if I can't?" He said the words soft, so soft she wasn't really sure she heard them. "What if I don't want to?"

She'd met trouble face to face with a money-comes-first type. She wasn't looking for a repeat performance. She stepped just out of reach. "May I remind you that you're here on a temporary basis, ready to jump ship in a New York minute? I suggest we muddle along like we have been, avoiding one another while maintaining a polite distance." She raised her eyebrow. "Politeness means not being a surly bear, snapping and growling every chance one gets."

"The surly bear disappears when I'm near the kids, right?"

She had to hand it to him; he was on his best behavior when the kids were around. Sweet. Funny. Compassionate. She started across the broad porch toward the SUV. "You're surprisingly good with them."

"Why surprising?" He grabbed the bag he'd set down and followed.

"I don't think most Wall Street types make racing cars on the carpet and pick-up sticks a priority."

"How many Wall Street types do you know?" He paused when they reached the wide, open steps leading down to the street. "I can't imagine it's too many."

"One was enough."

He held her gaze, thoughtful. "He didn't play by the rules?"

"In retrospect, I should have set much firmer rules. I know better now."

"So that makes me a bad guy by association."

She wanted to say yes and lump all successful money marketers together, but was Colt a bad guy?

She'd seen enough of him to recognize the wounded soul within. But lots of folks had wounded souls and actually did something positive as a result. "I've got to get the lunch stuff home."

"I'll help you put it in the car." And then he made the subtle move that wrangled her heart just so.

He shifted the bags all to one arm and took her hand to help her down the steps.

Nothing big, no grand Manhattan-style gesture, just a gentleman helping a lady to her car.

He released her hand to open the back of the SUV and stow the sacks of produce inside. She instantly missed the feel of her hand in his. The grip of his fingers, strong and sure, cradling her smaller hand. It felt like a promise to keep her safe from harm—the kind of silly, fun, feminine thought cops rarely allowed themselves, but for this moment she did, and it felt wonderful.

"Colt."

"Hmm?" He pushed up the brim of his old black hat and didn't offer the dazzling grin he flashed freely. This smile was calmer. Sweeter. Special.

Her heart didn't want to calm.

She forced it to because nothing about this could end well. He'd leave, she'd leave, Noah's sensitive nature would be messed up, and her mother would aim "I told you so" looks in her direction. "Don't start things you can't finish, cowboy."

"I never do."

She was pretty sure he took it more like a challenge instead of the warning she intended. He swung open the driver's door for her, held it as she stepped inside, then closed it behind her. He moved aside as she pulled away, but when she glanced back in the rearview mirror, Colt Stafford was still watching.

Red flags popped up in her brain, but her heart would have none of it because the minute Colt took her hand, he grabbed hold of a piece of her heart as well. She knew better than to allow herself to travel that road again. She'd be foolish to allow the two-sided attraction to grow, and she'd put a firm lid on *foolish* a few years back. No way was she going to reopen that box now.

Colt watched Angelina drive away, and for the first time since everything went bad, he wondered if there was more than money at stake in his circumstances. Maybe . . . *just maybe* . . . he was supposed to be here. Of course the idea was ludicrous and got shoved aside when he heard the crusty voice from the broad mercantile porch behind him. "You're back."

Colt didn't miss the slur, which meant Johnny Baxter had tied one on quite early in the day. He stepped onto the sidewalk and tipped his hat slightly as he continued to move toward his truck. A quiet acknowledgment wasn't going to be enough for Johnny. He followed Colt along the walk, then grasped the porch rail at the far end and spat as Colt reached for the driver's door of his truck.

The spittle landed shy of the car. Colt hoped Johnny would be content with making his opinion known and moving on.

Johnny wasn't all that bright.

He moved down the porch stairs, shaking a finger in Colt's direction. "Just like the old man, ain't ya? Takin' and keepin' and squanderin'. He done it with land and pushin' folks out. You did it with honest folks' money. A chip off the old block. And now you're home, a raw pup, tail tucked. And that ain't no surprise to anybody hereabouts. Old man sick, the failure son comes home to run the place into the ground. Same old, same old."

Colt held back, but just barely. It took everything he had not to drive a fist into Johnny's sneering face, and he might have done just that, but Sheriff Rye Bennett came across the porch from the other direction. He gave Colt a slight shake of his head as he descended the stairs, then stuck out his hand when he drew close enough. "Welcome home, Colt."

His move defused the situation, but not Johnny's wrath. "Like always, it ain't what you know, it's who you know 'round here. And everybody wants to saddle up with the Staffords. Even the law." Johnny shuffled off, spewing words not fit for anyone's ears, his feet scraping the worn concrete path.

Rye sighed, then turned back to Colt. "He's gotten worse. He's rarely sober and blames your father for everything he's lost—his farm, his wife, his estranged kids, and his job."

"Heavy list."

"Things have a way of trickling down," Rye noted. "If he hadn't lost the farm in that drought, he might have stayed married and not become an alcoholic. One change affects the other. That wasn't Sam's fault, but his arrogance in bidding on four spreads in the face of others' failures left some rough feelings."

"That was twenty-five years ago. You'd think folks would move on, wouldn't you?"

"Some, yes. Others, no." Rye waved down Center Street. "You know how it is here. With folks who go back several generations, stories don't fade, they grow with time. In their minds, the proof is right there in front of them, day in and day out. While so many places fell apart, the Double S flourished and grew."

"And my father wasn't exactly subtle about any of it." He watched as Johnny turned right on First Avenue. "But we're still talking a long time ago, Rye. We were kids."

"Brats, riding and roping and falling out of the saddle." Rye fake-punched Colt's arm. "And now we're here again."

"You were on the force in Chicago, weren't you?" The last Colt knew, Rye was a big-city officer in Chi-Town.

"Yup."

"Did you hate the city?" Colt found that thought surprising, but why else would someone come back to Gray's Glen?

Rye scoffed. "Loved it. Something going on all the time. But when my mom died, I had a choice. Either come home and raise Jenna and Brendan here, or take my two middle school siblings into the crazy of Chicago and pretend I could keep an eye on them while I worked. That made it a no-brainer."

Rye's mother was gone? Regret hit Colt as he stood with his old friend. "I didn't know about your mother, Rye. I'm sorry."

"I appreciate the sympathy," Rye said. "It came fairly quick and a surprise to boot. Good for her, worse for us. If you really want to *know* stuff," he added, "you'd have to come home once in a while."

Nick had said the same thing. Both were right. Colt hauled in a deep breath. "I'll do better."

Rye snorted.

"Thanks for the vote of confidence," Colt said.

"No problem."

"How are the kids doing?" Colt asked.

"It's been eight months, and every stinking holiday and anniversary puts Jenna in tears and makes Brendan want to punch people," Rye told him. "He's running track this spring—if spring ever gets here—and I'm hoping that helps. He needs a goal, an end game."

"He needs his mother," Colt said softly. He knew that no amount of outside activity could take the place of someone who loved you best.

Rye didn't pretend otherwise. "I know. You comprehend that more than anyone. But I can't do anything about that except try to be here for them. It doesn't help that there's so much garbage kids can get into these days. I feel more like a guard than a brother."

"That's probably a hazard of the trade when you put on the uniform. Why don't you bring the kids over for dinner this Sunday?" Colt suggested. "The temperatures are rising, which means mud, but mud means softer weather. I can get them up on a horse. Give them some paddock practice. Nothing like big animals and getting dirty to train a kid's brain the right way."

"They'd love it," Rye replied. "What time? I've got to get them to church at ten, so the afternoon would be better."

"Angelina and Dad will be coming into town for church too. Come by around two," Colt said. "I'll run it by Angelina just to make sure."

"Sounds good. And when I get tempted to hang around after dark, kick me out, okay?"

"You've got a curfew, Rye? Is that one of the new town regulations?"

"If it was, I could hound the mayor and get it fixed. No, it's the homework thing. Life with kids. Weekend homework is always a last-minute, throw-together thing for Brendan. Jenna's is done by supper time on Friday. Brendan's is a struggle every Sunday night."

"That brings back a memory or two." Colt chucked him on the arm. "I've got to head out, but thanks for coming over here when you saw Johnny. I appreciate it."

"I was actually more interested in protecting him. Yeah, he's a jerk, but coming back here, I can see how one thing affects another in a small town. It makes me want to be a better person. Raw deals can make or break people."

"So you think his problems are my father's fault too?" Colt asked. "Don't forget that Johnny went belly up on that property months before my father made it part of the Double S."

Rye's answer offered a more mature perspective. "It's not about Johnny. It's about choices, good and bad, and timing. Johnny's made some bad ones, but you have to wonder how things might have turned out if Sam hadn't been such an arrogant jerk about everything back then."

Colt didn't have to wonder. He knew firsthand how different things might be. "Can't argue that." He shut the door and poked his head out the window. "See you Sunday."

Sam Stafford's tough guy attitude had built an empire-styled ranch that raised the national bar on beef standards across the United States. But in the process he sacrificed his family, had few friends, and was hated by many. Sam said he wanted to make amends, well . . .

Colt grunted as he drove through the picturesque western town. Sam could start with the normal folk, the everyday people who called Gray's Glen their home. Making things right here would be a start because Sam's actions nearly three decades back left a trail. Some good, a bunch bad. And it was up to Sam to set things straight, but as Colt thought of the pale yellow tinge to his father's skin, he wasn't any too sure Sam would have time to do it.

Colt paused by the long, curved breakfast bar late that afternoon. Angelina kept her face averted. Colt had stepped into dangerous territory earlier, and he'd done it with the skill of a master. Flirting with her, slipping past her defenses. She removed the big silver mixing bowl from its stand, set it down with a thud, then disconnected the dough hook attachment. Bread was more trustworthy than Colt Stafford could ever hope to be. End of story.

"I invited Rye Bennett and his brother and sister to come over on Sunday and have dinner with us. I hope that's all right."

Angelina slapped the big round of bread dough onto the counter and pummeled it without looking up. "No permission needed. I'll plan accordingly."

"I wasn't asking permission. I was being polite."

"Then your manners have been noted."

She kept working the bread, ignoring him, knowing the attraction and recognizing the futility. She smacked the bread onto the board for one more quick turn, and if she gave it a heartier pounding than usual because Colt was standing right there, all the better.

"Will your vehemence toughen the bread or make it even more delicious?"

"Time will tell." She refused to look up. She'd warned him off earlier, and she'd meant it, but Angelina was a woman first and a cop second. Avoiding the depths of Colt's blue eyes was in her best interests.

"Mommy!" Noah raced into the kitchen, then skidded to a stop when he spotted Colt. "You're here! You're home! I've been waiting for you all day!" The uptick of excitement in her little son's voice at seeing Colt and the joy of having him close to her were wearing down her defenses and creating new questions. Noah loved being on the ranch. He'd fallen in love with the three ranch dogs, BeeBee, Kita, and Banjo, and he thought playing hide-and-seek in the huge house was the best game ever. Why shouldn't he think so? He'd been sheltered for as long as he could remember. Seeing him spread his wings and have the chance to be spontaneous was a blessing. Could he do this in Seattle?

Not the same way. Not if she rejoined the narcotics squad.

"Whatcha got, bud?" Colt stooped low. A smile tugged sweet laugh lines into place and his profile lightened. "What's this?"

"A new monster truck." Noah whispered the words, as if they were too cool to say out loud. "It came in the mail."

"So red is your favorite color?"

Noah shook his head. "My *very most* favorite are green trucks. Like yours," he said. "That's what I want to d-d-drive someday." He held the new truck aloft. "But r-red is l-l-like my other most favorite."

"Well, thank you." Colt reached out and gave her son a hug, the kind of hug a little boy needed. Big. Strong. Manly. Then he picked up Noah and the truck. "How about we play with this once I get cleaned up? Mommy's making supper—"

"I'm so hungry." Noah used his most dramatic hungry voice. "I don't th-think I can wait until supper. Not really."

"Well." Colt turned toward Angelina. "Would you mind if Noah had a quick supper while I get washed and changed? That would give us more time to play."

He had to know she couldn't refuse such a simple request. It seemed he was adept at using his kindness toward Noah to break down her reserve, which meant she should be even more careful around him. But seeing the two of them together, faces turned toward her, eyes imploring, weakened her resolve. They formed a picture, an image of how families could and should be if grownups stopped messing things up. "Sounds like a plan."

"Oh, th-thank you, Mommy! Can I have peanut butter bread? With sugar on it?"

"Yes. And then you and your buddy can race cars. All right?"

Noah and Colt bumped knuckles as Colt set him down. "Eat up. I'll be back soon, okay?"

"Okay!" Noah climbed onto one of the chairs, clearly excited. "I want to be a cowboy just l-like Colt when I grow up."

She wanted to snort. Noah's declaration was rather funny considering Colt had fled to a place and career about as far away from the Double S and ranching as he could get. But when she glanced up, she was glad she'd kept her snarky attitude at bay. The look on Colt's face, as though touched by her son's declaration, mushed her heart once more.

Stop looking at him! Stay back! Maintain your distance!

The internal warning was right, but her conscience only took her so far. When the heart stepped in, caution longed to fly out the window.

Colt moved forward, toward her.

She stepped back. There was absolutely no reason for him to come her way.

He moved closer. The scent of rugged outdoorsman hung about him—hay, barn, horse, cow—all wrapped in a hint of spring air and sporting flecks of mud. "Out of my kitchen. You're a mess."

"Hurry up, Mr. Colt! I want to play."

"Okay, little guy. In a minute." Colt made the promise as he drew close enough to touch her but didn't. He simply stood there, watching her, letting the warmth of the stove and the moment wend around them. "I never used to like coming into the kitchen, Ange. Other than food, there was nothing that drew me back to this house. Or this table. That's changed now." The simplicity of his words set her heart into quick motion again. "I don't know what kind of difference you made in your old job, but you've made a big difference here, and I wanted you to know that."

She took particular care in spreading peanut butter on Noah's bread so Colt wouldn't see how his words affected her.

"You've helped my father become a lot more human than he used to be."

"God's timing and an open mind," she told him as she drew a heart on the open-faced sandwich. "Your father was ready for both."

"Or was it fear of the unknown? Hedging his bets? Amazing how health issues can bring folks to their knees, isn't it?"

Skepticism weighted his words. She chose to ignore it. "Be careful. I wouldn't shrug off God's plan quite so quickly." She sifted sugar across the top of the bread, then began slicing a crisp green apple. "It was the influence of God's timing that brought you back here when your father most needs you."

"Bends in the road are a given on Wall Street. Stocks go up; stocks come down."

"Then you might want to consider another line of work." She raised her eyes to his and held his attention. "You have a legacy here. And a beautiful home."

He started to object, but she raised a hand. "You may dismiss it, but you cannot deny it. It always comes down to choices. Yours. Mine. Your father's. God will put new turns in our paths, but it's up to us to choose which path to take—ours or his."

"When I factor investments, there's always a plan involved," he argued. "If I were to buy into the idea of God's timing, then I'm not the one planning. He is. I like being in charge, Ange. It suits me."

"It suited your father too."

He cringed.

"'Two roads diverged in a yellow wood,'" she quoted softly. "Robert Frost had great insight and gentle wisdom. Looking back, we see our choices through different eyes. Each choice hones us, and, right or wrong, we carry the consequences of those choices into the future." She handed him the plate, and when he looked down, his expression made her heart fall a little bit harder. Something far away had caught him up. Something sad and sweet. "You made a heart on his bread," he said after a moment.

"Yes."

Colt studied the peanut-butter heart, then swallowed hard. "I think my mom did this for me. When I was little."

Her chest constricted, thinking of his childhood pain. His mother gone, his father distant.

"It's nice, Ange." His expression took on that of a little boy who had lost more than he ever should have. As he took the bread to Noah, he added, "I'm glad you and Noah are both here in the house. It's good."

Just that, a simple declaration, but she saw the truth in his words when he set down the bread in front of her hungry little boy. He wasn't just performing a task; he was serving her son with care. "I'll be back in a few minutes. Eat up, okay?"

"I will!"

Noah's excitement had him taking huge bites already, and Colt laughed. "He's a keeper."

"Yes he is."

Colt strode away, looking as good from behind as he did from the front, mud specks and all. It startled her that the sight of him, tall, rugged, roughed up by a contingent of circumstances both in and out of his control, made her long to soothe him. Talk with him. Hold hands and take long, measured walks up the hills and get lost in the forest for a while.

"With God all things are possible."

She believed that, but all the sweet words and challenges didn't change what brought her here. Two fathers. One who didn't care that he'd sired a beautiful gift from God. And the other laid to rest because she'd done her job the way she was supposed to.

She'd been running hard and fast, creating distance. But now— maybe it was time to explore more paths.

Noah waved his cup in the air. She corrected him with a look and said, "That will get you nothing, young man. Manners, please."

"May I have some chocwote milk, please?"

"Choc-o-late." She stressed the pronunciation as she poured.

He repeated the word earnestly as she handed him the half-filled cup, then grinned up at her. He was the image of content-ment, a miniature cowboy, tucked at an oversized ranch table. "I l-love it here so much, Mommy. I th-think we should just stay here forever, you and me and 'Buela, and we can help the cowboys every day. Okay?"

"That's one smart boy you have there." Sam saved her from a response as he came into the kitchen from the far end. He palmed Noah's dark hair and met Angelina's eyes. "Has a good head on his shoulders."

"Of course you think so because he supports your cause," she retorted. But then she smiled. "You look more comfortable today. Are you feeling better or putting on a good show?"

"Both," Sam admitted. "I think I'm getting better, and then a wave hits me and I'm pretty sure I'm worse. Who's to say?"

"I know it's tough to have the ranch operations taken out of your hands. Why are you up and around right now? Resting so that liver can heal is crucial. Do you know how much energy it takes to create new cell tissue?"

He laughed, then gripped his side. "Don't make me laugh."

"Go rest. This isn't a wrenched arm or a bloodied lip. This is organ damage and possible organ failure. Take it seriously, Sam."

"I am taking it seriously," he countered, "but when a man might be running out of time, there are other things to take seriously as well."

"Then rest so you have the energy to do them. If you like I can help you make a list of what you'd like to do, okay?"

"Don't need one. Got a conscience. It's just rusty. I'll figure this out." He walked down the side hall toward one of the first-floor guest rooms, listing slightly to the side.

Give him time, Lord, please. Let him make amends; let him get healthy enough to make amends.

Her phone buzzed. She saw Tony's name and picked up. "I expected you'd be calling soon."

"I promised to call if I didn't hear from you. Just keeping my word to my partner. You thinking about our conversation?"

"I am." She paused as Noah slurped his milk when the brim of his kid-sized cowboy hat got in the way. "But I'm caught in the middle, Tony. I explained that."

"Only because you're being indecisive," he replied. His perspective made it a black-and-white proposition. Hers had shades of gray. "Your mother deserves a chance to come home, Mary. So do you."

"I can't leave now." She kept her voice soft so she wouldn't be overheard. "We're in the thick of calving and Sam's ill. I can't leave him short-handed, and it's the worst possible time to train a replacement."

"You're putting me off."

"Only by necessity. It's how it is."

"Call me when you're ready."

"Tony, I—"

He interrupted her with a heavy sigh. "Mary Angela, you weren't meant to spend your life cooking for a bunch of backwoods cowboys and washing their clothes. Scrubbing their toilets. Think about it. Hey, sorry, gotta go." He hung up, and she held the phone for a moment before setting it down.

His parting words stung. Did her job lessen who she was? No. Any job worth doing was worth doing right. Her parents had taught her that. Her mother had sorted fruit for local farmers as a new immigrant. To make extra money, her father had worked at a car wash when he was new to the SPD. And once she'd gone off to elementary school, her mother had worked in Seattle hotels cleaning rooms and suites. The job didn't make the person; the person made the job.

"Mommy, I th-think I'm full."

"You did great." She tossed him a wet washcloth and watched as he scrubbed his face and hands. "And so independent. Bring your dishes to the counter, and you can go play."

"Yes!" Noah lifted the small plate and empty cup, then carefully walked them around the table and set them on the counter. "Bye, Mom!" Within seconds, the sounds of pretend engines filled the great room as monster trucks tangled with Matchbox cars and the occasional piece of furniture.

Isabo came into the kitchen, smiling. "I will help with supper now that the ironing is complete. He is having fun, yes?"

"Yes."

"And it is good for Noah to have others around now. To get to know other people."

"Having more people makes it harder when you have to say good-bye." Angelina lifted the big can filled with basmati rice. "I hate the thought of that."

"For him? Or for you?"

She sent her mother a look of warning as she took a bag of corn from the freezer. "I'm a big girl. I can handle myself."

Doubt marked her mother's expression. "When one is caught in the middle, it is hard to know which way to turn. Should we risk the old or embrace the uncertainty of the new? Since I did not raise my daughter to fear anything, I am hopeful she will see both clearly."

"Oh, I see them clearly, all right." Angelina indicated the noisy front room as Colt came down the stairs to join Noah. "Uncertainty versus uncertainty. Just different sorts, and I'm not a fan of either."

Her mother pressed her lips together but said nothing, and that was just as well. For the moment they were on a beautiful ranch at a grueling time of year. Once the urgent press for safe deliveries was over, she would reassess. In the meantime she'd pray for sorely needed guidance because right now she had no idea which path to take or what criteria to consider in making her decision.

EIGHT

I can't leave now. We're in calving season, and it's the worst possible time to train a replacement."

Angelina's words, spoken softly so as not to be overheard. But Colt had managed to do exactly that. He gripped the square laundry basket more tightly and waited silently on the back stairs.

Her profile looked stern, and when she argued her point, a deep V formed between her eyes.

She's leaving.

When she'd said his name . . . Tony . . . Colt let out a breath he didn't know he was holding.

Of course there was someone else. Why wouldn't there be? It was foolish to think Angelina didn't have a life beyond the Double S. He retraced his steps to the second floor, set down the laundry basket, and walked to the front staircase. Plainly, whoever she was arguing with wanted the situation changed immediately, and to her credit she'd refused to buckle. He had a glimpse of the roads in the wood she'd talked about earlier. It seemed her choice of roads did not include staying here.

As he turned the corner and made the final descent, he spotted Noah on the carpet, watching the stairs hopefully. The minute he saw Colt, he raced across the broad entry and skidded to a stop in Colt's arms.

Holding the little guy felt right.

He carried him to the jumble of toy cars, loving the feeling of having Noah close. What kind of stupid moron builds a relationship with a strong, beautiful woman like Angelina, makes a child with her, then dumps them?

Someone self-serving and arrogant, kind of like the guy you were in danger of becoming.

That truth humbled him.

He'd been dogged and ruthless at times. He'd skated close to the edge of "me first, forget the rules"—a fairly easy thing to do on Wall Street.

Maybe this career upset wasn't the worst thing in the world. What if coming back to the Double S was a lifeboat he didn't know he needed?

He sank to the carpet with the boy and crashed small trucks into unsuspecting Matchbox cars.

Noah's squeals and shouts reminded him that not everything in his childhood had gone bad. He and Nick and Trey had played like this, indoors and out. They'd done so much together. When had he decided the bad outweighed the good?

Maybe it hadn't. Maybe he had let the dark moments of anger shroud the joy of being a ranch kid with free rein to go wherever, whenever, riding range and flirting with the local girls.

A soft sound of music filtered out of the kitchen. Angelina, humming as she finished the preparations for dinner. The sound and the boy's excitement combined to fill Colt with something new and distinct.

Contentment.

But she's leaving, he reminded himself.

Nick and Hobbs shattered the moment as they burst through the back door, Murt right behind them, arguing the merits of Simmental and Angus cross percentages. In the scuffle of feet, voices, hand washing, and shouts of laughter, Colt's resolve stumbled. Despite the interruption, the good memories took hold of a solid spot within, and Colt couldn't remember the last time he'd felt that good. But he knew one thing: it was a very long time ago.

"I don't have to do it your way, Murt." Nick's voice was rock hard as he set a pot of gravy on the table with a thump thirty minutes later. "I don't need your advice. It's too little, too late. I've been working on these embryo-transplant programs nonstop while you decided to take an eighteen-month honeymoon, so don't spew numbers at me like you're some kind of knows-more-than-anyone expert. I'm the one who helped break ground with this, and I'll be the one hung to dry if it goes bad."

Colt stopped with a fork full of food halfway to his mouth.

Hobbs watched Nick, then his eyes darted to McMurty and back again. Angelina's face went taut with disbelief, and Colt was pretty sure steam would start puffing out of his father's ears at any moment.

No one dissed Michael McMurty when it came to matters of beef production. The guy had helped pioneer the seed-ranch philosophy of breeding the best cows and bulls for propagation, not slaughter. To be called out by someone less than half his age would have meant a good thrashing back in the day.

McMurty turned to Nick, and while his expression stayed placid, his eyes chilled. "I know you've got your share of problems with the girls right now, Nicholas, and I expect that's got you flummoxed, but I'm gonna ask you to stand down. Angelina worked all afternoon on this meal, and I don't intend to let mine be ruined by a case of the stomach grumbles I don't need or deserve."

Nick glared at him across the table, then stood. "Don't talk down to me. Don't presume you know what I'm doing, going through, or up against, and if I wanted the whole world to know my business, I'd send out a group e-mail." He shoved his chair back, the sound of wood scraping stone marking his exit, then strode to the door, banged it open, and charged through.

Colt turned to McMurty. "What was that all about?"

Murt kept his attention on food and only food. "Not for me to say, like you heard. Ask him."

"He's got no call to be at you like that, Murt." Sam started to rise, but Colt put a hand on his arm.

"Give him time."

"I—"

"You want to charge out there and tell him Murt did nothing wrong and how Murt's responsible for a huge part of our success— all of which Nick knows."

Sam sank back into his chair.

"He needs to figure out what's got him so angry," Colt said. "And from the sound of it, he's been making like things are fine with the girls when they aren't."

Murt's expression agreed. Sam's didn't.

"There's not a thing wrong with Cheyenne and Dakota," Sam said. "They're wonderful."

"Their mother walked out on them nearly three years ago," said Colt. "She's off with another man and has no contact with her daughters. Mother abandonment is a huge thing for a kid to deal with. And because Nick's mother also walked away from him, this scenario is especially tough for him."

"That was over a quarter century ago," Sam protested.

Angelina cleared her throat. All eyes turned her way. "A child's heart is a tender organ. The gaping hole left by the loss of a parent is not a quick fix, nor usually forgotten. Let's not forget that we carry many of those childhood hurts into adulthood."

Sam must have seen her point. "I hate that you're almost always right."

She rolled her eyes at him and directed a hand to the others. "Eat while it's hot. I think most of us know that Nick's been shoving the girls' problems under the rug. My guess is that things have grown more out of control. And like his father Nick prefers the illusion that everything he does is going well. I'd suggest that history repeating itself will not be in anyone's best interests this time around."

Isabo appeared in the doorway with a freshly washed little boy wearing cowboy pajamas. Noah greeted the table full of somewhat grizzled men with unbridled excitement. "'Buela wanted me to wear my pirate jammies because they were clean, but I said I had to wear my cowboy ones because they're like Colt's!"

Hobbs smirked. "Colt, you got jammies like that upstairs? With all them little horses and kabobbles on 'em?"

"And cowboys too young to grow beards?" Murt asked, grinning. "Mebbe I'll get me a pair."

Noah looked from one to the other, confused. "I fink . . ." He stopped, took a breath, and worked his jaw. "I th-think he does. Don't you?" He turned toward Colt, and his look implored the big cowboy to tell the truth, the whole truth, and nothing but the truth.

Colt stood and pinched the edge of the red, brown, and yellow print flannel. "I did, bud. I had some just like this when I was a little cowpoke like you. I think they might have been the very same ones, in fact."

"Really?" Noah's eyes went wide with delight. "You think we have the same jammies, Mr. Colt?"

"I think we *did*," Colt emphasized, and when he opened his arms, Angelina's son half jumped into his embrace. "They don't make cool jammies like this for us big guys."

Noah pulled back, astonished. He put a little hand on each side of Colt's face. "Are you kidding me?"

"Wouldn't do that, bud." Colt smiled into the boy's hazel eyes, then bumped foreheads with him. "But if they made 'em in my size, I'd grab me a pair, just so we could be twins."

"I bet my mom will l-look on the computer to see," Noah said. He gave Colt a big hug and a smacking kiss, then wriggled to get down and raced to his mother. "Can you go see, Mom? See if they make jammies just like mine for Mr. Colt?"

"I will." She hugged the boy fiercely, gave him a big kiss, then raised her eyes to Colt. In that look he read a warning. "We'll check tomorrow, okay?"

"Okay!"

Noah dashed off with his grandmother following. As Colt handled the guys' good-natured ribbing about his nightwear, he couldn't miss the concern on Angelina's face. Was it because of the phone call? Knowing she'd be going soon? Or was it because the little guy liked him, and this Tony guy might not like that? Well, too bad for Tony, because Noah was taking hold of Colt's somewhat rusty heart and not letting go.

Ask her to stay.

He shoved the idea aside because that would be the height of selfishness. He wasn't staying any longer than he had to. Why would she? Why should she?

Plans get changed all the time. Why not yours? Why not now?

That couldn't happen. He rinsed off his dishes, loaded them in the dishwasher, and went outside to have a look around the far barns. Cold, crisp March air cleared his head but did little for the confusion in his brain. How could he manage to help his brother, his nieces, his father, and Angelina's situation when everyone held their cards tight to the chest?

Spring stars blinked above, a haze of galactic sparkle. He felt small in comparison, but as the curve of a gibbous moon peeked out from behind a random cloud, he realized he wasn't so small. The universe was just plain big.

The wonder of that stirred a yearning inside him. The blanket of stars and moons and planets and flying intergalactic debris loomed above him, thick and vast.

There was little visible sky in Manhattan. Actual night sky was a rarity in a city famed for its photogenic skyline. Light from competing skyscrapers polluted the darkness, so even if he was lucky enough to be on a rooftop patio, seeing many actual stars wasn't the norm.

Here it was expected. That realization had Colt looking up, wondering about the whos, whats, wheres, and hows of everything. Head back, he remembered stargazing as a little boy, not much bigger than Noah, peering up at the heavens with his mother. "Where did they all come from? Who made them?" he'd asked as she kept her arms looped around his middle. She'd let him climb to the top rail of the fence, so high that he was almost afraid, but not quite, and when she'd wrapped her arms around him from behind, he wasn't afraid at all.

"God, Colt. God's in his heaven, and he's watching over you and me."

"Over Daddy too?" He remembered tipping his head back to look at his mother. Even though he tried to bring it up, her image didn't come to him now. All he had was a shadow and a voice.

She'd laughed. He remembered how much he loved hearing her laugh. *"God especially watches over Daddy! He knows that daddies have a lot to do watching over families, so God watches over them especially well."*

"But not more than you, right?" He'd choked down the worry. If God spent so much time watching dads, when would he have time to watch over moms? *"He watches over moms the most, doesn't he?"*

"Of course." He remembered the soft kiss of her lips to his arm and the scent of her skin—kind of like cookies and flowers and

clean clothes all mushed together. *"He watches over moms most carefully because they have wonderful little boys like you."*

Later that night he'd dozed off, feeling good about everything. Believing God had it all under control, watching here, there, everywhere.

The next day he'd sucked up his fears, marched off to preschool, and kissed his beautiful mother good-bye. And then he never saw her again. Which meant either she was wrong and God didn't watch over mothers at all or that God was pretty clueless. Unseen, unheard, and totally untrustworthy.

Colt hadn't had a thing to do with God since. But here, tonight, gazing up at the heavens, his mother's voice came back to him. Her belief in the words she'd said to him pushed him to a new thought—maybe Colton Samuel Stafford ought to reexamine his belief systems.

And for the first time in over three decades, he considered doing just that, starting with church the next Sunday.

"Everybody ready?" Colt jogged down the stairs Sunday morning, straightening his tie. He adjusted the suit coat he'd worn the first night back, tucked Noah into his sturdy little winter jacket, hoisted him, and moved toward the kitchen. "We're going to be late if we stand around here. Hobbs warmed up the car. He's got it parked just outside the back door."

"You're going to church with us?" Surprise and pleasure brightened Sam's eyes.

"I am." He turned his attention to Angelina and smiled for no reason, and her heart fluttered in response.

"It will be wonderful to have such a full pew," Sam said.

"I'm so 'cited!" Noah flashed his mother a happy look over Colt's shoulder, as if he'd won a round of Candy Land. Angelina wanted to warn him that this was church—not a playground—but paused when her mother rounded the corner from the hallway joining the kitchen.

"I haven't been to church in so long!" Isabo looked around, radiant. "This is a blessing, so nice! All of us, together." She fell into step alongside Sam, adjusting her quick steps to his more measured ones as they followed Colt out the door. "If this church has candles, I shall light four," she continued as she pushed through the door. "One for Martín, one for gratitude, one for peace, and one for Stafford generosity."

Colt tucked Noah into the SUV, then stood by the rear door, ready to help his father into the warming vehicle if necessary. The fullness of his expression as he waited patiently for his father stirred Angelina's heart.

Isabo rounded the SUV and climbed into the backseat as Noah clicked the buckles of his third-row booster. When Angelina reached the car, Colt swung the front passenger door open for her. The look he gave her was so tender and sweet that despite all efforts to stop it, her heart went soft.

She could resist the gritty financial negotiator side of Colt Stafford, but there was no resisting this Colt—the gentle, caring guy, the true cowboy within. His charming behavior was touching too many sweet emotions—which meant Colt had just upped the stakes exponentially.

"I will help get food ready for our company later," Isabo said as Angelina settled into the front seat. "That way we don't fall behind. I had forgotten the joy of cooking for so many!"

"You sure do know your way around a kitchen, Isabo." Sam laced his words with thick gratitude. "Angelina obviously learned from the best."

"In such a kitchen as yours, there is no hardship in cooking," she said. "So much space, so many ideas, and the men, so happy. Their thankfulness makes cooking an honor, Sam!"

"Do you think Nick will come over with the girls?" Colt asked.

Sam shook his head. "Don't know. He was in quite a state the other night, and he's come straight in and out of the barn since, so he's got a stick—"

"A bee in his bonnet," Angelina quickly corrected.

"Sorry," Sam said. "Maybe he will, maybe he won't. And if something's wrong with the girls, he most likely won't be asking for help either because he's stubborn as a mule."

"Wonder where he got that from." Colt kept his eyes on the road but sounded almost amused. A nice change for a guy who'd been wearing bitterness like comfortable shoes. And he was right—the apples hadn't fallen far from the tree in Stafford-land.

As they passed the Carlton place, Sam asked, "That's where the gal lives who brought the cake, isn't it?"

"Yes. She's a single mom with three little kids. She works night and day to make a go of this Christmas tree farm."

"Single mom?" Colt looked puzzled.

"Widowed."

The crease in his forehead deepened. "I know it's been awhile, but I don't remember anybody named Carlton living in the Wheeler place. And I can't imagine the Wheeler place went up for sale and didn't become part of the Double S. I expect there's more to this story." He stopped the car at a stop sign and met his father's eyes through the rearview mirror.

"The Wheelers were losing the place," Sam replied. Reluctance deepened his voice. "I wanted it. They knew that. They didn't want me to have it and sold it quietly to Carlton. And then he—"

Angelina interrupted him as she offered an encouraging look at Noah. "You'll get to meet the Carlton kids in church, Noah. Belle's your age. Her brothers are older. Cheyenne and Dakota will be in church too."

"This will be so fun!" Anticipation brightened his eyes as he studied everything they passed. "I didn't know going to church would be so fun, Mom!"

Colt leaned her way as they slowed for the next stop sign. "He and the reverend might have different definitions of fun." He winked, then addressed his father. "They sold the property out from under you? That's kind of harsh."

"I'd made offers. They'd have rather gone broke than accept them."

"More than harsh then." Colt waited for slow, long beats as he made the turn into the town center. "What did you do to them?"

When Sam didn't answer, Angelina did. "Sam leased the grazing rights to the property that had been between the Wheelers and the Double S, then bought it. In addition to that, he punished the Wheelers for not accepting his offer by using his full share of the water rights, leaving them very little, even though he had plenty of fresh water from Gray's Creek."

"It was a knee-jerk thing to do, and I'm not proud of it," Sam admitted.

"Wow." Colt looked genuinely surprised. "I try to embrace a wider margin of anonymity before I mess folks over. Not the ones living next door."

"That was a long time ago," Sam countered. "I haven't done a thing to that new young woman's family." Sam brushed off the past as if it were that easy. "I eased up on the water and changed my grazing patterns. That way she had clean, fresh water for her trees as needed."

"In five years her trees will catch up to where they should have been," Angelina mused as if that was nothing. "In the meantime—"

"I'll write myself a note about that." Sam withdrew his phone, tapped a moment, then started to put it away.

"Silence it," Angelina said.

"Eh?"

"Your phone. Put it on silence or turn it off because you don't want it to ring in church."

"Of course not." He did as she asked. "I'll make it up to her. Somehow. You said she's got three kids?"

"Two school-aged boys and a little girl. Good kids."

"I'll fix it, Angelina. One way or another." He tucked his phone away in his coat pocket. "I'll make it right. I promise."

Heads turned as they walked into the gray and cream stone church. Colt looked straight ahead, holding Noah firmly in his arms, but Sam nodded at people left and right as if he were a regular. When only a few folks dipped their heads in welcome, Colt figured almost eighty percent of the congregation pretty much hated Sam Stafford. That wasn't a big surprise, but it meant his father had his work cut out for him.

Sam slipped into a pew on the right. Colt assessed his choice. *Near enough to the front to be seen and close enough to the middle to appear humbled.*

As if.

Colt stepped back to allow Angelina and her mother to enter the pew, then followed with the boy.

"This is church?" Noah looked around, surprised. "Where are the kids?"

"Sitting with their families," Angelina whispered. "Being quiet."

Noah glanced around. "When do we play?"

Colt coughed on purpose. Angelina's quick look warned him to keep his opinion to himself, then whispered an answer. "Afterward. Right now it's quiet prayer time."

"For everybody?" He burrowed closer into Colt's side. The big cowboy couldn't deny how nice it was to have a little cowpoke seek shelter in his arms. He bent to explain what was going to happen even though it had been a long time since he'd darkened the door of a church for a regular service. The guitar player in the front left began picking out notes. As the congregation stood and began singing the beloved, familiar tune, Colt leaned close to Noah's ear. "Do you want to stand on your own or would you like me to hold you?"

The boy snuggled closer.

Colt's heart melted further. He toughened it quickly. He was starting to get comfortable with this old/new routine. Early to bed, early to rise, great food, a beautiful woman who wore faith like New York women wore black blazers, and the feel of a child tucked close beneath his chin.

Yeah. He could get used to this if he let himself, so he wouldn't allow that to happen.

An hour later, after the reverend brought the service to a close, Noah jumped off Colt's lap when two school-aged boys raced across the aisle toward them. He stared up at the bigger boys, almost dancing with excitement.

"Miz Angie, I did just what you said, and I closed my eyes before Mom turned out the light," the smaller boy said, "and I wasn't one bit scared!"

"And I made sure the cat had food and water every day," asserted the bigger boy proudly. Behind them a petite little girl dimpled as she peeked around the bigger boy's arm.

"And I only wet the bed once this week," she whispered. The look on her face, like dry sheets were the world's most amazing accomplishment, reminded Colt of Trey when he first came to the Double S. Trey's mother had been Sam's younger sister. She was a party girl who married a drug user, and by the time Trey was a toddler, his clueless parents shared a deep addiction. A bad mix of street cocaine killed them both, leaving three-year-old Trey orphaned. Sam brought the little guy to the Double S—a scared, sad bedwetter who'd been neglected by the two who should have loved him most. Sam adopted Trey, making him the third motherless child to call the Double S home.

The Staffords had been a poor substitute for normal, but at least Trey had clean sheets each night, a home on a thriving ranch, and the affection of several housekeepers over the years. Not perfect, no. But not as bad as living with drug-addicted parents in a hovel in Oakland.

He made a mental note to call Trey once they got home, see how he was doing. He'd let their relationship slide, and that was wrong. He was the oldest. He should be the mainstay.

Angelina closed the distance between them and bent to the little girl's level. "Belle, that's wonderful! I'm so proud of you! And now I have someone I want you guys to meet." Angelina embraced the little girl with one arm, then drew Noah close on the other side. Her long dark hair fell over her front shoulder into an oblique beam of stained-glass light. The refracted ray sent colors shimmering across her shoulders like crazed, dancing, animated fairies. She looked up, and the rainbow patch shifted to her cheek.

Colt couldn't breathe. Holding Noah through the service, seeing Angelina and the children, surrounded by the sights and sounds of the past he'd walked away from, he had a sudden and desperate need for air. He broke the connection, turned, and headed for the door.

"Colt, you remember Mrs. Iudicci, don't you?" Sam had stopped just ahead, blocking his path.

It was either frog-leap his father or pause and suck it up while exchanging pleasantries with the former elementary school nurse. "Of course." He stuck out his hand, wondering why he'd thought coming to church was a good idea. He'd walked away from this, all this, long ago, and he had no intention of getting caught up in the suffocating small-town atmosphere he'd labeled "unimportant" when he graduated from Wharton. "It's been a long time, ma'am."

She clasped his hand in both of hers. "Too long!" She smiled up at him and then his father before releasing his hand and admonishing him. "Now we just need Trey back."

Sam shook his head. "Not likely, I'm afraid. He's busy—"

Colt cleared his throat, and his father stopped midsentence, then sighed.

"What I mean is," Sam confessed, "I was a jerk when he wanted to explore music and move to Nashville, and he probably wants nothing to do with me. Understandably."

That his father admitted this to the elderly woman was astonishing. She reached a hand to Sam's shoulder and said, "A man who sings of love and forgiveness with the grace of Trey Walker Stafford won't let too many more suns go down without setting things right. Trey loves God. It's plain in everything he does. He'll be back."

"I hope so." Longing and exhaustion thinned Sam's voice.

Colt put a hand under his arm. If you'd asked him a few weeks back if he thought he'd ever be helping his father out of church on a Sunday morning, he'd have fallen down laughing. But here he was.

Obviously he didn't know as much as he thought he did. "We've got the Bennetts coming for dinner, Dad. If we don't get back to the ranch, they'll be visiting an empty table."

"I won't keep you," Mrs. Iudicci said. "Go with God and enjoy this beautiful day."

The sun's higher angle promised spring. Water dripped from gutters and trees, and the thick blizzard snow had diminished to thin lines on north-facing slopes. Beneath the church's overhang, tiny green spikes from hearty flowers tested the warmth, tempting fate this early in the year.

"Mr. Colt!"

He turned. Angelina and their widowed neighbor were walking his way, deep in conversation.

Not Noah.

He raced along the sidewalk, then launched himself into Colt's arms when Colt bent low. "Hey, bud. Whadja think?" Colt jerked his thumb toward the emptying church as the two women drew closer.

Noah threw his arms wide. "I l-loved it so much! Not at first." He leaned close, whispering. "I don't really like being quiet, but when those big boys said hi to me, it was so much fun!"

"Well, it's pretty special when a little dude gets noticed by the big guys, I agree." He hugged the boy close. So close. For just a moment the roles were reversed, and it was Cole being hugged outside the pretty stone church, caught and cherished in the loving arms of his mother.

He sighed, and when Angelina drew close, he turned.

She smiled at the boy, or maybe it was the sight of him holding Noah that inspired her look. He'd be okay with that.

He turned more fully toward the woman with Angelina and extended his hand. "I'm Colt Stafford, Mrs. Carlton."

She looked uncertain, then accepted the gesture. "It's Lucy, please."

"Lucy." He smiled down at the three kids, all of whom seemed to have taken a sudden vow of silence. "Nice to meet our nearest neighbor. You did all right in the storm, I hope?"

Surprise flitted across her face, as if the last thing she expected was to have a Stafford ask after her well-being. "We managed, thank you. The boys helped me shovel out."

Regret hit Colt square. He'd never considered checking on neighbors, helping them move the heavy, wet snowfall. "I'm sorry. I should have thought of that, ma'am. Next time, for sure."

"Which, hopefully, won't be until next year," Angelina said. "I'm ready for a change of seasons."

"Me too." Lucy glanced up. "The higher sun feels especially nice."

"It does." Angelina stooped to say good-bye to Lucy's brood. "I'll bring Noah over on Tuesday, okay? We'll have a little time together before I need to get back and make supper."

"Okay!"

"Sure!" The boys looked excited at the prospect. Colt found out why when the younger one asked, "Will you bring us cookies again? Because they were really good, Miss Angie!"

"It's not polite to ask!" The older boy smacked the younger boy's arm. "You're embarrassing Mom."

"Am not!"

"Are too!"

Colt turned back to Lucy. "Rye Bennett is bringing Brendan and Jenna over this afternoon for dinner and some time on the ranch. Would you like to bring the kids by?"

Lucy squirmed. "No, but thank you. It's very kind of you to ask—"

"I'd like to go!" Now it was the older boy having his say. "How come we don't ever get to do anything?"

Lucy gave him a mother-knows-best look. "Perhaps another time. And that's not how you talk to your mother. Ever."

"I've been wanting to see the big house for a very long time." The second boy groaned the words in a most convincing fashion, as if he might run out of air by being denied his heart's desire.

"I'll wait." The little girl whispered the phrase and dimpled up at Colt. "I'll come over when Mommy says it's okay."

The boys didn't like being shown up by their little sister. Grumbling, they trudged off to a minivan that had seen its best day a decade before. Lucy watched them go, and when they were safely in the van, she turned back. "I appreciate the invitation, Mr. Stafford."

"Colt."

She accepted that graciously. "Colt. Though I'm not sure everyone in your family would embrace our presence."

She meant his father. Colt breathed deep. "You'd have been right a few months ago. Let's just say Angelina has managed to have an unexpected effect and there's been a change of heart up at the Double S."

"That would be an answer to a lot of prayers," Lucy told him softly. She glanced at the valley town surrounding them. "This should be a great place to raise a family, but divisiveness makes poor seed ground. I'd love to see the community working together. Not split apart."

"I agree." Angelina hugged Lucy good-bye. "I'll see you on Tuesday. I won't have too long to visit. Long enough for Noah and Belle to play and for him to have a few minutes with the boys."

"You take the time you need," Isabo said as she approached them. She'd gone to the bank of flickering votive candles in a secluded corner of the rustic church while Sam had walked ahead to the SUV. She came alongside them in time to hear Angelina's last words. "I'll make supper, and Noah can have time with other children. As it should be. But now we should go because Sam looks so very tired."

"He does." Colt held Angelina's door open for her, then circled the car to do the same for her mother. "We'll see you again, Lucy."

"Of course." Lucy waved good-bye and took Belle's hand before walking toward her van. Once everyone was in the SUV, Colt deliberately waited to make sure Lucy's van started. It did, but from the sound of it, it wasn't going to start much longer. He pulled away, made a U-turn, and headed back up the hill toward the ranch, but his brain was busy dissecting what he'd seen so far.

Gray's Glen needed jobs. It needed an energetic shot in the arm to get the wheels moving faster and without mishap. Jobs and small businesses were the rootstock of a successful community. But how to get them was another question altogether. Two small manufacturing plants had closed down long ago. The sprinkling of successful shops were long-established, family-owned businesses.

He mulled the situation as he made the turn up the ranch drive. He pulled up to the side porch and glanced at his father in the rearview mirror. Sam's head lolled to one side. He jerked it back, fighting sleep, but Colt was pretty sure fatigue would win this round. He stepped out, rounded the car, and helped his father into the house. Should Sam be so exhausted by something as simple as attending services? Colt didn't think so.

He helped Sam to his room, and when his father had collapsed onto the bed and fallen sound asleep, Colt went upstairs to call his brother Trey.

"Colt? What's up? Is everything okay?" Surprise and concern hiked Trey's voice, because having Colt call him in the middle of the day . . . or ever . . . wasn't the norm. If anything, Colt would shoot off a text now and again.

"Does there have to be something wrong for me to call you?"

"Generally. What's going on?"

"I think it's time for a visit, Trey."

A long moment of silence followed his words, then Trey's voice came through softer. "Dad's that bad?"

"I'm no doctor, but this injury and illness are taking a toll, and I don't see him getting better."

"He left a message on my voice mail the other day. Just to talk, he said. I never got back to him."

"Well." Colt breathed deep. "It's probably a good idea to make that call, Trey. There've been a lot of changes around here."

"As in?"

"He's sick and he's found God. He says he intends to make

things right on multiple levels, which tells me the Grim Reaper's got him scared spitless."

"The late harvesters," Trey muttered. "They always come back to bite you in the butt."

"Huh?"

"A parable about not expecting equality. Jesus. Bible. New Testament. You remember that stuff, don't you? A smattering, at least?"

Trey was the kind of Bible thumper Colt could get along with. Never shoving, always musing, quietly inspirational, and genuinely funny. Sitting there on the edge of the bed, he realized how much he missed his younger brother. What a jerk he was for letting so much time slip away. "I remember. Why don't you show up here and remind me some more? I could use a dose of your common sense, Trey."

"That's no surprise," Trey replied, and he sounded downright cheerful saying it. "I'll make arrangements."

"Arrangements? What arrangements?"

"A room, a place to stay. The Glen Hollow Inn is still nice, isn't it?"

"You'll stay right here," Colt ordered. "There's plenty of room, and this is your home."

"I got tossed out when I moved to Nashville, remember?"

Colt scoffed. "We've all gotten tossed out. Big deal. Stay here, Trey. Really. The only way to get a feel for what's going down is to be in the thick of it. Dad's illness, a bossy new house manager who makes everyone pray before meals. We're right up your alley now."

"I'll consider it," Trey promised. His voice deepened. "And

honestly, Colt, you're surprising me. You sound . . ." He paused as if groping for words. "Different. Almost happy. I didn't expect that. I like it."

"Bad connection," Colt replied smoothly. "Come visit, climb on a horse, and we'll see if we can attract some pretty girl action."

Trey laughed out loud. "I can do without the girl action. I'm ready for a little time off."

"That's right, you've got scores of women throwing their phone numbers at you, waiting at the back door to scream and wave and faint. I forgot how rough that is."

Thick silence met his teasing, and when Trey replied, Colt heard the longing in his voice. "It's not about numbers, Colt. It's never been about numbers."

"I know, bro. I was messing with you. Come hang out here for a bit. We've got the best food in the world, Nick's girls need to meet their famous uncle—"

"Unlike you, Nick actually came to my Seattle concert last year—with the girls."

"I went to the one at Madison Square Garden three years ago," Colt shot back. "Nothing holds a candle to MSG."

"Because it was practically next door, with the least possible effort expended," Trey reminded him. "I'll get back to you about coming. But you're right, Colt. It's time to set things right, and God doesn't work on man's schedule. He's got his own calendar, and it would be plain stupid of me to run out of time."

NINE

"*You have made us for yourself, O Lord, and our heart is restless until it rests in you.*"

Restless. Yes. The perfect word with an imperfect solution. Saint Augustine sure did know what he was talking about, Angelina decided. She gripped the top rail of the fence and watched as Jenna worked a horse in the adjacent arena. Brendan hadn't wanted to ride, but when Hobbs offered to take him uphill in the ATV, he'd jumped at the chance to climb aboard. Rye came alongside her, holding an insulated cup of coffee. "Your mother is a wonderful person. She gave me coffee and a monster-sized hunk of pumpkin roll."

"Did she mention she accidentally tripled half the ingredients, so she had enough for six full rolls once we discovered the mistake and fixed it?" Angelina slanted a smile his way. "We've got three to eat and three in the freezer."

"Don't much care why she's generous," Rye drawled. "Just that she is. Nice that she's staying here with you guys, Angelina." He winked and sipped his coffee. "And the mystery kid's a total bonus."

"Rye." She sighed. "I knew you'd call me out on this because you're good at your job." She watched as Noah clung to the saddle horn, then said, "He's only a mystery to you. Not to me. That's what counts, right?"

"Hey." He shrugged, gazing outward. "I don't know what your story is, but here's what I do know. I came back to town at the worst possible time in my life. I left a job I loved in Chicago because this is where I was needed. Folks told me about you—the housekeeper up at the ranch who makes a difference."

She flushed and looked away.

"And then I got a report of an unknown little kid being treated by Doc Humphreys last fall. Brought in by his Hispanic grandmother."

"So much for HIPAA rules," Angelina muttered as Colt led Noah around the far corner of the ring.

"Doc said nothing. He and Sam go way back. He'd never throw Sam under the bus. It was a not-so-well-meaning local who thought the kid and his grandma might be illegals."

"Like that's a rarity at apple-harvest time. And all Hispanics look alike, of course."

He ignored her remark and leaned against the fence. "I asked around. No one knew anything. It didn't seem to be a big deal, so I let it go. Now, four months later, we've got new folks living at the Double S. A grandmother and grandson—a kid you never mentioned. When mothers don't mention kids, it makes a cop wonder why."

With her family out in the open, the reason for secrecy disappeared. "I'm a cop," she told him. "*Was* a cop," she corrected herself.

Rye snorted. "Tell me something I don't know."

Surprised, she started to turn his way as Colt and Noah drew near.

"Mom! L-look at me!" Noah pseudo-shouted to her, following Colt's direction to keep his voice soft. "I th-think this horse likes me a lot!"

She fist-pumped the air, quietly cheering him on. "I'm sure she does." She looked at Colt, but he wasn't looking at her. He was staring at Rye as they passed, a back-off-my-girl expression on his face.

"So that's how it is." Rye pushed back his faded cowboy hat and looked sideways at her.

Was it? She'd been telling herself she didn't want that. Didn't want *him,* the financial guy. Yet watching him with Noah, she realized maybe she'd been lying to herself. She left her confusing thoughts and went back to the former topic. "How did you know I was a cop?"

"Simple observation, sweetheart. You're always packing, you've got the cop eye, and you never have your back to the door. So then I asked myself, 'What's a cop doing washing dishes and slinging hash on a ranch? What happens to make someone toss the badge aside and take up a spatula instead?'"

She wasn't about to launch into that topic now. "Life changes things. This"—she breathed deeply as she watched Colt and Noah make an easy turn around the paddock—"is peaceful. Look how happy he is."

"I see that." Rye watched as Colt swung himself up behind the boy and urged the horse to a faster gait. "But if you'd come here for peaceful, you would have had your kid and mother with you. I figure that something happened somewhere. I'm not prying, Angelina."

She disparaged that with a look, and he shook his head. "I'm not.

I just want you to know that if you need anything, the sheriff's department is here for you. More than one person told me about how you stopped by to see my mother before she died."

"Your mother was a good woman. Kind and caring. And those kids had enough to deal with. I was happy to do it."

"When folks do things like that in small towns, people notice," Rye said. "You need anything at all"—he aimed a look across the paddock—"let me know. And if Colt isn't smart enough to know a good thing when he's got it, I'll be glad to pick up the pieces when he heads back east."

"Rye Bennett, are you flirting with me?" She looked right at him.

Rye winked. "I'm not stupid enough to get in Colt's way, but he's a Stafford, and they're uncommonly dense about what they want."

She sighed because she'd seen that firsthand, but since she didn't know what she wanted either, that made them evenly matched.

"Can we go faster, Colt? Like real fast?" Noah peeked up at the big guy behind him, eyes wide with excitement.

"A little faster," Colt promised. He winked at Angelina and urged the mare into a faster clip, and when Noah laughed out loud, Colt grinned.

Sweet longing grabbed hold of her.

This is what she'd wanted for her child. A loving man dedicated to raising Noah with her. She'd chosen poorly and that was her fault, but why was she tempted to repeat the error in judgment? She pushed back from the fence. "I'm going to help my mom with dinner. And Rye, thanks for the kind words. I appreciate them."

He met her gaze, then tipped his hat briefly. "Meant every word, ma'am."

She strode back into the house, perturbed at herself, Colt, Noah's father, and life.

"What's happened? What's wrong?" Concern deepened Isabo's voice as she looked up from the roasting chickens she'd taken out to baste.

"Nothing. I'm just ticked off at the world in general. Choices, good and bad. Lack of choices, good and bad." She yanked off her hat and scarf and flung them onto the bench inside the back door.

"I think it is because you do not wish to leave here," her mother said, eyes down.

"Don't be ridiculous."

"I am not ridiculous; I am fairly sensible." Isabo kept her tone mild, a trick Angelina needed to practice more often. "But I see what is at hand, and there are looks that pass between my daughter and Sam's son."

"No law against looking," Angelina said as she scrubbed her hands. "We've got two different agendas, and I will never let myself be fooled by a smooth-talking money mogul again."

"I think you have to actually *have* accessible funds to be considered a mogul," offered Colt from the doorway.

Chagrin and embarrassment made her voice gruffer than she intended. "You followed me in?"

"My little cowpoke needs to use the facilities, ma'am." He rubbed Noah's hair, dropped his hat onto a pile of other hats, and set him down in the kitchen. "And then I promised him hot chocolate."

"Well, kick those shoes off and head down the hall, partner." Noah laughed at her lame attempt to talk western, tossed his shoes aside, and raced down the hall to the bathroom as she redirected her attention to Colt. "Thank you for riding with him. You gave him the thrill of a lifetime."

"I expect it was the smooth talk that did it." He winked, using her words against her, and backed out the door. "Temperature is dropping. I'm going to call Jenna in and have the horses put up. Feels like a blow coming on." He strode away as a gust of wind whistled beneath the side porch eaves.

"He is not one to hide his interest. I like that," Isabo said as she slid the double roasters back into the oven. "A man who stakes a claim is more likely to be trusted."

"There is no claim to be staked. You know it. I know it. He knows it."

"He will never accept that," Isabo replied. She dropped potatoes into the kettle of water with infuriating calm, one after the other. "He is not that kind of man. Like his father, when he sees something he wants, he finds a way to get it. You can see that as you look around this home, this land. It takes a person like that to accomplish what they've done. You have Colt thinking of new things and old. He weighs what was with what could be," Isabo noted. "This is good."

"You're assuming too much, Mami. He is simply dealing with the ghosts of old memories, the loss of his mother, his father's anger, and attempts to make things right."

The sound of the front door opening cut their conversation

because everyone on the ranch used the back door. Then Nick came in with both girls, and as he attempted to close the solid wood door, a brisk wind snatched it from his grasp and smashed it against the wall. He grabbed the door and pushed it shut as Rye, Hobbs, and the older kids came through the back door.

"Did you hear?" All traces of Nick's midweek animosity disappeared as he faced the men in the spacious kitchen and dining area.

"Hear what?"

"Two weather systems have merged off the coast. They've upgraded the wind force to hurricane levels."

Rye withdrew his keys and started for the front door. "Jenna, Brendan, gotta go."

Jenna looked disappointed but started to follow him. "Okay."

Brendan stepped in the other direction. "Why can't we stay for a while? For supper, at least. You promised."

"If there's trouble coming, I've got to get things moving." He held up his radio as an emergency broadcast signal blared the recognizable warning. "When things get dangerous, I'm on duty. It's my job," he said as Colt came into the kitchen through the back door.

"It's always about your job," grumbled Brendan. "It's not like you'll even be at home. You'll go off to work, and Jenna and I will be stuck alone with no food and nothing to do."

"Can they stay here?" Colt asked Rye. "Food's almost ready and that way you'll know they're safe. You'll be free to work, and we could use Brendan's help if there's fallen trees or moderate damage to the ranch."

"After last year's wildfires, we've got mudslide dangers in multiple areas if we get hard rain," Nick said. "Angelina, is it okay if the girls stay here while I work? I don't want to ask Cassie to watch them if there's trouble at the house or we lose power."

"It's fine." She winked at Cheyenne and Dakota as Sam came down the hall.

"Another storm?" Sam asked.

"Welcome to spring," Hobbs said as he put in calls to the other men. "One season comin', another goin' means just about anything can happen and often will. A blizzard one week, a deluge the next."

"The thaw's softened soil layers," Sam reminded them. The frustration in his face said he hated not being able to layer up and join them as they guided cattle toward the safer sides of the rangeland. "Big wind and soft ground can uproot spruce real quick."

"And when you add gale-force winds, no side is really safe." Colt turned as Murt came through the side door to join them. "Murt, thanks for coming right over. Can you and Hobbs bring the ATVs up?"

"We sure can. I brought Joe along; he's ready to jump in." Murt's teenage great nephew came through the door just then, dressed for work. "The missus is none too happy with me for leavin' when the kids are there for Sunday dinner, but weather's weather I told her. If this storm is anything like Columbus Day back in '62, we've got a fight on our hands, and me and Joe aren't ones to miss a good fight." He clapped a hand firmly against Colt's arm. "How you doin' missin' that climate controlled office on Park Avenue now, Colton?"

Colt shoved his hands into thick gloves. "Ask me again in three hours. Let's go."

Colt turned, then swung back. He sent Angelina a look across the room that said more than words, a look that hit her heart. "Take care. And tell my little buddy I had a lot of fun workin' circles with him."

"I will. Go with God, Colt."

"Yes'm." He tugged a double knit hat onto his head, then pretended to tip a nonexistent cowboy brim her way. "I'll call."

Two simple words, spoken just to her in front of everyone.

The men heading into the hills were too busy to make much of it right then, but she saw Sam's eyebrow hike up and heard her mother's soft hum, which communicated that both had noticed.

Rye disappeared out the front door. Brendan and Joe went out to secure anything loose around the stockyards, and Angelina set Jenna to work overseeing a reluctant Cheyenne's homework. If the wind was bad, it might mean another round of days off for the kids. But just in case it blew by with little notice and there was school in the morning, getting weekend homework done was worth risking Cheyenne's glare.

"Pinch me. Tell me I'm not dreaming," Jenna stage-whispered after dinner when a burst of ice-cold wind blew through as the front door opened from outside. "Because if this is a dream, I'd be okay with never waking up. Seriously."

Isabo crossed the kitchen toward the open door to the great room, concerned. "You are wide awake! Why do you think you are to dream? What kind of nonsense—? Oh." She paused at the entrance to the kitchen, turned, and motioned Angelina over. "I think you need to call Sam."

Cheyenne looked up from the floor of the great room, homework spread out before her. So did Dakota. They stared too, and it wasn't until Angelina made it around the corner that she understood.

Country music superstar Trey Walker Stafford had come home.

He waved to Cheyenne and Dakota as he shut the door, then made Jenna half swoon when he flashed her a stage-worthy smile. When his eyes landed on Angelina, he took off his cowboy hat, set it on the newel post, and moved forward, hand outstretched. "I'm Trey."

"Angelina, your father's housekeeper." She clasped his hand.

"I've heard a lot about you from Nick." Trey smiled right into her eyes. "He says you've been downright good for my father, so I'm mighty grateful. And when I talked to Colt earlier, he said it was past time for a visit, so here I am."

Colt, again, drawing folks back. How was it that the one who left the flock the longest managed to somehow bring people together?

Sam's shaky voice interrupted their introduction. "You . . . came."

Angelina turned, alarmed.

The falter in Sam's voice was caused by more than surprise or storm concerns. It was evident in the dusky pallor beneath pale skin. As he walked toward them, he listed hard to the right.

Angelina caught him on one side.

Trey took hold of the other. Angelina noticed that despite how badly Trey and Sam had parted years before, the youngest son's grip had a tenderness to its strength. "Couch?" he asked with a quick look to the great room beyond.

She nodded. Isabo raised a phone in question. Angelina nodded again, and her mother slipped down the hall to place the 911 call.

She didn't know if it was Sam's liver or his slowly mending ribs or something else going on, but she knew his deterioration in the last few hours wasn't anything she could handle at the ranch. Sam needed help and he needed it now.

Colt's phone vibrated. He yanked it out, saw the house number, and took the call. "Ange, what's up?"

"It is Isabo," her mother corrected him. "Your father is sick. We have called for help, but Angelina said I should call you."

Colt's heart went tight. So did his gut. Was this how it was all going to end, with his father fading away and nothing fixed? Had the great Sam Stafford finally run out of time? "We'll come right in."

"No. I've got this, Colt." A different voice took over the phone, a distinctly Stafford voice.

"Trey. You came."

"Grabbed a quick ride and just arrived," Trey replied. "Keep on with what you're doing. Dad will be calmer knowing you're moving cattle."

"Too many cattle and not enough time, but we'll do what we can. Put Angelina on." A moment of silence answered his command before Angelina's voice came through.

"Don't boss your brother around like that. Be nice."

Her words felt good because if Angelina was scolding him, Dad couldn't be at death's door. "What's up with Dad? Is it serious?"

"It looks serious, but I'm not a doctor, hence the ambulance call. Mami is staying here with the kids. The ambulance just rolled in. I'll call you." *Click.*

With anyone else, the quick put-off would have scorched, but with her, he accepted it.

Because you're falling for her.

He knew it. He'd known it from the beginning—well, maybe not when the gun was pointing at his heart, but not long after. She drew him. Worse? He wanted to be drawn. But what possible end could there be? His future wasn't here. It had never been here. And from the sound of things, neither was hers.

And yet as he backed up Yesterday's News to stop a rush of cattle from missing the gate to the eastern pasture, it felt right to be with the others on the windswept hillside. Moving cattle to safer ground and directing Banjo and Kita to gather up strays meant something. Other than making boatloads of money, when was the last time his work had meant something?

He couldn't remember, but right now he needed to focus on getting these pregnant cows into a lower pen and pray the fences held. Deep snow, mud, or high wind could wreak havoc with fencing, and loose cows weren't all that bright. He had no intention of watching their specially developed herd of seed cattle go to ruin at the hands of Mother Nature. Not if he could help it. As the wind rose, moaning through thick stands of hillside trees, Colt realized this outcome wasn't up to him. This one was between Mother Nature and God.

"Colt!"

He locked the second gate and turned toward the urgency of Nick's voice.

Thick black smoke poured out of the village below. From their higher vantage point, they could see Gray's Glen fanned out along the valley floor, surrounded by a patchwork quilt of farm fields and pastures. This evening the postcard image was marred by wind-fed smoke and fire. He urged Yesterday's News to follow the other men down the hill at a much faster clip than was safe and pulled up in the stockyard. "Brendan! Joe!"

Joe rushed out of the barn, Brendan on his heels. "Take the horses and see to the barn stock. There's a fire in town. It looks bad. We're taking the SUV."

"Got it, Colt." Joe wasted no time and quickly gathered the reins.

Nick jumped into the driver's seat. Colt grabbed shotgun, and Murt and Hobbs climbed in behind Colt. Brendan scrambled in the other side. Nick gave him an instant thumbs-down. "Brendan, go help Joe. You can't come down there. Your brother would kill me if anything happened to you."

"I'm fourteen. I'm not a kid. And folks might need help," Brendan insisted. "If you don't take me, I'll run down there anyway. It's got to be smarter to take me along, Nick."

Colt kept his mouth shut. The kid was right. Besides, he remembered being bullheaded at fourteen.

Nick must have come to a similar conclusion. Instead of arguing, he issued a stern warning. "Stay out of trouble and don't get killed."

He popped the car into gear and squealed the tires against the hard stoned surface as he turned it around.

Fire in densely forested land traveled fast, and wind-fed fire magnified the peril. Even though it wasn't fire season, the proximity of the village houses and businesses in a wind-tunnel valley meant a raging fire in high-wind conditions could spell the end of their picturesque town.

In the strained silence of the car, each of them understood what could lie ahead.

"The church is on fire," Angelina whispered to Trey in Sam's three-curtained cubicle at Slater Memorial. She pocketed her phone and grabbed her jacket from the ER chair. "They'll need help. Call me or one of the guys when you know what's going on with Sam, okay?"

Trey didn't quibble, but his interest sharpened. "What kind of housekeeper are you, Angelina? Because I noticed they didn't question the gun you've got tucked in your waistband at the hospital entrance."

"I'm trained for emergencies, and plenty of people pack heat out here." She grabbed her purse, then turned. "I'm taking the car. You'll be okay hanging out here until one of us can come get you, won't you?"

"We're fine." He clasped his father's hand and bowed his head as she parted the curtains to leave. Hurrying to the parking garage, she contemplated the differences among the three brothers. Trey owned his faith. It was clear in his eyes, his countenance, and the folded hands in prayer. Nick tolerated the idea of faith because he was a father and that's what fathers were supposed to do. Colt fought the idea of handing over his hard-won control to anything or anyone, a true questioner. Three brothers with similar lives, yet so different. Was that normal?

She didn't know. Her mother had lost several babies, born too soon, leaving her an only child.

She took solace in her faith and comfort in God's forgiveness.

Fifteen minutes later, when she approached the dark, smoke-filled town of Gray's Glen, prayer was the first thing she reached for. She wanted that for Colt. Something bigger than man and money to fall back on.

She parked the car in the convenience-store lot above the business district, shoved her hands into gloves, and pulled her hat snug over her head. She might not be able to fight a fire, but she could help with crowd control and public safety. She locked the car door, pocketed the keys, then raced toward the fire.

~~~

"Aim that hose there! No left, go left!" The fire chief barked a continuous stream of orders.

Two hose companies from surrounding towns made it into the burn zone, but tree fall blocked others from getting into Gray's Glen. That meant regular people helped fight the wind-fed fire until more help arrived. Downed trees, branches, and live wires would make access difficult, but Rye sent word that they were focusing on clearing the lower road into town. Until they were successful, it was the people of Gray's Glen versus a raging inferno. And the people weren't winning.

"Colt! I need you over here!"

Colt followed Todd Johnson's voice through the wind-driven smoke. The volunteer firefighter pointed to a pumper set up near adjacent buildings. "Open it full throttle and soak 'em."

Colt took his place behind two rugged firefighters to help steady the heavy hose. Smoke belched from the burning church. The ornate stained-glass windows he'd admired that morning were gone, all gone. Wind-whipped flames jumped through the air and set a churchyard tree on fire. Within seconds the majestic spruce was engulfed, and the spectacle of the dangerous evergreen torch pushed everyone back to a safer distance as crews sprayed water on the flaming tree.

"Pumper two, pumper two, redirect on church!"

The order came through the firefighter, and the men in front of Colt worked a cooperative pivot to aim their hose at the engulfed church while the crew on the opposite side focused on the tree.

Rancid air surrounded the volunteers. By rights, every one of these people should be in protective masks, but there were none. The extratropical windstorm lunging their way wasn't cutting them any slack. As of yet, not a drop of rain accompanied the wind.

"We've got people in the second house on Chelan Pass!" A firefighter barked the information across the static-filled radio as Colt peered toward his father's rental properties on Chelan Pass. The smoke was too thick for him to see anything. "Who's on Chelan Pass? Evacuate! Second house, evacuate!" The wind had shifted direction into a full swirl mode. Flaming embers landed on houses facing the rear of the fully engulfed church.

As a wind shift lifted the smoke around Colt, the church roof made a painful, agonizing groan. And then the tall arched roof crashed to the ground.

Gone. The church he attended with his mother, her hand holding his, now gone. Something inside—his heart maybe—ached to see it.

He shifted his gaze deliberately, fighting the pain. Gripping the hose, he retrained his attention on his father's rentals, just behind and above the church. When the wind cleared the smoke momentarily, a familiar figure raced past the low-level floodlights and up the steps of the second house on Chelan Pass.

Angelina.

What was she doing here?

He didn't have to ask the question. He knew the answer. And from what he'd gleaned about her so far, he shouldn't be surprised. But the thought of her in danger made him want to abandon the hose and race after her.

"Pumper two. We're back in. Redirect to the perimeter housing."

From the slightly garbled request, Colt knew they hadn't been able to save the tree. A quick glance confirmed it. The tree was nothing more than a smoldering caricature of its original self. In minutes, the seventy-foot evergreen had been consumed.

"We've still got people on Chelan Pass. Send evacuation crews now!" Todd barked the order into the radio. "We've got active fire on Chelan Pass. Active fire on Chelan Pass!"

The twisting wind had carried more than small embers in the

last thirty seconds. It took a section of flaming plywood, torn loose by the roof's demise, and sent it flying onto the porch roof of the second house on Chelan Pass—the house Angelina had just entered.

His heart fought a war within his chest. Had anyone else seen her go into the house? Could anyone spare a man to follow up? Where were the crews from the surrounding towns?

"What do we need most?" a voice behind him asked. "Dad's in good hands, and a cop gave me a ride back to town."

Colt turned. Trey was at his side. At that moment, his pesky, God-loving, music-crooning younger brother looked like a gift from God himself. "Take my place. We've got trouble on Chelan Pass," he yelled over the roar of wind and flames. The flood of water pulsing through the thick, heavy hose matched the push of blood through his veins. "I'll be back."

Trey stepped in behind him and grabbed hold. The minute Colt felt the weight of the hose lessen, he darted for the narrow neighborhood street cutting diagonally away from the church. He raced up the steps of the now-burning house. The porch roof flamed above him, the wood-seeking fire and gusting wind a formidable pair. He pushed through the door, calling Angelina's name.

Nothing.

He had no flashlight, but his cell phone did. He swiped it on, yelling as he raced through the bottom four rooms of the dark house, the bright, narrow beam flicking from spot to spot.

Still nothing.

He pounded up the stairs, and as he turned left at the top,

Angelina appeared in front of him. "¡*Gracias, a Dios!* Take this one!" She thrust a small boy at him, then raced back into the room she'd just exited. She came back in quick seconds, pressing a screeching, bawling girl against her chest. "Go!"

He went. They barreled down the stairs as the fire broke through the front wall. The little boy screamed in terror and gripped Colt's chest fiercely. The girl hadn't stopped shrieking, but when thick, waving flames licked the walls surrounding the nearest exit, the child went strangely silent. Colt glanced back. Intense fear claimed her face while dancing flames shifted light and shadow.

As they ran down the porch steps, the right-hand support gave way. The thrust of energy nearly knocked Colt off his feet. He turned, grabbed hold of Angelina's arm, and led them left, away from the flames.

A pumper rounded the corner from the northwest, followed by another. Firefighters jumped down, a mad scramble of organized activity as the roar of burning wood and radioed commands filled the normally quiet air of the sweet, small town.

"I want my mommy." The little boy in his arms whispered the plea as fire hungrily consumed their home. "I just want my mommy."

Colt looked at Angelina. She shook her head. She hadn't found anyone else in the house, but who would leave two small children unattended? He couldn't imagine such a thing. Tears streamed down the children's cheeks. Part of him wanted to cry along with them. Parents who couldn't take the time to be parents shouldn't have kids. He unzipped his barn coat, hugged the boy close, and pulled the edges of his jacket around him. "The evacuation site is the middle school. Let's get these guys there. You wanna trade up, Ange?" He looked at the little girl in her arms. "My guy's smaller."

"We're good." Angelina cuddled the crying girl against her. The child's tears inspired a sheen of moisture in Angelina's eyes. She didn't cave, though, and as she held the little girl close, she began crooning an old-time lullaby. They walked through the garish scene of burning buildings and flashing lights toward the only building with light—the generator-powered middle school.

His heart started beating an almost normal rhythm about half-way there. Angelina was safe. The children were safe. Behind them, in spite of the firefighters' efforts, the house was destroyed within the brief minutes of their walk through town.

Somehow, someway, Angelina and Trey had shown up at just the right time, and they had barely gotten the children out before it was too late. Was it the hand of God or coincidence or old-fashioned "everybody puts their hand to the plow" in times of need?

His mother would have given God credit. After coexisting with thousands of people in New York and knowing almost none of them, Colt put credence in the third option. Western folks stuck together.

But that meant it was coincidental timing that got Trey here in time and put Angelina on site at the critical moment when move-ment was spotted at the endangered house. Colt had experienced enough in life to believe things didn't "just happen." The circumstances that put two tiny lives in their arms caused him to consider the whole God thing might just be at work.

Whichever it was, Colt was mighty grateful for the outcome.

"Bring them in!" Annie McMurty pulled the heavy doors shut behind them as they stepped into the school's front entrance. She motioned toward the big gymnasium to their right. "We've got the emergency supplies set up in here. The Red Cross is on its way to help." The boy lifted his head from Colt's shoulder to look at Annie. Annie drew back in surprise. "Oh my word, Angelina, these are the MacDonald kids. They're Tim and Maura's youngest, but . . ." Her voice trailed in question, then stopped. She righted her shoulders and led them across the room to a quieter corner. "I'll get word to Grandma and Grandpa that Jason and Mandy are here."

"Thank you, Annie," Colt said.

Colt read the silent message that passed between the two women. Where were the children's parents? Why were they alone? Had Angelina somehow missed them in the dark house?

Annie reached out and stroked the little boy's hair. "Jason, are you hungry? Thirsty?"

Eyes wide, the little boy shook his head, popped a thumb into his mouth, and was sound asleep against Colt's chest within minutes.

"Mandy? How about you, honey?" Angelina leaned down to see the little girl's face.

The girl ducked her head against Angelina's jacket as Annie moved away to make the phone call.

An EMT came their way. He crouched in front of Colt and Angelina. "I need to check these guys for smoke inhalation."

Colt pulled the sleeping boy closer. "No need. We got them out before the house was engulfed."

"Doesn't matter. Where there's fire, there's smoke, even if you don't see it. And protocol. Gotta follow it, Colt, although I expect that still isn't your strong suit."

Colt looked closer at the EMT and recognized a high school classmate. "Brian?"

The EMT nodded. "I saw the escape. I'm mighty glad you guys didn't hesitate or we'd have had a different kind of ending." He turned to the little girl. "I'll get vitals on this one first." He smiled at the girl, reached over to check her pulse, and got a mouthful of sharp teeth on his hand as a result.

"Ow!" Brian snatched his hand away. "She bit me!" He sat back, none too happy, and stared at the girl.

She scowled right back at him. "Mommy doesn't want strangers to touch me. Go away."

Brian wordlessly questioned Angelina. "Your choice," she said quietly. "How badly do you need those vitals?"

"Not as badly as I need all ten fingers," Brian said. "You'll need to watch her carefully and let me know if her condition changes—even slightly." He reached down and gently took the sleeping boy's pulse while the older sister shot daggers at him with her eyes. "No smoke in the house when you entered?"

Angelina shook her head. "Not at first. I saw movement at a window and realized we had someone in there."

"So, sweetheart." Brian squatted low to face the little girl.

"Mandy," she told him, but she didn't look any too interested in carrying on a conversation with him or anyone else.

"Mandy," Brian said.

Colt had to hand it to him. He kept his voice even despite the healthy teeth marks she'd left in his hand. "What were you and Jason doing when the fire broke out?"

She puzzled on that, then made a face. "I don't know when it broke out, but when I saw the bright lights, we sneaked over to the window to look. And then I saw it."

"Why did you have to sneak?" Angelina asked softly. "Were you supposed to stay away from the window?"

Mandy hung her head. "Mommy said we were supposed to stay in bed. But when the red and blue lights started flashing, I got up. And then Jason got up. And then we went to the window and looked out." She lifted her head, her eyes round, remembering. "And then someone started knocking on our door saying, "Everyone out! Everyone out, now!" and I grabbed Jason's hand and we ran upstairs and hid under Mommy's bed. I didn't want the stranger to get us, and Jason doesn't know about being careful because he's little. I'm big."

"So you didn't hide from the fire, you hid from the stranger." Her version made sense to Colt.

She sighed. "Well, I was way scared of the fire, then of the guy, then the fire again. I just wanted my mommy to come home."

Annie returned. "Mom is on her way. She said the kids were asleep when she left to drop her older daughter off for her shift at the

diner on County Road 4, and when she started back to town, a
downed tree made her take the long way around. By that time the
fire had started in the church and the roads were all blocked off. She
sounds scared."

"She should," Colt began, but Angelina held up a warning hand.

"Single mothers don't always have the choices others take for
granted," Angelina said.

Colt read her meaning and grunted reluctant assent. Leaving
two sleeping children home alone for a ten-minute run to the diner
and back probably didn't seem like such a big deal under normal
circumstances, but normal had turned deadly in the space of minutes today.

A short time later when Maura MacDonald charged through
the south-facing doors, the anguished look on her face helped defuse
Colt's anger. Yes, she'd made a grievous mistake, but she'd learned
her lesson—the hard way.

"I don't know what I would have done if you hadn't been there."
Red-eyed, she cuddled Mandy while Jason slept soundly snuggled in
Colt's arms. "With Tim deployed, I do double duty. But that's no
excuse for leaving them while I took Nicki to work. What was I
thinking?" Tears flowed again.

Angelina's expression was one of compassion. "You were probably thinking that it would be nice to get six straight hours of sleep
now and again. Annie said you worked the overnight at the hospital
last night."

"Being tired is no excuse for being stupid when it comes to the safety of my children." Maura swiped a hand to her face. "Tim is going to be so upset by all this."

"Maybe." Colt touched Jason's soft hair. "But he's mostly going to be glad you're all okay. The kids are fine; houses can be rebuilt." He stood and handed the toddler off to Annie. "I've got to get back out there. When it's time to rebuild, we'll be there to help, Mrs. Mac-Donald. You have my word on it."

Angelina tugged on her coat, hat, and gloves as they walked to the door together. Colt held it open, and when she stepped through, he slipped an arm around her shoulders, pulling her close. It didn't feel nearly close enough because he was pretty sure his heart nearly stopped beating when she ducked into that burning building less than an hour before. "I could have lost you tonight."

"Colt."

He pulled her into the shadow of a small spruce grove. He knew they didn't have much time, but she needed to understand the depth of his emotion, and he had every intention of telling her. "I stood there, holding that hose, knowing I couldn't let it go, and watched you run into a burning house. For the first time in a long time, I had to put my trust in something other than myself."

"I'm trained to do dangerous things," she began.

"Yes. But not when I'm watching."

Amusement softened her mouth. Her very pretty, kissable mouth. Close. So close . . . He shifted his arm to hold her a little tighter, but she was still too far away for his liking.

"I had to hurry, so I did." She searched his face and seemed to take comfort in what she saw. "I knew you'd come. When I saw that porch roof flaming and smelled the smoke curling beneath the windows, I knew you'd be there. And you were."

He hugged her close, the feel of her knit hat and soft hair pressed against his neck. And then he had no choice, none whatsoever. He shifted back slightly. Her eyes met his, and he didn't hesitate or wonder if he should ask permission. He dipped his head and caught her mouth in a sweet, slow kiss, a kiss he'd been waiting for all his life.

Time stopped.

It couldn't stop, not really, because they were needed back at the fires, but it *seemed* to stop, as if to block out all the old and ugly as long as he was kissing Angelina. When he finally broke the kiss, he kept her close, wanting to protect her and keep her safe from harm.

Of course she'd probably shoot him for saying that, so he kept it to himself, letting actions speak louder than words.

"We have to go," she said.

"I know." He released her, but not before he pressed soft kisses to her cheeks, her eyes, her forehead. "I know."

He took her hand as they hurried across the school parking lot. "Promise me one thing," he said as they took the road back toward the smoke-filled town. "Promise me you won't do anything crazy, foolish, or dangerous when we get back down there, okay?"

"By whose definition?"

It was pointless. He realized that right away. Ange wasn't like any other woman he knew. "You've got a little boy to raise. Think first. That's all I'm saying."

"I know. But I realized something tonight." She paused, looking up at him. "I loved this. Being part of a rescue; being back in the action. It was like coming home."

He recognized the hunger in her eyes, the need to be who she really was—a trained officer. He heard the longing in her voice. He read the yearning in her eyes. They'd sort it out later, when they could think straight. Right now, there was work to be done.

Extra hose companies had arrived while they sat with the Mac-Donald kids, which meant better odds, but as Colt mentally calculated the damage, he knew today's hit to Gray's Glen might be insurmountable.

Four houses and two small businesses had burned in the time they cared for Maura's children. Nearby residential properties and businesses had suffered major smoke and water damage. Lives and livelihoods had been forever changed by the combination of elements. The beautiful historic church, where his father and mother had married, was now an empty shell of scorched stone walls. As he contemplated the skeletal structure of the church, he wondered how this had happened. He'd sat in that church this very morning, holding a small child, hearing words he'd long ignored, and now the structure lay in pieces before him.

Maybe that's the thing. Maybe you're supposed to help pick up those pieces. Put things back together. You've spent years working in the shadow of Ground Zero, watching people repair. Rebuild. Gather and pray.

Maybe now it's your turn, here, at home.

A curl of something warm swirled within him.

Angelina moved off to help Rye. Colt tracked down Trey and took his place behind his younger brother. As he followed the barked orders of the fire chief for the next several hours, his brain worked overtime. He'd come back to town a fallen man. He might not have access to personal funds to shore up the town's demise, but he had rugged hands, a good head, and a strong back. One way or another Gray's Glen would be rebuilt, and the Staffords would be right there in the thick of it.

TEN

*I*s Dad dying?" Trey faced the group of tired, dirty, fire-battling friends and family just before dawn, and the sadness in his eyes tugged Angelina's heart.

She chose her words with care. "Not from yesterday's issues. It seems the cracked lower rib resplit and punctured his lung. That's what caused him to need intervention. They're confident they've got that fixed, aren't they, Nick?"

Nick took a swallow of coffee and stood, cradling his mug. "Yes. But he needs to rest more to let the bones heal, and he's not the greatest patient in the world."

"Amen to that," mumbled Hobbs. "Ornery old coot is what he is, just like me. I ain't fixin' to go to my own reward yet, so I'm not keen on seein' Sam go neither. Bones heal, sure as shootin'. It's this liver thing that's got me wakin' up, prayin'."

"I noticed the yellow tinge to his skin," Trey said. "What are they doing about it?"

Nick turned to Angelina. "Can you fill him in so I don't sound stupid?"

Colt snorted, Trey grinned, and Nick almost smiled. Hobbs and McMurty settled back to hear the scoop.

"He's got liver cirrhosis caused by hepatitis C and too much drinking back in the day."

Murt shot a guilty look to Hobbs. Hobbs ducked his head, and she knew why. Sam had told her that he and the guys had gotten wasted many times when the boys were small.

"They've tried to arrest the progress of the disease, and that's key," Angelina went on. "If they can, he should do all right."

"If they can't?" Trey asked.

She didn't mince words. "He'll die without a liver transplant."

"But we're nowhere near that, are we, Ange?" Nick set down his coffee mug and tugged on his gloves, a signal to everyone that there was work to be done, sleep or no sleep. Last night's wind hadn't brought much rain, which had meant greater disaster to the town, but possibly less harm to the ranchers. Colt grabbed his gear while Angelina continued.

"I think we're closer than we've believed the last couple of months." She took a deep breath before continuing. "If it's not reversing itself or being stopped by their intervention, then there's no choice. Maybe the broken ribs are making liver healing harder or vice versa, but from the way he's been the past few weeks, I think there'll be some big decisions coming soon."

"Do they have him on a transplant list?" Trey asked. Standing with his brothers he didn't look much like Nick and Colt, but the strong jaw and steady gaze were similar. He might not be a biological sibling, but he couldn't escape the Stafford blood.

"Not yet." Angelina finished her coffee and stood as well. "But my guess is they will. When do you have to go back, Trey?"

He looked unhappy. "Tonight. I have two more winter tour dates. Then I'm done until next winter."

"No summer tour?" Nick asked.

He shook his head. "I needed a break."

"Aren't you supposed to be cutting an album?" Murt asked. "Annie read it in the weekly, and she was all excited about a new Trey Walker thingamabobber."

"Do they still call them albums?" Colt asked as he grabbed his hat. "Even though they're MP3s or CDs?"

"They do," Trey said. "And there are lots of folks out there who still think a 33$\frac{1}{3}$ vinyl outranks a CD anytime, anywhere."

"And they're the kind who probably don't appreciate microwave ovens," Angelina remarked, throwing them a wry look. "Let me know if you guys decide to end your work day early in order to catch some sleep. I can have a midday meal ready."

"Sleepin' in the saddle sounds 'bout right, right now," joked Hobbs. Then his expression turned serious. "You know, dealin' with that fire last night near broke my heart. My mama had me baptized in that stone church. But seein' you two"—he looked at Angelina and Colt—"haul them babies out of that burnin' house . . ." His voice caught as he fought back emotion. "Seein' kids like Brendan right there in the thick of things doin' whatever he was told, then comin' here to the big house where 'our' kids slept safe helped me. It give me a hope I haven't had in a lot of years. Not lackin' in God. My hope there's done okay. But in us. In Gray's Glen. And that felt mighty good."

"Shut up, old man." Murt gave Hobbs a horrified look and a

gentle shove toward the door. "You'll have us all kabobbin' like a clutch of old hens with your talk of hope and crap like that. Let's get to work."

"I think it's sweet," said Angelina. "I think you're right, Hobbs. It's time we all worked together to make Gray's Glen the town it should be."

She felt Colt's eyes on her but didn't dare look at him. They'd turned some kind of corner last night, saving little lives, working together, sharing kisses on the run. She could still feel the grip of his fingers, strong and steady, wrapped around her palm, holding firm. The warmth of his embrace, the texture of his mouth touching hers. So perfect. So . . .

And when Colt didn't follow the other men out the door, when he rounded that breakfast bar, slipped an arm around her waist, and drew her in for a sweet, long kiss good-bye, she didn't think at all. How could she when the pressure of his mouth and the safety of his strong arms made her feel delightfully whole and fairly invincible?

"I'll be back." He whispered the words, his forehead to hers, his voice husky. Touched by Hobbs's words perhaps. Or lack of sleep and smoke inhalation and amazing kisses . . . and then Hobbs's words.

He left her with one last, lingering kiss to her temple, so tender and good it left her weak kneed. After the door shut firm behind him, she walked into the front room, sat, and hugged a pillow to her chest.

"Now I see through a glass, darkly . . ."

But what did she see? And who could she trust? Ethan had left her and their son without a backward glance. She'd lost her dad not long after. Her mother's longing to go back to Seattle seemed in sync with the department's invitation to welcome her back. So why let things get convoluted? Wasn't simple better? Safer? Because she'd gone through the whole broken-heart thing and had no reason to repeat the debacle.

"Fear not," Isaiah proclaimed often. She'd believed that when she accepted the badge of a policewoman—until life turned upside down.

The rooster's crow heralded the approaching dawn. The big white Aracauna cross didn't like strong winds. He'd cowered in his chicken house, waiting for the air to mellow, and now it had.

Footsteps sounded upstairs.

She sighed, tucked away troublesome thoughts, and returned to the kitchen. According to the latest reports, there would be no school again, probably for days. The town was blacked out, and the middle school would be a shelter until at least Wednesday. That meant more time with Nick's girls and Rye's brother and sister. Later in the day she'd take the long way around to the hospital. Sam would be chafing, wanting an update, wanting to come home. From the looks of the men, not one of them would be allowed through a hospital door until they'd showered and shaved and put on clean clothes.

She needed to talk to Sam alone anyway. He might be contentious and tough with others, but he'd taken good care of her and her family over the last two years. He'd become like a second father to her, and she'd tried to bless him in kind, but the stark truth had been cemented when Colt kissed her a little while ago—she couldn't

possibly stay here once Colt left for New York. Not when every corner and crevice would remind her of Sam's oldest son and what
couldn't be.

Maybe her plan for a new start back in Seattle was exactly what
she needed.

"Any wind damage on the west face?" Nick asked as Colt and Hobbs
rode up alongside him.

"Shed's gone." Hobbs snorted. "The wind mighta done us a
favor on that one. Nice insurance claim for an eyesore building past
its prime."

"That's it? The west barn and yards are fine?"

"Whoever thought to put the stockyard on the east side of the
barn deserves a raise," said Colt. "The young seed bulls huddled up,
and the barn broke the wind. They didn't seem spooked at all."

"Murt's idea when we re-fenced." Nick gave the mottled cattle
dog a quick whistle. BeeBee darted around the far cows' legs until
they went Nick's way. "It wouldn't have worked so well in the open,
but on the windward side of the hill it makes perfect sense."

"We've got over three hundred market calves to deliver yet." Colt
backed Yesterday's News out of the way. "What are the chances of
cutting me loose in a week to help rebuild the town?"

Nick, Hobbs, and Murt exchanged looks. "Once we've dropped
most of 'em, I think we'd be fine," Murt said. "You got the urge to
get handy?"

"I want to help."

Nick sharpened his expression. "You remember how to drive a nail? Because I don't expect you've practiced in a while."

"Like riding a bike. Or a horse." Colt urged Yesterday's News up the hill. "Let's get these gals moved. When we're done I'll ask in town when they expect to begin demolition and cleanup."

"Rye said not till all the smolderin's done," Hobbs said. "So likely a few days. But maybe we could get a town meeting together and talk about what's what."

Colt looked at Hobbs. "What do you mean?"

"Three of them properties that burned were Stafford owned. Your dad bought up half a dozen places on Chelan Pass a bunch of years back. With him being sick and all, he might not want to rebuild."

"Why wouldn't he want to rebuild?" Colt asked. "Where would those people go if he doesn't?"

When Hobbs looked anywhere but at him, Colt understood. "Because cold, hard insurance cash is more bottom-line friendly than rebuilding so people can get back into their homes."

"I ain't sayin' he wouldn't help. I'm just sayin' that might make a difference."

Hobbs was right. Hadn't Colt made plenty of decisions the past nine years based on bottom line alone? He hadn't bothered with neighborhood pleas, employees' hard-luck stories, or outcries on Facebook. He'd forged ahead doing what needed to be done to maintain the financial integrity of his investors' holdings.

He couldn't hate his father for the very sin that felled the son. But Colt was determined to support the town with or without Sam's financial assistance. On top of that, he didn't intend to waste a whole lot of time sitting around a conference room talking about it. Staffords didn't talk a thing to death. They acted. And right now, that was a good quality for the father to have passed on to his son.

⁓⸺⤫

"I can't die yet." Sam sat more upright as Angelina walked through the door to his hospital room that midafternoon. "There's too much to do. What a stupid, bad time to get kicked around by a cow. And now the town's in a ruckus, nearly burnt down—" He glared at her as if waiting for her to appease him.

She sat down next to him, took his hand, and bowed her head.

He sighed, impatient.

She squeezed his hand, and not all that gently either. "Knock it off. Listen to your heart, your faith, and your body."

"My heart says I'm running out of time, my faith's on an unpaved road, and my body's pretty well shot," he retorted.

"Ay yi yi." She looked skyward as if seeking celestial intervention. "Has it occurred to you that God may have given you an amazing opportunity to help others in the form of this natural disaster?"

He rested against his pillows, considering her words.

"Your sons have gathered around you for the first time in almost a decade. They want to help you. And now the town's been grievously hurt. Maybe God's message is for you to sit back, heal, and let the younger generation rise to the occasion."

"I don't like sitting around doing nothing."

"That's apparent by the fact that you managed to pop a rib loose and deflate a lung. How do you expect your liver to heal if you can't breathe?" she asked practically. "Last I looked, oxygen was a requirement. Not a choice."

He sighed. "I know you're right. But I want to be home. All three of my boys are here. That's been a long time coming."

"Trey has to leave tonight."

Sam's face fell, and the true emotion of the moment made her soften. "But he's coming by to see you—"

"In case I kick the bucket while he's gone," mumbled Sam, aggravated.

"He's coming to see how you're doing," she corrected and took his hand into hers again. "He told me that you sent him off to help last night. How you insisted you'd be fine."

"I figured the town might need another strong back and pair of hands."

"You were kind and generous and right." Her assurance seemed to calm him. "He's coming to say good-bye and to tell you he'll return for a longer visit when his winter concert tour is over."

"You think he will?"

"I know he will," she said. "He said so, and he's a man of his word. And really nice, by the way."

"Maybe too nice."

She shook her head. "There's no such thing, Sam."

"He hung in longer than he should have when his wife started using drugs again. Some things refuse to be fixed. I saw it with his mother and his father and others along the way. Sometimes you have to know when to cut loose."

"A smart guy like you knows that addictions wear on the head, the heart, the health, and the soul. There's nothing easy about over-coming them. You did some heavy drinking in your time. In light of your current circumstances, I would think you'd have more empathy."

"Drinking was bad enough. Drugs?" He shook his head. "I never understood the risk. A person with half a brain could see the danger involved, so why do it?"

"Temptation comes in many forms." She tightened her grip on his hand because she needed to broach a different topic he wouldn't like. "You know I've gotten an offer from Seattle. I wanted you to know I'm seriously considering it."

"You really want to leave?" Sam's surprise was followed by concern. "Why? Is it money? Because I can pay you more. I'll match whatever they're offering. We need you here, Angelina." He hesitated, then admitted, "I need you here."

She knew this would be hard, but she hadn't realized her heart would actually ache. "I loved my job on the force. I excelled at it, like my father before me."

"I get that part," said Sam. Reluctance deepened his tone. "But you're good on the ranch too, Angelina. And that's not a given around here."

"I also love being on the ranch," she said, "overseeing things, bossing around a bunch of somewhat clueless cowboys. And I love living here. It's got to be one of the beautiful spots on earth, Sam."

That earned her a slight smile.

"But it's not what I was meant to do." She sighed. "Responding to last night's emergency made me realize that I worked hard to excel on the force because I wanted my dad to be proud of me."

"And he was."

"Yes. But I think if he were here now, he'd say, 'Chica, what are you doing? Are you afraid to be who you are, who the good Lord meant you to be?'" She raised her eyes. "And he'd be right. I need to wear the badge again. I need to feel like I'm doing what God designed me to do. And I need to see to my mother's happiness, to take her back to what she knows best. I'm all she has, and I can't send her back alone, away from her only grandchild. That would be wrong." She paused. "I won't leave for a while. I'm going to see you through this sickness."

"No need, I'll be fine."

Disappointment shadowed his face. Gruff, he pulled his hand away, but Angelina wasn't ready to let him slip back into the dark den of anger he'd called home for so long. "Don't do this."

"Do what?" he asked, stubborn as one of those yearling bulls on the ranch.

"Get all mad and pull away from people. Isn't that what got you into so much trouble with your sons? Each time one of them needed to get away, you made them pay."

"I never claimed to be easygoing." Sam squared his shoulders, then stopped when the gesture caused more pain. "Easygoing doesn't build a legacy like the Double S, and it doesn't put food on the table."

"But it can help foster good family relationships." She reached out and hugged him, ignoring his grumpy demeanor. "I love you, Sam. I love the Double S. But there are other responsibilities calling me. You understand that. And I want your blessing."

"You can't just roll into people's lives, change them up with all your talk of faith and hope, then leave them. That's not how it's done, Angelina."

"But isn't that the strength of faith?" she asked him. "To weather change because we believe? By faith we stand firm."

"Tell that to a group of hungry cowboys at the end of a long, hard day when the kitchen's empty and the oven's cold," he grumped. After a moment he reclaimed her hand. "You're not rushing into this? You promise?"

"On my honor. But it wouldn't be right to keep this to myself, because it affects a whole lot of things."

"Darn right it does. I haven't had to worry about much of anything other than cattle and horses since you came on board, and that hadn't been the case for a lot of years. But there's something else I've learned these past two years, a lesson I forgot a long time ago," he said. "To put other people's happiness ahead of my own. I forgot it with Christine, and then it was too late. For a long while I just didn't care."

"You care now, Sam."

"Yes."

She squeezed his hand lightly and stood. "I've got to get back. Mami is cooking dinner, but I want to help Cheyenne with schoolwork. She's Stafford stubborn, that one. And there's an emergency town meeting tonight."

"So soon? Why?" Sam frowned. "Something's not right." His brows furrowed as he went into thinking mode. "Tell the boys we need to be there. If there are decisions to be made, we need to be in on the ground floor."

"What's the matter with you people that you think rest is un-needed? The whole town could use a good night's sleep, that's what I'm thinking. And I'm guessing if someone's pushing for a quick meeting, it could be because they know you're in the hospital and won't be in attendance."

"And three of those properties are part of Stafford holdings. You'll give the boys my message?"

"I will."

"One more thing," he said. "What about Colt?"

"What about him?" She kept her eyes and voice void of emo-tion—no easy feat.

"A blind person can see—"

"Don't go there, Sam," she warned. "Off limits."

Being a Stafford, of course he refused to listen. "I've seen the way Colt looks at you." His words put her right back in Colt's arms that morning. "What if God's plans take you in that direction? Do you listen? Or still go?"

"Dulce María, madre de Dios, ¿Qué estás pensando?"

He answered smoothly, "What am I thinking? That my son has come home. He cares for you. What better way to spend the time I have left than seeing a son happy? That's my dream, my goal right now. I want to see each one of my boys happy before I die. I think that means you need to stay."

"Stop trying to micromanage everything and everyone, okay? Colt's got no intention of staying, and I have no intention of being left behind ever again." She stood, slung her purse over her shoulder, and bent over him. "Don't give the nurses a hard time and don't cough. Or sneeze. Or laugh. Let your ribs rest and mend."

"You'll come tomorrow to get me?"

"Yes. And Trey will stop tonight on the way to the airport. So take a nap now. That way you'll be awake when he comes through."

"You're bossy."

"Which is why we get along. See you tomorrow."

"Angelina! Kittens!"

Nick's youngest daughter should have looked guilty when she drew Angelina's attention toward the barn an hour later. Her comfortable expression meant sneaking into the barn while her father was distracted was becoming a new and bad habit, because a first grader shouldn't be creeping into a cattle barn alone. Angelina hurried across the stone yard and followed Dakota into the barn. "You know you're not supposed to come in here without an adult."

"Cheyenne does it."

"That doesn't make it okay, sweetums. That just makes you both naughty."

Dakota looked up, her face imploring. "I had to follow Callie, Angelina, otherwise I wouldn't find the babies. I love them so much. They're so cute." She squeezed her little hands as if unable to contain the glee, looking too sweet and innocent for anyone's good.

It was true that the barn cats were evasive when it came to their kittens. If a nest went unfound, they'd have a slew of feral cats

running around instead of being adopted by happy country families. In that way Dakota had done well. "Where did she have them?"

"Back here!"

She followed Dakota to the far west corner of the second barn,
and when they tiptoed behind some stored equipment, she caught
Dakota by the shoulder. "You know your way around here way too
well, 'Kota. You've been sneaking into the barn way more than you
let on, haven't you?"

The girl sent a guilty look her way. Angelina bent lower. "This is
no place for a kid to wander. There's dangerous equipment everywhere, there are huge cows that aren't exactly the most easygoing
creatures when pregnant or protecting a newborn calf. Your grandfather is recovering from three broken ribs right now from one of
those angry mamas, and he's an experienced cattleman. What if
something happens to you?"

"I don't touch anything," Dakota protested. "I just follow the
kitties. And sometimes I pet a horse. Or a baby cow. But I never go
in the pens."

"You mustn't do this." Angelina settled a stern look on her. "I
can't keep you safe when you're out of sight behind closed doors. If
you want to come and see kittens or calves or this year's foals, come
get me. I'll bring you, okay?"

"Sure."

Her quick answer sounded like token appeasement. Who would
watch this daredevil child if she left? Who would see the seriousness
of her desires to learn the ways of the ranch? Not her father. He was
steeped in denial.

"There are two calicos and one stripey and one orangey. I don't know which one I want to keep, but I think the stripey is my first favorite."

"Oh. They're so very tiny." Angelina leaned over the straw bale and peeked at the new babies. "How precious."

"I know." Dakota's small hand clasped hers. "I'm always the happiest when I'm out here in the barn, Angelina. I wish I could stay here forever."

"Dakota! Where've you gotten to?" Nick's voice bellowed from the ranch yard adjacent to the house.

Dakota sighed, unhappy. "Good-bye, Callie. I'll come see you and the babies soon."

"But not without a grownup."

"Okay."

"Promise?" Angelina stooped low. "Because otherwise you won't be able to stay at Grandpa's."

Dakota's eyes went wide, distraught, and her sadness made Angelina want to give Nick Stafford a good shaking.

Dakota had a natural interest in farming and horse work, and the Double S was part of her future legacy. Sure, she was little, but both girls had a curiosity and affinity for the ranch. In the heart of central Washington, most kids were playing rope-'n'-ride as soon as they could walk.

"There you are." Nick folded his arms as they exited the barn. "What were you doing in there?"

"Looking at kittens." She whispered the words in a sweet, tiny voice.

"She had them?" He turned his attention to Angelina as Colt approached on horseback.

"Four of them," Angelina said.

"I wanted to pick mine. You did promise us, Daddy."

He sighed, defeated. "I suppose it's fine as long as you girls take care of it."

"Them."

"Them? What 'them'?" he asked as Colt swung down from his horse.

"You promised we could each pick one," Dakota said. She folded her arms to mimic his stance. "You remember, right?"

"I remember being hoodwinked. I don't recall agreeing."

"Well, it's the right thing to do," she said, very serious. "Unless you get me a horse, Daddy. Then Cheyenne can have the kitten."

"Nice ploy, kid." Colt reached down and bumped knuckles with her, then lifted his eyes to Angelina's, and there was no missing his spark of interest. "Care to show me the kittens, Ange?"

"I expect you're too tired for kittens right now." She stepped around the two men and the horse. "We need to make the town meeting tonight, so I'm going to help Mami get an early dinner on the table."

"I got your text about that," Cole said as he loosened the saddle on the big chestnut gelding. He withdrew the saddle, settled it on the fence rail, and turned back to the horse. For just a moment he stood there, alongside his mount, chin down, as though he and Yesterday's News were having a silent heart-to-heart. "Although why they're meeting so quick is anybody's guess." He drew the reins forward and led the horse into the paddock as he spoke.

"We go together," Nick said. "If Isabo doesn't mind having the girls here. I want to see what the rush is when the ground is still smoking."

"Your father is wondering the same thing and asked if you would both be there. As for watching the girls, I'll check with Mami, but I'm sure it's no problem. She's enjoying their company tremendously."

"There's Stafford land involved and Dad in the hospital. How often do you get an opportunity like that?" Colt's tone suggested there might be other agendas afoot.

"My guess is someone's hoping we're too busy to take notice," Nick said. "It's the perfect time to take advantage of our father when he's too sick to stand his ground. So we'll stand it for him," he added. "I told Hobbs he didn't have to go. He's fine with sleeping now and taking the next watch on the mothers. Murt and Brock will help too, and Murt said Joe can sign on full time for the season. Then we can sleep tonight after the meeting."

"I'll go get cleaned up," Colt said. "Nobody wants me at a meeting smelling the way I do. With the power still out in town, you and the girls will stay here tonight, won't you?"

"Yep. Plan to." Nick reached down and clasped Dakota's hand. "But I'll have to remind Isabo that these girls like to sneak into the barn."

Guilt kept Dakota's eyes averted.

"Maybe Brock can show Cheyenne and Noah the kittens," Colt said.

"You think he would?" Dakota turned toward Colt and her face lit up. "After supper?"

"If he can't, don't go in there alone," Nick warned. "You understand me, Dakota Mary Stafford?"

"Yes sir."

Angelina flinched inside. She could rat the kid out, but her father already knew she'd adopted her sister's covert missions as her own. Surely he knew that was partially his fault for making everything off limits.

Dakota raced ahead, her excitement an example of everything good about raising kids on a ranch. Rebirth, industry, fruit of the land, and the labor of human hands. So much of what was proclaimed in the Bible came from farmers and fishermen. Buying food from sterile modern grocery stores tended to distance people from the source.

Colt caught her hand. She turned, surprised. He held a clutch of white phlox, just beginning to open. "I found these on the south slope where they kind of appeared overnight, so I tucked a few in my bag. These little guys like sun but they don't mind some shade, and they're not fussy about dirt. I thought you'd like them."

She didn't just like the clutch of baby blooms in her hand. She loved them. The thought of the wildflower beds ready to blossom reminded her of running the creek banks as a child. She held the miniature bouquet, the softer spring breeze gently ruffling them. When she didn't say anything for long moments, Colt rocked back on his heels. "Stupid, right?" He shoved his hands in his pockets, and as he started to take a step back, she shook her head and raised her eyes to his. "Not stupid. Beautiful."

He noted the sheen of moisture in her eyes right off.

Colt might be able to handle a bunch of lying, cheating, conniving, suit-wearing Wall Street types, but he couldn't handle a woman's tears. Avoiding them made it worth staying single all these years, but when it was Angelina with damp eyes, he didn't have the urge to run and hide until the tears passed.

Instead he just wanted to make things better. "Hey, hey. Don't cry."

"I'm not." She swiped a hand to her cheeks, one at a time, and laughed through her tears. "I never cry."

"I can tell."

"I don't," she said, and he knew she was winning the battle by the increased authority in her voice. "Unless it's a really good old movie I've seen a dozen times. In which case, all bets are off."

"You like them." He indicated the spring blossoms.

"I love them. I used to run the creek slope behind our house when I was young. I'd pick these for my mother, and every year she acted thrilled and surprised when I'd show up with a fistful of little white phlox." She brought the bouquet up to her face and breathed. The sight of her long dark hair, the white collar of her turtleneck sweater, and the bouquet of white flowers made him think of weddings and pretty music and a beautiful bride, images he'd never entertained before. But he envisioned them now, watching Angelina.

Maybe Murt was right. Maybe he'd been brought here for some-thing that had nothing to do with money and everything to do with life. But that frame of mind would mean a full one-eighty change of direction. Was he ready for that? Would he ever be ready for that? He wasn't sure, but with Angelina standing before him, the thought of staying seemed downright nice. "You're beautiful."

She flushed. Looked down.

He reached out and brought her chin up. "So beautiful."

"Colt . . ."

He should kiss her again. He was aching to do just that, but the harmony of voices from the kitchen meant supper was being laid out. "I'm heading up to shower. We can revisit this later."

She didn't look convinced, but she did look intrigued. He'd take that as a partial victory. He reached behind her and opened the door. When she walked in holding a bouquet of upland phlox, Nick, Murt, Brock, and Isabo exchanged glances. They all knew she didn't find them growing in the yard. Which meant someone brought them to her.

She said nothing, but as she crossed the room to get a small vase, she hummed softly.

Isabo kept her eyes averted, pretending nonchalance. The men exchanged quick looks. Nick's jaw went tight—remembering, maybe, when things with Whitney were good?

Colt didn't know.

But when Angelina put the small round vase of white flowers on the shelf above the sink, the glow of the white blooms against the red-checked curtains brought him hope for more simple joys to come.

ELEVEN

"Well, Angelina, haven't you got the two handsomest escorts in all of Gray's Glen?" Wandy Schirtz's happy face greeted them as Colt held the middle school auditorium door open for Nick and Angelina that evening. "If I wasn't a happily married woman of forty-odd years, I'd take one of those lovelies off your hands."

"Take that one." Colt popped a thumb in his brother's direction, then reached down to grasp Angelina's hand in front of everyone. "And teach him some manners, will you, Mrs. Schirtz?"

"There's a powerful amount of fixing to be done, so we'll just add that to the list," she replied. She studied the blighted town a few blocks below. "We've got our work cut out for us, boys."

"That we do." Nick moved through the door and then did something so sweet that Angelina wanted to go smack his ex-wife for a whole host of reasons, but mostly for not appreciating what a downright nice man Nick Stafford was. He put an arm around Wandy's shoulders, gave her a half hug, and said, "Nothing we can't handle, of course. And if that husband of yours ever leaves you a widow, I'll come calling, okay?"

She blushed like a schoolgirl. When Nick planted a son-like kiss to her temple, the elderly woman smiled through damp eyes. "You be sure to do that."

He walked in behind them as Angelina tried to wriggle her hand free from Colt's grip. Face placid, and without a glance down, Colt didn't let go. He moved forward, bringing her along. She knew he was doing it on purpose, because if there was one thing she'd discovered about Stafford men, they did everything with purpose.

He led her to sit in a group of open seats to the right of the podium. Nick sat next to his brother as a large group of other locals filled in around them.

The mayor brought the meeting to order. They started to follow the customary rules for meetings, but one of the old-timers stood up several rows back, his hat in hand. "Mr. Mayor, yesterday was a long day and night, and this one's draggin' deep already. Can we just let Eileen take the minutes while we move ahead without all the legal malarkey?"

"I second that motion!" shouted a voice from the back.

"All in favor, say 'Aye,'" someone else called. When the room rang with approvals, the mayor smacked his small gavel against the sound block.

He mopped his brow despite the cool room. Reluctance shadowed his normally easygoing face. He hauled in a breath and addressed the small crowd. "You all know why we're here. We've got some big decisions comin' up and not much time to weigh them. We lost several complete buildings last night, including four homes on Chelan Pass, Sal's Auto, Curly Jo's beauty shop, and the church. Six other buildings sustained significant smoke and water damage. Now I know we've got two other churches in town." He gave a deferential nod to the priest and pastors sitting on the far left. "And I respect each one of them, but Grace of God Community was the first church hereabouts. Half of us were either baptized there or married there or said our good-byes to someone we loved there.

"We won't have accurate figures for a week or so, but the rough estimate on rebuilding leaves the church deep in the hole."

"The hole?" called out someone from the back. "That church has been full paid for decades. How can we be in the hole?"

Small sounds of surprise and dismay echoed around the packed room.

The mayor offered the crowd a reluctant grimace. "The insurance policy hasn't been updated in all that time. There was no mortgage on the property, so there was no legal reason to increase the coverage. And without much money in the weekly offering, adjusting the coverage never got done. Which means the insurance won't cover much more than the teardown and cleanup."

Silence reigned for long, drawn-out seconds. Folks looked around, stunned. An undercurrent of angry muttering began to round the room, a room filled with disappointment and emotion and sleep-deprived people. Just as it looked like the anger might escalate, Colt stood.

He'd worn his cowboy hat into town, and he held it in his hand, against his chest. When folks saw him standing, things went quiet again. "Most of you know me." He glanced around the room, making eye contact.

Some acceptance greeted his words, accompanied by a few caustic looks.

"And most of you know I've had some ups and downs of late as well."

Mutters of agreement followed. Colt turned and faced the crowd, still gripping his hat like he was saying the pledge of allegiance. "I don't have any money of my own available right now to help out the rebuilding efforts. All I have to offer is the work of my hands. In a week or so my brother won't need me as much on the ranch. So when that work's done, I want to be here in town, helping folks rebuild. Because that's what neighbors do. They help each other."

"Colt." Ben Schirtz stood, getting straight to the point. "I appreciate your words but doubt if you really understand what's going on here. The past few years have been tight for most in this town. In light of that, I don't expect too many of these fine folk increased their insurance coverage at the same rate as inflation. And if folks don't have insurance or funds to cover the losses, they'll probably go belly up." He wagged his head. "And if them properties of your father's aren't rebuilt, then right there that's a bunch of folks left without a place to live."

"I hear you, Ben," Colt said. "And I don't disagree. But I'm saying we shouldn't go too far toward making big decisions this quick. It's amazing what folks can do together when they put their minds to it."

"You figured that out in Manhattan, Slick?" A burly man stood up in the back. "Because while you were whooping it up and spending other people's money, the rest of us were doing the daily work that needs to get done out here. Your talk is all nice and fancy-schoolboy pretty, but out here what counts is the day to day, and I haven't seen a lick of Stafford day to day in this town in a long time."

"That's about to change."

Nick's quick voice of agreement pulled Colt's attention around.

His brother took his place alongside Colt, and for the first time since coming back home, Colt felt like a born-to-the-saddle Stafford. "Colt and I are planning to throw in whatever time and physical effort we can to help make things right again."

"Can't make right what was never right to begin with," someone said. "No turning back that clock."

Colt wasn't sure who made that contribution, but he accepted the reality. "You're right. Our ranch has been on disconnect from the town for a long time. But no longer."

An old woman called out, "You boys are cute enough and you seem sincere, but when you're talkin' years of Staffords ignoring most of what goes on in this town, it's like chaff on the wind. It don't mean much. We've got real folks here with no money and not much in the way of insurance. My guess is the older ones will retire and the younger ones'll leave. It's happened before, which is why there's so few of us left. There comes a point where folks have to move on, lookin' for jobs and a place that welcomes them."

Colt heard more than dire acceptance in their voices. He heard despair, as if the raging fire and the loss of businesses and homes was too bitter a pill to swallow. He remembered feeling that way as a boy, the weight of so much on his shoulders. So why did he feel he could do something about it now? What made him think he could foster change, especially with his track record?

"What do you plan to do, Stafford? Especially with a good share of your your money tied up in a real neat bow with the Manhattan District Attorney's office?"

Colt turned to face the speaker's challenge. A former ranch hand locked eyes with him, a man who'd tried to take a cut above his salary when delivering their genetically crafted, meat-producing cattle to customers. His father had let the foreman go instead of putting him in jail. Unfortunately the man wasn't exactly swimming in gratitude.

Colt stayed firmly away from the past and focused on Gray's Glen's future. "If I have to go into the forest and cut down trees myself to make a log cabin church, I'll do it. If I have to have Josh"—he motioned to Josh Washington, the tall, bronze-skinned local contractor sitting across the room—"put in some pretty windows without stained glass, I'll do it. If I have to trade cattle for doors and grain for flooring, I'll do it because my mother loved that church. She took me there every single week of my life until she died. She's buried in the Grace of God Community Cemetery. So do I have what it takes to make a difference? The answer is yes. I do."

"I remember your mama." Wandy Schirtz rose from her chair. She bustled up the aisle toward Colt and grasped his hands. "Such a kind, giving woman. Always smiling at folks. I have missed her a good long time, Colton Stafford. But I swear I just glimpsed her again in her beautiful son. Welcome home, Colton. I'll be the first to stand by your side and help with that church building because God does not care what it looks like when all's said and done." She shook her head, solid. "He cares that his people come together to worship and pray and play. Sign me up on Colt Stafford's work crew." She sent a tart look toward the mayor. "I might not be good with a hammer, but I'm mighty good with a soup pot, and I've got a freezer full of food that's not getting any fresher. Ben and I will do whatever it takes to help Colton see this through."

"I'm in," chimed a voice from the back. "I don't mind bringing down trees and making a log cabin church. I think it would be right cozy. If Staffords are offering the wood, I'm offering my time."

"I'll help too."

"Count me in!"

"Add my name, Mayor, if you can write that fast."

"Hold your horses, hold your horses." The mayor banged the gavel and raised his hand for order. "I'm going to have Rye put three sign-ups on the side table there—one for helping with the church, one for the town, and one for food. You all figure out where you'd like to help. If you've got time to help on all three, well, good. Once we have the rubble cleared later this week, we'll meet again to make a plan and set it in motion—one way or another, it seems." He tipped his glasses down and peered at Colt and Nick, still standing. "You boys ready to take this thing on?"

"Yes sir."

Nick punched Colt's arm and none too lightly either. "I'm with him."

The mayor's jaw eased, but he didn't look one hundred percent convinced.

But he would be, Colt decided as he, Nick, and Angelina waited to put their names on the work lists. He would be.

Colt was tied up talking to the mayor and his wife, and from the look on his face, they were extending a warm welcome. As Angelina and Nick headed toward the far door, a woman's voice hailed Nick from behind. "Mr. Stafford?"

Nick turned toward the fortyish woman walking their way. "Yes?"

The woman put out her hand and looked Nick in the eye. "I'm Rachel Willingham, the principal of Cheyenne and Dakota's school."

Nick looked trapped, and Angelina was pretty sure if she hadn't been standing between him and the exit door, he'd have taken off. Although he stayed put, he didn't look the least bit comfortable. "Nice to meet you."

The woman looked doubtful. "Well, it's most likely not nice, I'm sure. I've been trying to contact you for some time, and you've been quite adept at avoiding me."

Guilt stamped itself across Nick's features. Angelina took a step away. "This sounds private. I'll see you outside, Nick."

"Thank you." The principal acknowledged Angelina's grace, but Angelina didn't fool herself that the woman was going to go lightly on Nick. Principals didn't like being blown off when she was a kid. She was pretty sure that hadn't changed over the years.

She went outside. Until yesterday the people of Gray's Glen took the fresh scent of forest air for granted. No more. The stench of wet, smoldering wood filled the air, a fetid smell she'd like to forget but never would. Colt found her there a few minutes later. "What are you doing out here?"

"Thinking."

He tugged her jacket closer around her. "It's damp and chilly. Isn't that what zippers are for?"

"I hear hugs can keep you warm too."

He slid his arms around her waist, his grin warming her as much as the embrace. "Now we're talking. Where's my brother?"

"Inside getting lambasted by the girls' principal."

"Why would anyone pick a night like tonight to do that?" Colt drew back, surprised. "Wasn't there enough emotion going around that room?"

"Ask him," Angelina said as Nick came through the door looking none too happy. "If you dare."

Nick didn't just stride across the planked wooden sidewalk leading to the parking lot. He stalked, pounding over the aged boards. Colt slid a sideways look to Angelina. "I don't reckon I want to open that can of worms."

Angelina silently climbed in the backseat of the SUV. Colt took the front passenger seat and flipped the keys to his brother. "Here you go."

Nick grabbed the keys, started the engine, and stopped.

Colt looked back at Angelina, then at Nick. "Want me to drive?"

"No."

"Want to talk about it?"

"No."

Colt waited about five seconds, then sighed. "Well, then get the lead out and get us home. We're all done in. And maybe in the morning you won't feel like punching somebody in the face."

"I don't punch women, but I'm okay with decking men. And you're right here."

"Did you set up a meeting with the principal?" Angelina asked.

"Don't need to."

"Then that's good, right?" Colt asked. "No big deal."

"She wants my kids to see a shrink."

"A . . . what?"

"A psychiatrist. Or a therapist. Psychologist. Whatever these head cases call themselves these days."

"All three, I believe," offered Angelina from the backseat. "And didn't Cheyenne's teacher talk to you about this at the parent-teacher conference last fall?"

"I ignored it then. I can ignore it now." Nick shoved the car into reverse, backed up, then squealed tires once he thrust it back into drive. "There's nothing wrong with my girls that a little time won't cure. It's not like we're the only family in the world to split up."

"What's so bad about having someone to talk to?" Colt asked. "I'd have liked that when I was a kid. I sure wasn't talking to Dad."

"And that's the difference." Nick sent a cold look Colt's way. "My kids can talk to me about anything, anytime."

"Oh. Well. Good."

Angelina thought for half a moment that Colt was going to let it go. Of course he didn't.

"So that's why they sneak into the barn to be around the animals because they love the ranch and want to learn and you won't let them do anything more rigorous than ballet."

"Shut up, Colt."

Colt ignored him as the rare camaraderie the brothers shared in the town hall evaporated. "Cheyenne sends pictures of pretend horses to her friends so they'll think she's got horses, just like they do on their ranches."

"She does no such thing. And there's no reason for them to learn the ins and outs of ranching. It's not like a girl will ever run the Double S."

Angelina stared, appalled. "Women run all kinds of enterprises now, Nick. Get out of the Dark Ages and stick a toe into the twenty-first century. You're being ridiculous."

"My kids. My choice."

"I'm confused," Colt said. "So she wants the girls to talk to someone, but why? What's happening at school for her to make a recommendation like this?"

Nick didn't say anything for over a minute, and when he did, he thumped the steering wheel with his left hand. "Cheyenne isn't doing her work."

"Still?" Angelina frowned. "Cheyenne used to be an excellent student. How long has this been going on?"

Nick flinched and she sat back, appalled. "Since last fall when they first talked to you? You mean she's blown off half of last semester and half of this one? She's going to fail her grade?"

"It's a strong possibility."

"Nick." Angelina wasn't sure what to say, how far to go. She'd known both little girls for two years, and she'd taken on a lot of their care. She loved them. But the reality of Cheyenne refusing to do schoolwork for months and Dakota doing whatever she pleased when she thought no one was looking spelled more than trouble. It reeked of disaster. "I don't even know what to say."

"Then it's best to say nothing." Nick brought the car to a screeching halt in the stone barnyard. "I'll figure it out in my own way and my own time, like always."

"Except you haven't." Angelina leaned forward and put a hand on his shoulder. "It's been nearly six months, and it's getting worse. What's so wrong with kids needing someone to talk to?"

"They're not crazy, that's what."

"No one said they were. But when your mother leaves you high and dry—"

"You think I don't know that?" He turned toward Angelina and included Colt in his harsh look. "I'm the Stafford whose mother walked out on him, remember? Yes, your mother left." He directed this straight at Colt. "But it wasn't her choice; it was a horrific accident. Mine left because none of us mattered more than her own self-interests. So I probably comprehend this scenario better than anyone. Which means I can handle it on my own, without any help. Understand?"

Colt got out of the car and raised his hands. "Got it. Right now I'm thinking the girls might not need someone to talk to as much as their old man does."

"Shut up, moron."

Nick didn't go near the house. The girls would be asleep and would stay at the ranch until power was restored to their house in town. He got into his pickup truck, turned it around, and headed down the hill at a quick clip.

Angelina hugged her arms against her chest, watching him go. "This isn't good. I had no idea that things had gone this far. I know Cheyenne's been a passive-aggressive brat about her homework, but I didn't know she'd gone to this extreme. What's Nick thinking? That this will all go away and take care of itself?"

"Guess so. Because that's exactly what he did," Colt said. "And he thinks it worked out fine."

"In some ways maybe it did. But when his mother left he was immersed in something he loved," Angelina said. "This ranch, this business, growing up Stafford. The very things he won't allow the girls to do."

"Hey, I agree with you. But you saw his reaction. Not much talking to him."

"Oh, I saw it all right. Stubborn and doggedly focused, like his father and brother." She yawned, exhausted. "From the looks of the town, we've got plenty to do for spring and summer, and with the ranch work and kids needing help, I'm wondering how much Nick can take before he breaks."

"You planning to stay and help?"

"At the moment I don't have much of a timeline," she returned. "Not until your father's better and we're on an even keel here."

"Even though your mother wants to go home?" He paused before opening the back door and faced her. "Can you stay if she goes?"

"No." She held his gaze. "She needs me. She sacrificed a great deal just to have me, Colt. Four times my parents had hoped for the child of their dreams, and four times my mother lost baby after baby, all born too soon, tiny souls and graves she had to leave behind in Ecuador. When they came to America, she got pregnant one more time. Here, with good care, she was able to have a successful pregnancy. She gave me life. I can't just walk away from that."

Colt seemed to consider her every word.

"I've also made a promise to your father, and I don't break my promises. But what about you, Colt?" She pointed to the phone on his belt. "If New York issues an 'all clear,' or your other funds become wildly successful, do you catch the first plane east or stay here and get your hands dirty building a church?"

"I don't break promises either."

Easy words, the kind of words she'd heard before . . . but tonight she'd seen a major difference between Colt and Ethan. Colt didn't offer lame assurances, looking to gain career footholds. He'd offered the people of Gray's Glen the work of his hands, a genuine Christian gesture.

Ethan would never have done that. So maybe her mother was right. A smart woman didn't use past mistakes as an excuse to stay stuck in the past. She learned from them and moved on.

She yawned again and didn't resist when Colt slipped an arm around her shoulders and pressed a gentle kiss to her temple. "We need sleep. In the morning we can sort out what kind of promises we made under the guise of exhaustion."

"Possibly a rude awakening."

"Not if it means we're both going to be around for a while. A guy could get used to that, Ange."

His words reassured her because, even though it was impossible, she could get real used to it too.

Angelina was right, Colt realized as he drove to the burned-out town two days later. Bearing responsibility for people you cared about raised the emotional stakes. He'd come back to Gray's Glen because he had to, but as he made the descent into the haggard town, he realized he'd committed to help because he *wanted* to. No one was more surprised by that than Colt Stafford.

His father had been released from the hospital and now was home, resting uncomfortably. Narrowed choices were still frustrating the older Stafford. After all this time, he finally wanted to help others and help the town, and he was stuck at home in ill health. But there was nothing wrong with Colt's health, so he headed into town, determined to make a difference.

Center Street looked desolate despite the afternoon sun. Big equipment had been parked after a hard day's work, ready to continue demolition in the morning. The results of their work today had intensified the stench of wet burned wood. The blocks-long visual of overwhelming destruction prickled his physical and emotional senses. A town the size of Gray's Glen didn't need much to tip it into misery.

He'd watched coolly from his comfortable New York office as small companies folded and little towns struggled when bigger firms or banks pushed in and drove them out of business. Now he was part of that downside, and Colt wasn't a downside kind of guy. One way or another, he'd help make things right. He parked opposite the cordoned-off church, climbed out, and approached the debris field.

The church property was half cleared. Construction barriers and yellow caution tape blocked off the perimeter. Colt ignored them, stepped over, and surveyed the damage close up.

"Colt, shh. We're in church, honey."

He heard his mother's soft reminder like it was yesterday. He remembered walking out of the church, his hand tucked in hers, when he longed to run and race free after sitting quietly—well, *not* so quietly—inside. She lifted him, holding him tightly as cars moved about the parking lot. She smiled into his eyes and said, "You can run all you want at home, I promise. But there are too many cars here, Colt. You could get hurt."

"Why do we have to come to stupid church anyway?" Had he scowled when he said it? Had he pouted? He couldn't remember. He just remembered the look on her face, as if calling church stupid hurt her feelings. "Daddy doesn't come. I want to stay home with him next time!"

She held his gaze for what seemed like a long moment. "We need to pray for Daddy, Colt. Every day, okay? Because even the busiest daddies should take time for church."

"Do I have to?"

She'd nuzzled his cheek so softly and so gently he could almost feel it now. "It would make me happy."

"Okay."

Colt faced the ruin before him and could honestly say he'd never once prayed for his father, and he was pretty sure his father hadn't sent up prayers for him until lately, so did that make them even or just evenly stupid?

The latter, Colt decided. He turned to go, when a voice called his name.

"Colt? That you?"

"Mrs. Irvine?" Colt crossed the cinder-strewn grass and took the elderly woman's hand. "How are you? How's Coach doing?" Bob Irvine had coached the Gray's Glen high school basketball program for nearly three decades before Colt, Nick, and Trey played and for several years after. "Gosh, it's nice to see you."

Sweet wrinkles dimpled her face when she smiled up at him. "And you. I heard you and your brother are going to help put things back together. So when I saw you standing there, I wanted to come over and say thank you."

"Are you living in town now?" The coach and his wife had lived on a two-lane south of town, a small property filled with an odd shake of animals and a mishmash of fencing. "You still have Coach's menagerie?"

"Gone," she told him. Her soft voice sounded sad. "Bob's in Ellensburg now. They've got him in one of those memory care centers. That's a nice way of sayin' they don't let him wander. He's got the Alzheimer's, and I couldn't take care of him, the critters, and the place. About six years back, when he started to get sick, we moved here." She pointed to a small gray village house behind him, east of the square and untouched by the fire.

"Easier for Coach that way?" Colt asked, but was surprised when she shook her head.

"I thought it would be, but once he got in town, he spent the next three years trying to find his way back home. Only home was gone, of course."

His heart heavy, Colt envisioned the scenario. "Can he have visitors, Mrs. Irvine?"

"He can, but he doesn't remember much of anyone or anything these days. It's best to go early in the day. He gets nervous-like when dusk comes, so I go in the morning and talk to him."

She and Coach had never had children, so the boys in the basketball program had become their brood. "Mrs. I" had attended every evening practice and every game, supporting Coach and the kids with her cookies and her presence over the thirty-plus years he worked for the high school. "Was Ellensburg the closest place for Coach?" he asked.

"Well, Gray's Glen is small and getting smaller, so there isn't much in the way of nursing care hereabouts," she explained. "And Bob bein' such a homebody, I wonder if I could have made his last years better by stayin' put. But it's too late to fix that now." She studied the burned-out church and sighed. "So much loss, so much sorrow, and time marches by. Well! I didn't come over here to make things worse; I came by to say thank you for wanting to help. It does an old heart good to hear it."

"It will be my pleasure," he said and meant it. He took her arm and escorted her back to her little house, slowing his pace to match hers. The gray house needed work. The roof looked worn. Peeling paint mottled the four porch supports, and while the front steps looked warped, the back steps were solid and firm. "Nice stairs back here."

She smiled. "Josh Washington came by and put those in last year when he was between jobs. You know he lost Susan to cancer. So now he's got those kids of his on his own. With the hard times here in the valley, he's not had much contracting work. It was real nice of him to come by and take care of this." She patted the sturdy hand-rail. "We've got good folks here."

A few weeks ago Colt would have scoffed, seeing the "good folks" as insignificant compared with the high-powered men and women in the financial world. Shame flamed within as he thought how he'd dismissed a lot more than Sam Stafford with his ignorance. He'd negated all the other relationships he'd built in this town as if they didn't matter. But seeing Mrs. Irvine, hearing about Coach and Josh showed him they did matter—very much.

He'd wanted to punish his father by staying away and ended up hurting others in the process. Like Josh. He and Josh had been good friends throughout high school two decades back, playing varsity basketball together under Coach. To hear that Josh had lost his wife to cancer deepened Colt's shame.

"Do you need anything, Mrs. Irvine? Anything I can bring you?"

"Oh no." She pretended all was well, but he couldn't miss the sorrow in her eyes. "I'm fine, really. Things certainly aren't how I envisioned them a dozen years back." She glanced about, a little lost.

He opened his arms and drew her into a hug—not because he was a hugger but because she needed one. When her eyes filled with tears, he had to blink back moisture himself. "It was good to see you, ma'am. I'm glad you came over to say hello."

She pressed her hands against his arms and offered him a look of gratitude. "Me too."

He waited until she was safely inside before he returned to the church. He walked up and down the street, studying the remains of the church and the rest of the town. He had his phone out, tapping notes into it as he went, and bit by bit a plan came to mind. Nothing huge in and of itself, but there was always hope that it could begin a domino effect.

When he was done, he climbed into the SUV and headed back to the ranch. He called Nick and asked him to stay at the ranch until he got there, then he called his father's cell phone. "Dad, are you awake?"

"I am now."

He sounded more amused than cross. Meds, most likely. "I need to talk to you and Nick about an idea I have. An idea that might help the town."

"You close to home?"

"About to pull into the driveway."

"I'll meet you in my office."

"We'll be there." He parked the SUV and went inside.

"You must have called from just up the road," Nick said when Colt walked in. Cheyenne was sitting on a stool, her schoolwork fanned out on the breakfast bar. A pencil lay alongside the papers. Nick fixed himself a mug of coffee and faced Cheyenne. "Study those spelling words and then write them three times each."

She looked down, sullen, then propped her chin in her hands and said nothing.

"My homework's all done, Daddy!" Dakota called from the living room carpet where she'd gathered four baby dolls and propped them on a clump of pillows. "We're having a party."

"It's easy to do homework when it's baby stuff," Cheyenne muttered.

"I've got tickets for the new princess movie coming out," Colt announced. "But all homework has to be done and checked for two weeks."

"Can we have popcorn, Uncle Colt?" Dakota asked, excited.

"Absolutely."

She fist-pumped the air. "Then I'll get mine done for sure!"

Colt was one hundred percent certain she'd earn her ticket. Cheyenne's outcome was more doubtful.

Glum, Cheyenne picked up the pencil and stared at her paper. If Colt was a gambling man, he'd hedge his bet when it came to Cheyenne Stafford. She was stubborn and mad at the world—two traits he remembered real well.

He let Nick lead the way into Sam's office then shut the door behind them. "I've got an idea."

Sam was already seated behind his desk. "The phone call was a clue."

"Is it about the ranch?" Nick asked.

"No."

Nick sighed deeply and strode toward the office door.

"Where are you going?"

"I'm all in on the ranch, and I pledged my efforts to the church. But in case you haven't noticed, I've got two kids who need the occasional father. I can't do anything more and maintain my sanity."

"Sit."

Nick hesitated a moment, then sat himself in one of the leather wingback chairs. "All right. I'm listening."

"When I was in town, I ran into Coach's wife."

"It's a shame about Coach," Nick said. "It's hard to see such a vital person go downhill like that, but at least he's safe now."

"Safe and forty minutes away," Colt said. "And Mrs. Irvine looks mighty frail to be making that drive daily."

"So your suggestion is what? Bus service?"

Colt pulled out his phone and showed them a picture. "These are the burned-out properties on Chelan Pass."

"Yes." Sam drew the word out slowly as Colt slid to the next two photos on his phone.

"And here is the property you bought on speculation six years ago, at the opposite end of town where that small tool-and-die place used to be."

Sam looked at the pictures. "And your point is?"

"We flip-flop the locations. We take this location here"—he pointed to the upper end, close to the churches and the mercantile and the smattering of small businesses along Center Street—"and we build a small over-fifty community complete with an adult-care facility. Not a full-scale nursing home but an adult living center with a memory care unit. A street of shops at ground level"—he swept his hand across the sidewalk-facing windows—"to replace the ones damaged in the fire. And apartments above. As people age, they can stay in their hometown and have friends and neighbors nearby."

Nick looked skeptical, but then Nick wasn't the most observant of human beings, so Colt ignored him. "Then we rebuild your rental houses on the west end of town. No one can argue too much about that since the properties are already zoned appropriately. The residents will be closer to school and the playground. The younger folks who usually rent your properties are more capable of going up and down steps to get to the store."

"And we're doing this because we want Coach to be close to his wife?" Nick asked. "That's a mighty big thank-you, isn't it? Couldn't we just send him a card?"

Colt would have thought the very same thing a few weeks ago. Something had changed. Wait, not something. Someone. Him. He made a face at Nick. "Very funny." Colt tapped the phone back to the original picture of the burned-out buildings. "We're doing this because the Double S owes this town after decades of shrugging things off." He locked eyes with his brother, then with his father. "It's the right thing to do, and it's a plan that not only helps others, but will pay off the initial investment easily. An adult-care community would bring jobs to the town and offer an anchor and a place for our aging citizens to live. This frees up affordable housing for younger families, which in turn creates momentum and brings growth. On top of that it will bring the Double S a much-needed tax deduction for next year."

Nick acknowledged that, but Sam bristled. "You checked my books?" He squared his shoulders, and when Colt just looked at him, he sighed. "You probably didn't need to, did you?"

"That's for amateurs," Colt replied. "I simply looked at the numbers and production ratios beside beef futures versus the ratio of seed cattle to—"

"I get it." Sam looked impressed. "Building nursing homes—"

"Adult care communities," Colt corrected him.

"Right, well, we're out of my range of expertise here. Since I'm not one to leave a job half done, and your brother's busy enough running both sides of the cattle operation, if something happens to me, who oversees this project?"

"First, I'm hoping nothing's going to happen to you," Colt told him, and his sincere words put a look of hope in his father's eyes. "But I intend to oversee the project if you decide to do it."

"This is going to take awhile," Sam warned him.

Colt nodded. "I'm all in."

Sam gazed up as if wanting to say more but kept silent. Nick's expression was flat. Either he wasn't listening or he didn't like it.

Colt knew what he was promising, and he kind of surprised himself. But the minute the full picture of the project came to him, he knew the idea had merit. "If it's all right with you, I'd like to contact an architect I know. He designed a similar project four years ago. It's been quite a success."

"What kind of rezoning are we looking at here?" Sam asked.

"From what I recall, the zoning on the upper piece should be fine for the planned community, and then if we do single family residential on the lower end, we won't need any additional permissions there either."

Sam nodded slowly. "That makes it easier for the town council to approve the plans." He cleared his throat and pushed his chair back from the desk. "Are we done here? I need to get my meds, or Angelina will have my hide." He stood too quickly. When Colt reached a hand out to steady him, he frowned but accepted the help. "I hate being weak."

"Illness and weakness are two different things," Colt said. "FDR won a world war from a wheelchair, and no one considered him weak."

Sam grunted, regained his equilibrium, and started moving on his own. "You can get a set of the blueprints that quick?"

"I can have the originals overnighted. They'll need tweaking to make them more western friendly, but we can do that later."

"Good." He patted Colt on the shoulder and headed down the hallway with more purpose in his step.

Nick led the way to the kitchen looking rather glum, edging out of Angelina's way as she entered from the opposite side.

"What?" Colt asked Nick. "You hate the idea that much?"

"It's not the idea," Nick confessed, his expression shifting until he looked more admiring than angry, a nice switch. "It's that the stupid prodigals get all the kudos. I've spent the last ten years working night and day, and you show up and start talking diversifying investments and community service crap, and all of a sudden you're the good son. How does that work exactly?"

Angelina stashed the girls' snack bowls in the dishwasher and reached for a dirty plate. "If you two are looking for biblical confirmation, I believe the parable of the lost sheep is as good as the lost son. God mourns the loss of a believer as a mother mourns a child. He looks and looks until he finds his own and gathers the lambs in his arms."

"Can we get lambs, Daddy?" Dakota bounded in, throwing herself at her father. He picked her up so they could be face to face. Fresh from a bath and cozy in pink pajamas, she was the picture of sweetness. "I would love to help with little lambs."

"I said yes to the kitten. Don't push it, kid."

She grabbed his cheeks and gave him a kiss on the end of his nose. "I will love Stripey so much, Daddy."

"You picked the striped one?" Colt asked.

She looked up at him, puzzled. "The orange and black one, Uncle Colt."

"The calico."

She bobbed her head. "She's so beautiful, isn't she?"

"She is. But you're naming her Stripey?"

"Just like my old kitty that died. He was Stripey One. This will be Stripey Two."

"Except the old kitty actually had stripes, stupid." Cheyenne came in from the great room looking pretty haughty for an eight-year-old.

Hobbs and Brock came through the back door just in time for the argument.

"We're naming the cat Snickers and that's that," Cheyenne said.

"Are not!"

"Are too!"

"I don't know what it matters. Cats are so persnickety that they don't come to a name, no how," Hobbs noted.

Angelina changed the subject without saying a word as she set a whipped-cream-frosted cake on the counter.

"Is that cherry cake, Angelina? Please say it is." Brock sat down on the nearest stool.

"Yes."

"Well, cherry cake sure beats fightin' over cats in my book and probably in most others as well." Hobbs took a seat alongside the younger cowboy. "I saw you settin' them layers earlier, and I was hopin' that was what you were makin'." He gave her a big gap-toothed grin. "It's one of my favorites, Angelina."

"We didn't have time to make one in February when Sam was sick, so I thought we'd welcome spring with it. Girls, you've had yours, so head off to bed, okay?"

"Why should we when there's no school tomorrow?" Cheyenne crossed her arms, defiant. "If my mother was here, she wouldn't worry about me going to bed at eight o'clock when there's no school."

"Well, she's not here," Nick said, "and I am. When Angelina tells you what to do, just do it. Without the sass. Apologize. Now."

She flipped her hair, muttered "sorry" in a barely discernible voice, and stomped down the hall and up the stairs.

Dakota gave her father a big hug, then hopped down to give one to everyone else in the room as well. When she finally skipped happily down toward Grandpa's room, Colt whistled lightly. "'Kota knows how to work a crowd, doesn't she?"

"She sure does," Nick said. "And while she appears to be more cooperative, she's as stubborn and manipulative as Cheyenne. She's just smart enough to do it with more grace."

Colt didn't dare ask Nick if he'd considered the principal's request. He didn't want to open a can of worms. Besides, the sight of whipped-cream frosting on cherry cake put everything else on hold. Or maybe it was the beautiful woman serving the cake.

He rounded the breakfast bar and came up behind her. He wanted to get her alone. Explain his decisions. Tell her his plans about helping the town—but not in front of the guys. He needed to nail down a few loose ends before he went too public. Another trait he shared with his father: he liked a plan set in stone. Less disaster and embarrassment that way. But he wouldn't mind telling Angelina, letting her think about him being here long term . . . so she might consider staying.

Angelina moved to cut Colt a slice of cake. He came up behind her, laid his hand over hers much like a groom would do on a wedding day, and broadened the knife angle for a much bigger piece. Was his thinking matching hers? Grooms and weddings and sharing cake? Most likely not, and his next words proved it.

"I'm really hungry."

A lesson learned. She was pipe-dreaming about ever afters, and the cowboy was yearning for cake. "So it would seem."

Her mother bustled into the kitchen, still energetic after putting in a long day of work, work she wouldn't have to do if she were back in the city. Isabo ticked off on her fingers the chores she'd done. "I have taken the last load of laundry upstairs, all folded and ready to be put away. Ironing is done, and I will get up early to begin breakfast. I am going to do some sewing in my room for a little before sleep. If you want to sleep in tomorrow and catch up after the crazy times of this week, it is fine, my daughter. I am sure you are tired after so much going on."

Guilt hit as she finished cutting Colt's cake. Isabo had taken on several of Angelina's duties since moving to the ranch house, and the aftermath of the fire's destruction put more work on her. In Seattle, her mother wouldn't have to concern herself with cooking and cleaning for a crowd. She could relax and take on civic duties as she'd done before. Have lunch with friends, walk the piers. Her mother loved being near the water. Tucking her this far inland went against her grain. "I can do breakfast, Mami."

"There is no need, but if you wake up, we can do it together," Isabo said. "Good night, everyone."

A chorus of good-nights followed as Angelina handed Colt his monster-sized piece of cake.

"Your mother has amazing energy," he said.

"Too amazing."

He didn't dig right into the cake with the fork she handed him. He set it down and focused on her. "You don't want her help?"

It sounded foolish when he said it, because who wouldn't want a hand running a busy house that had so much going on? This week alone, her mother's help had been invaluable. She couldn't have helped Sam or the town if Isabo hadn't been taking care of things on the ranch. "It's not that I don't want it; it's that she'll never relax when there's work to be done. She has to be in the thick of it, helping."

"How is that bad, exactly?"

Brock and Hobbs finished their cake. They stood up, said their good-nights, and headed out, leaving her to face Colt's question. But the answer wasn't as easy as Colt made out.

He didn't get it because Staffords thrived on work, work, and more work. She respected their work ethic, but hadn't her mother done her share already? Earned her reward? "This is supposed to be *her* time," Angelina explained. "This should have been her retirement with my father. It was all planned out so they could travel, see things together, do things together. And now that he's gone, it's all changed. She's spent the first two years of widowhood going stir-crazy in a cabin. I want her to be able to embrace life now. Her life, her choices."

"Does she seem unhappy to you?" Colt asked. "Because I think she likes taking charge, being at the heart of things, bossing men around. A family trait, it seems," he added, smiling.

"She doesn't seem unhappy," Angelina agreed. "She seems . . . busy. Really busy."

"Have you asked how she feels about it?"

She hadn't, so his question annoyed her. "I've got this, Colt. With my father gone, I'm all she has, and I take that very seriously. I believe I've mentioned that already."

"But if you guys don't talk about it, how do you decide who wants to do what?"

Was it a question of *want*? Or a question of *should*? "There's nothing to discuss. Whatever she needs to make her life complete, I will give her."

"So if she leaves . . . you leave?" He still hadn't bothered with the cake, as if working this out was more important. "It's that simple? Or are you leaving because you want to get back to the force and you're using your mother as an excuse?"

"I don't need an excuse, Colt." She faced him square. His questions hit a nerve, but what right did he have to question her when he intended to leave too? Did he think a few shared kisses—wonderful, mind-clearing kisses that shouldn't have happened—gave him rights? Because if that's what he was thinking, he was sadly mistaken. "My parents did everything they could for me. They cared for me and loved me from the beginning. That might be hard for you to understand," she continued, and right at that moment she didn't care that her harsh words might wound. "But that's how it was. They sacrificed for me, their only child. Now it's my turn."

"You think I don't understand sacrifice."

She shrugged, silent. How could he comprehend something he'd never known? Yes, he knew what it was like to lose a mother, and that had changed his life.

For Angelina, it was different.

Isabo Castiglione wore sacrificial love like a mantle of grace. Now Angelina was determined not to let her mother down. She placed plastic wrap over the remaining cake and slid the tray back into the refrigerator. "Good night, Colt."

She walked away, torn, tired, and grumpy. And he'd never even taken one bite of the stupid cake to see how good it was.

Angelina was right—kind of. He didn't know a lot about sacrifice, but he could learn, couldn't he? If his father could embrace a change of heart in his fifties, Colt could certainly manage it twenty years younger.

He placed a call to his friend in upstate New York and asked him to overnight the project his firm had designed three years before. And then he opened his laptop to double-check current zoning areas in Gray's Glen and the road heading west. When he approached the townspeople, he wanted a firm layout in mind.

Angelina didn't trust him. Was that because she saw him as a player or because she'd been played? He guessed both, which made him want to be a better person sooner.

He had the crazy urge to go wake her up and tell her he was staying put, right there on the Double S, but caution kept him where he belonged, upstairs, working on his plan. He saw what happened with Nick's mother and then Nick's wife. Loving ranch life didn't come naturally to everyone, and what right did he have to mess with Angelina's plans?

None.

He worked until he had to sleep, and when he woke up, he grabbed coffee and went to the barn. There was work to do on the far ranch border. Moderate weather and rain had given too much leeway to big animals and fence posts—even sturdy ones like theirs. He'd spend the day tending fence and wishing he was a better person, because if he was, maybe she wouldn't be so all-fired ready to pack her things and leave.

Midmorning his phone rang. He spotted the New York number and answered, surprised.

"Selma?" The newly named CFO of Hutchison-Mills Investing hadn't spoken to him in over two years. Not since she'd left the Goldstein Group. "This is unexpected. What's up?"

"We want you here, Colt. I want you here. At Hutchison," she said briskly. Selma rarely wasted words and always went after what she wanted. "I can't believe Goldstein was stupid enough to let you go over the Tomkins fiasco. I'll sweeten whatever deal anyone else is offering, but I want you back here, ASAP."

The horse neighed, then shied away from the fence because Colt wasn't paying proper attention. He brought the horse to a halt before his split attentions caused trouble. "You're making an offer? Why?"

"You haven't been on your computer, I take it?"

Not to check e-mail or stocks because he'd been running on pure adrenalin and not much sleep since the fire. "No time. Tell me in short, understandable phrases because the connection up here isn't the best."

"Major fund increase due to shift in export taxing, and unheard of increases in medical because of cancer treatment breakthroughs. On top of that, recent earthquake activity has shaken up the energy world and is likely to become the next big hashtag, one that will make climate change look minimal after the politicians take sides. You're suddenly sitting pretty, and my guess is that when you do access your e-mail, you're going to have a dozen offers. Whatever they offer, I'll offer more. And I want your team too. We're ready to deal, Colt. We can ignore the past and work toward the future. Together. Just as it should be."

Leave it to Selma to put her own spin on things as long as they were in her favor. "You mean the past where we were a couple and you cheated on me by trading up to the Chief Operating Officer at Hutchison? The idea of working with you and the guy you dumped me for doesn't exactly tempt me, Selma."

"The past is over. Done. Finis. We're the future, Colt. Hutchison wants you and doesn't care what it takes to get you. He sees your brilliance. He got burned by Tomkins himself."

That was news to Colt because Hutchison's name wasn't on the fallout list of investors. "He used an assumed name."

"A market fund name. He didn't like Tomkins and didn't want an open association. He still got burned—for a similar amount. However, when you've got funds showing millions in the debit column, Tomkins becomes small change." Colt could see her sitting bolt upright, dressed impeccably in her designer clothes. "This gives you the chance to get back in the game," she went on, "back to what you do best. Make tons of money and watch Goldstein squirm for letting you go."

He wanted Goldstein to squirm. His old boss was a greedy, egocentric kingpin in the world of hedge-fund finance, and he'd thought nothing of making Colt the fall guy. Colt had accepted the blame initially because he felt there was some merit to the assessment. But hearing that market shifts were pulling him back on top gave him a different kind of head rush.

"Don't make me come out there, Colt. Get on a plane. Make this easy for both of us."

"I'm supposed to drop everything here and come crawling back?"

"Not crawling, Colt. Marching in with your head up."

"I doubt that's going to happen, Selma, but I'll check my e-mails when I get back to the house. I've got work to do right now. I'll get back to you soon. Thanks for calling."

He hung up.

That would infuriate her, he knew. In retrospect he should have sent her a thank-you note for breaking up with him two years back. She'd been part of the inner sanctum, groomed to rise to the top— and she had. Selma fit into this world of hedge-fund movers and shakers, the cool, calculating, not-much-conscience, minimal-life-outside-of-work type people.

He wondered if he belonged in that world anymore. Maybe he never did. Maybe the whole thing was to prove to his father that he could be successful in his own right. He wasn't sure if that should make him proud of himself or ashamed. But he felt a little of both.

Whether or not he belonged, if Selma was correct about the current shifts, and Colt's personal investments were recovering as she intimated, he would be wise to set aside some time to adjust his personal portfolios.

Nick rode toward him looking grim, but that seemed to be the norm these days. "If your break's over, can you scout the canyon with Brock?"

"Will do." He pulled a knit face mask over his mouth. "Stupid wind."

"Wet ground, cold wind, bad combination," Nick acknowledged and then rode west to check fencing.

Colt found Brock on the other side of the tree-dotted pasture where Hobbs joined them on the four-wheeler. Together they moved to the canyon. Most cattle stayed upland on their own, but there were always a few mothers who sought the privacy of the breach to have their young. By the time he and Brock had brought in six cows and three babies, the afternoon was done and he no longer felt the least bit cold. Driving cattle up the ravine worked up a sweat. With BeeBee's help, they herded the group into the next fenced area, penning the last of the missing cattle.

"That's it then." Hobbs slapped them each a high-five. "We done it with only two casualties, boys. That's less'n ever. Don't it feel good?"

"It does," Colt said, and Angelina's parable came to mind. There was distinct satisfaction in finding those lost cows and newborn calves, then herding them to safety. The thought that he and God agreed on something felt good and strange, all mixed together. "It feels darn good, Hobbs."

He turned Yesterday's News around, and he and Brock walked the horses across the broad upper pasture. Hobbs drove the four-wheeler ahead of them, opened the gate, then relatched it once they'd passed by. They repeated that twice more, and by the time they descended into the barnyard, a late afternoon sun had broken through the clouds and the wind was dying down.

He thought of what he'd be doing in New York at this time of day. He'd be living in his office, crunching figures, overseeing deals, figuring achievement percentages. In hedge funds, the status quo was never enough. If you weren't moving forward you were losing ground, always behind. So different from riding the range, gathering calves, and putting up horses.

As he dismounted and began to unsaddle Yesterday's News, he heard a sweet, familiar voice drifting through the open door of the barn. The sounds from Angelina and the children made New York seem thin and distant.

Once more he wondered if this abrupt change was some sort of eternal plan to show him the difference between the Manhattan Colt Stafford and the cowboy he saw in the mirror these days. Selma's phone call had riled a wealth of emotions. His cynical side would love to go back to New York, make a fortune, and see his former boss squirm. He couldn't deny the underlying satisfaction in that.

But another part was ready to turn his back on the whole thing—as long as his personal investments were secure. There was something indefinably nice about the fresh ranch air, seeing life from a saddle perspective, and waking to see Angelina each morning. The sound of her voice emphasized how important she'd become to him. A coming home he hadn't expected but needed. He stopped at the house, picked up the long tube he'd had overnighted from Hueber Architectural, and set the plans in the backseat of the SUV. He'd run these down to Josh Washington's place and get the contractor's advice about his idea, but first he needed to see Angelina smile over baby kittens.

He crossed the barn, determined. One way or another, he wanted a future with this woman. He needed to court her in earnest because whenever he thought of the Double S and settling down, he saw

Angelina by his side and Noah in his arms. Now he just needed to convince the woman in question.

"Angelina!" Cheyenne pointed at the striped kitten. "When I pet the kittens, this one seems happier than the other ones. Do you think he likes me?"

From her spot on the floor, Angelina gave the nest of kittens her most serious attention. She heard more than kitten love in Cheyenne's question. She heard the heart of a child whose mother walked out on her. She read in her face a little girl searching for reasons . . . and something warm and fuzzy to cuddle. "I think it could very well mean that, darling."

Angelina's chest tightened when Cheyenne slanted a sincere smile at her. A beautiful child, hiding so much emotion, pretending things were all right, hanging on to anger like a bull rider wrapping his hand in the rope.

Who would watch out for Cheyenne and Dakota once she left? Who would encourage their imaginations? Their love for animals, patriotic Popsicles, and princess gowns?

Dakota crooned to the tiny calico as Colt approached from the far side of the barn. "I've been hoping you'd show me these kittens, Ange."

"And here they are."

He settled on the straw next to her and lifted the fluffy orange fellow. The baby cat opened its mouth with a quick *mew* but calmed when Colt drew the wee thing to his chest. "There, there, little guy." He lifted his beautiful blue eyes her way. "Is Noah sleeping?"

"Yes. Lucy brought her kids over to play, and they wore him out. We missed our earlier playdate because of the fire, and Noah wasn't about to let me forget it."

"I like tenacity in a kid, but I wish someone would make me go take a nap." A wide yawn punctuated his statement.

"You can take one if you want, Uncle Colt." Dakota kept her voice uncharacteristically soft. She peered up at him. "I'll wake you up for supper, okay?"

"I'd love to take you up on that offer, sweet thing, but I've got some things to do in town." He settled the tiny orange kitten into the box, then stood straight and tall, looking strong and self-assured.

"We've got to get back to the house ourselves," Angelina said to the girls. "Schoolwork." She ignored Cheyenne's pout and started to stand. Colt reached out a hand to help her. The touch of his fingers, the clasp of his hand around hers felt right. So right. She tried to avoid his gaze, but he bent just enough so she couldn't and then smiled at her. *For her.* "Come on, ladies. Out of the barn."

Dakota started to fuss, but Cheyenne quickly changed her attitude. Angelina figured that meant she wasn't all that worried about leaving her kitten behind because she wasn't afraid to sneak in and out of the barn at will. As the girls preceded them, Angelina looked up at Colt. "Did you fit in on Wall Street as well as you do here?"

He stopped at the barn's edge and tipped his hat back. "Used to." Hills swelled and fell around them, stretching into the broad expanse of fertile farmland, greening with hinted spring. He slipped an arm around her, a half hug she didn't know she needed until he did it. "You think I'm fitting in here? Because I'm thinking that too."

"Yes I do."

"Good." And then he kissed her, as if kissing her before he drove into town was the most natural thing to do. When he finally broke the kiss, he leaned his forehead to hers and sighed. "I've been thinking about that all day. How 'bout you?"

"I, on the other hand, have been keeping my mind on my work."

"Really?"

The disappointment in his voice forced her to be honest. She didn't want to admit it because admitting her attraction would make it harder to leave. But in fact, that day she'd thought of little else. "It's possible I thought about kissing you. Once or twice."

He laughed and kissed her once more—a soul-stirring, you-and-only-you kind of kiss, the kind that erases rational thought. "Need anything from Hammerstein's while I'm in town?"

Such a simple, normal request. She shook her head. "How can I possibly think of something as mundane as groceries after that?"

Her answer pleased him. He squeezed her hand and climbed into the SUV, and when he pulled out and drove away, a part of her heart made the trip with him.

He spoke sweet words as though all this meant something to him, something deep, but he'd left once and spent long years away. She knew how the temptation of something fancier, grander, and riskier called these financial types. Legal gamblers, that's what they were. Yes, she was guarded because she'd seen the reality. Cunning investors didn't just play to win. They played for the fun of the game.

If the financial district of New York City decided it wanted Colt Stafford back? He'd go because, no matter what he said, he'd left the game half complete, and that wouldn't sit well with Sam Stafford's firstborn son.

~⟶€ℰ⟶

"Colt." Josh Washington opened the door wide for Colt a quarter hour later. "Right on time. Come on in, let's see what you've got."

Colt followed Josh into the garage office, opened the tube, and laid out the plans he'd ordered from the architectural firm. "I need your opinion."

Josh whistled as he pinned the plans to his draft board display. "Wow."

"Yeah."

"What's your plan, Colt? Location? Timing?" Josh studied the specifications. "This is an amazing setup—but I think you know that."

"I thought so, but I needed an expert opinion," Colt replied. "I was thinking west end where the fire-damaged buildings will be torn down. The Staffords own just shy of twenty acres there and we've got access to full utilities. We'd need parking for the adult living center, street-level businesses here, here, and here." He pointed to several places on the plans. "With senior apartments above the businesses. And possibly patio-style homes on the parcel of land just west of ours."

"Have you secured that land yet?"

"Yes." When Josh looked skeptical, Colt admitted, "I used a proxy buyer. They signed the contract a little while ago. That gives us enough room to expand the senior living opportunity and still be close to services and amenities." He pointed north. "My agent also put in a purchase offer on a six-acre plot, which would give us enough room for a proposed future clinic. But first, a place for older folks to live so they can stay in town."

"This is a big project."

"It is," Colt agreed. "That's why I'm here. I need expert advice on this before the town gets wind of it. I knew you'd shoot straight. Who should I contact? Who can be trusted to do this right?"

Josh studied the project, then pulled out his phone. He scanned his contacts and jotted down a number. "Tim Slater, Slater Commercial Construction out of Wenatchee. A part of me would love to tackle this, but it's out of my league. Tim's the kind of construction guy who can polish this idea brighter than a new penny." Josh moved to his computer screen, hit a few keys, then pulled up photos of a small business park. "This is Slater's most recent project. He came in on time and on budget."

"You don't mind me calling him in?" Colt faced Josh. "I don't want to step on toes, but I'm anxious to get this started."

"Why?"

"I ran into Mrs. Irvine, and she told me about Coach, how she had to send him to Ellensburg for care."

"You want this done so Coach can come home."

"Yes."

His answer seemed to satisfy Josh. "You bringing these to the town meeting?"

"I am."

"I'll stand with you," he said. "But what about the houses that burned? Between your rentals and second-floor apartments above businesses, we've got six displaced families. That might not seem like much," he continued, but Colt interrupted him.

"It's a lot to them, I'll wager."

"Yes, sir, it is. The Red Cross has them put up in a couple of spots, but it's temporary."

"Well, I'm hoping you'll take on this next part of my idea. Let's take a walk." Colt opened the door and led the way down Center Street, past the skeletal church and the business district, until they came to the old tool-and-die building. "My thought is to do the housing rebuild down here. According to the town zoning, we've got plenty of room for a cluster of single-family homes. Simple but nice."

"Like the old Craftsman style?"

The bungalow-style homes were exactly what Cole had in mind. Their classic construction style would fit well into Gray's Glen. "Yes. I'd want them small enough to keep the rent affordable, with enough green space to make them family friendly. That way they have closer access to the park and playground, businesses, churches, and schools."

"Now you're talking a job I can handle," Josh declared. He stuck out his hand. "I'm in."

"Good."

"We're talking some serious investment money here, Colt," Josh said frankly. "On both ends of town. Is your father willing to back this? He hasn't had much to do with the town in a long while."

"He's making up for lost time, Josh. Me too."

"That's good enough for me." Josh indicated the sorry-looking lot and the rusted metal building. "Do you have a layout plan for these houses?"

Colt shook his head. "You understand the dollars-to-square-foot ratio better than I do."

"I'll call Etta Davis." Josh pulled out his phone and took various pictures of the broad lot. "She'll know exactly what kind of layout to use to maximize benefit to cost."

"Perfect. Can we meet once she's got a plan?"

"You stayin' around long enough for that?" Josh sounded surprised. "I thought you'd be heading east once things picked back up."

"A sick father, a family business, an ailing coach, a beautiful woman, and a really cute kid changed my plans," he told Josh. "I'm here for the long haul. I'll be the go-to man on this."

"I'm real happy to hear that." Josh clapped him on the back. "Welcome home."

Colt had grown accustomed to agreements being much more complicated back east. Having integrity be the norm felt mighty good again. He grinned and chucked Josh on the shoulder for old time's sake. "It's good to be here."

"Angelina?" Isabo called her name softly late the next morning. "There is someone here to see Colt."

"So why are we whispering?" Angelina slid a tray of cookies out of the oven. "It's the first decent day we've had for laying fence. They won't be back down from the range for hours. Can you show him in here, Mami?"

"Her."

Her. Well, then.

"Whatever. I'm rather preoccupied here for the moment." Her mother disappeared, and the sound of high heels on slate tile announced the woman's approach. They'd reopened schools that morning, and Angelina thought she'd have a full day to play catch-up around the house. She knew that possibility vanished the moment the leggy blonde strode into the room carrying a leather attaché case.

Immaculate. Tall. Gorgeous, wearing a killer designer dress, wicked-hot boots, and black-rimmed glasses—the kind a superhero wears when trying to blend in with normal society.

But nothing about this woman said *normal.* Angelina wiped flour from her hands and moved toward her. "I'm Angelina, the house manager. You're here to see Colt?"

"I am." The woman tapped the attaché with some of the most amazingly perfect manicured fingernails Angelina had ever seen. "I've got paperwork for him." She gave Angelina a cool smile. "I was going to overnight it, but I decided to overnight me instead."

Tiny hairs rose along Angelina's neck. It took real work to ignore them. "He's not expecting you?"

"He was expecting the paperwork—our contract—not the personal delivery. But I've always found that Colt was easier to convince in person." She smirked as if she knew a whole lot about Colt, in person. "So here I am."

Angelina fought back an adrenalin surge. "Is this a contract for the housing development?"

One perfectly sculpted brow rose slightly. "The contract is for Colt's new position in Manhattan with Hutchison-Mills Investing."

Colt's new position in Manhattan?

Angelina's heart buzzed. Raw emotion scaled her spine, but she kept her face placid and her tone even. She'd kill him later, happily, but this woman would never see the effect of her words. Angelina was too skilled a detective for that. She'd predicted this from the beginning. So why did the reality hurt so much?

"Have we got company, Ange?" Sam's voice drew Angelina's attention as he came down the hall. He spotted their visitor. If he was surprised, he didn't show it. "I see we do."

"Sam, this is—" Angelina marked time purposely, then shrugged. "Actually I have no idea who this is. She's come to see Colt."

"Selma," the woman cooed. In a move that said buttering up rich men was an intrinsic skill, she rounded the table and extended her hand to Sam. "Colt and I are old friends, and now we're business partners again. You must be his father. It's a pleasure to meet you."

Sam shook her hand but zeroed in on her words. "Business partners?"

"Yes. We worked together several years ago. We parted badly, unfortunately, but that was a different time. Colt's brilliance in maneuvering funds is renowned, and we've extended him an offer he couldn't refuse."

Sam's eyes narrowed. He glanced toward Angelina. She couldn't miss the flash of sadness in his eyes, but he composed himself before he brought his attention back to Selma. "This must be sudden."

"Yes." Selma smiled as if pleased that he understood, but Angelina knew the woman had no clue who she was dealing with. "We work quickly in New York," she explained as if old westerners dawdled their way through life and couldn't possibly understand the ways of a big city. "It's the mode."

"Sam." Angelina drew his attention before he could go apoplectic. "Since Colt won't be back for hours, and then we're going straight to the town meeting . . ."

He got her gist. "Where are you staying, Selma? I'll have Colt contact you as soon as we have things square here."

"Staying?" Selma didn't look surprised. She looked stunned. "I can't stay. I just need to see Colt and be on my way. Hopefully with him following right behind."

In a coffin, Angelina thought as she started slipping warm cookies onto cooling racks.

"Tell me where he is, I'll go meet him, and then I'll head back to that little airstrip in Yakima."

Sam looked regretful and went total "down-home" cowboy on her. "I would do just that, ma'am, but they're up top today. Ain't rightly no way of gettin' hold of 'em till they come back down, there bein' no cell reception up in them hills and all."

"Surely I can take the rental car up there?"

"No roads, ma'am. The boys went up on horseback and four-wheelers. Hopefully they'll come down the same way."

Selma didn't look upset. She looked downright furious as she glared at her watch, then set the envelope on the table. "I can't believe this."

"Mommy, can you take me to see the kitties now?" Noah dashed into the kitchen from the great room. "*Daniel Tiger* is all over, and I would l-l-love to see the baby kitties again. Please?"

"I will take him." Isabo pulled on a barn jacket, then tugged a hoodie over Noah's head. "We will check for eggs, as well. The longer days are making the hens more productive."

"Thank you, Isabo," Sam said.

"I am, of course, happy to do it." She darted a look of question toward Angelina, but right now Angelina had no answers. All she had were questions—and thoughts of assault and battery.

Sam stared at the official-looking envelope on the table as if hoping it might disappear.

It didn't, so Angelina picked it up and moved toward the door. "I'll put this on Colt's desk and let him know you were here. Does he have your contact information?"

"Oh, honey." Selma leveled a woman-to-woman look at Angelina before offering a Cheshire Cat smile. "He's got *all* my information."

Angelina refused to be baited. "Good." She opened the door. "Have a safe flight."

Selma hesitated, but a little chime from her phone drew her attention. She pulled it out, scanned the message, and looked immediately distraught, as if Wall Street might fall into the Hudson without her presence. "Tell Colt I'm sorry to have missed him and I'll see him in New York."

"Of course." Angelina shut the door quickly and turned toward Sam. "You didn't know about this."

"Obviously not. You either?"

"Colt has no reason to update me on his comings and goings."

Sam snorted.

"It's true," she insisted, but was she trying to convince Sam or herself? Maybe both. "We knew this was going to happen, which makes it our fault for thinking otherwise."

"He made a promise."

What could she say to that? Nothing.

"He stood in my office and told me he'd stay here to see projects through. What could have changed in forty-eight hours?"

"What generally changes a person that quickly, Sam?"

Sam's expression faltered because he'd set this example for over thirty years. "Money."

The timer signaled the next tray of cookies done, but when Angelina opened the oven, there were no cookies. She'd forgotten to put the next trays in.

Colt was leaving, Sam was brokenhearted, and the stupid cookies weren't baked.

Hot tears stung her eyes. Her throat went thick and tight. *Stupid, stupid, stupid.* She knew better, knew better from the beginning. She had plans to help her mother; he had a triumphant return to New York on his radar. Why did she let herself believe this time would be different? That he was different?

"I'm going to my office," Sam said.

She couldn't bear to read the disappointment in his face. She set the mixing bowl into the sink. "I'll bring you coffee, Sam."

He didn't answer, and she didn't press him. She was short on words and long on disillusionment, so she understood. Nothing she could say would help, so why talk?

She slid the cookie trays into the oven, set the timer, then took Selma's envelope upstairs. She walked through Colt's doorway,

resisting the urge to throw the envelope across the room. She set it
on the desk, grabbed a handful of tissues, and blew her nose.

She wouldn't let him get to her.

Too late.

She swabbed her eyes with a fresh tissue and took a deep breath.
She'd been reckless—a silly second mistake—but at least she understood the rules of the game now. She'd handle this like she'd handled
many tough cases in her time on the force. Day by day, step by step,
putting pieces together. Now she knew there was no place for Colt
Stafford on the game board.

As she returned to the kitchen to monitor the cookies, she pulled
out her cell phone and dialed Tony's number. He answered on the
third ring. "Hey," he said. "Tell me this is the call I've been hoping
for. You finally back in the game, Mary Angela?"

She didn't let herself think of hopes and dreams, vanished so
quickly. "I have to get Sam back on his feet, but yes. I'm in."

"Good!" Enthusiasm brightened Tony's voice. "I'm conferencing
right now, gotta go. You just made me happy, Detective. Talk later."

He would be happy with her back on the job. Her mother would
be happy back in Seattle. And it wasn't that she didn't like the city or
her job; it was—

She sighed as she slipped the last batch of cookies onto the cooling rack.

Seattle wasn't the problem. She was the problem, and she needed
to erase the pipe dreams she'd entertained recently. Her, Noah, and
Colt, finding a home on the Double S . . . because it wasn't about to
happen.

TWELVE

No time for food. Pressing to finish. Back just in time for meeting."

Colt sent the text, then repocketed his phone.

"You letting Angelina know time's tight today?" Nick asked as he and Brock unspooled fresh wire to Colt's fence post. "Hate to have her make something and no one's there to eat it."

"I told her not to worry about dinner."

"I hope Isabo doesn't mind watching the girls again. I should have mentioned it to her this morning." Nick waited while Brock applied the fastener before he looped his wire in place. "I don't mean to take advantage, but the girls really like her."

Colt glanced at his watch. "They're already at the house, so I expect she's got it figured out. I know you've got a neighbor who keeps an eye on them after school, but who watches them when you go out?"

Nick frowned as he worked the second strand into place. "I don't go out."

"Oh, man." A hint of warning came with Hobbs's words.

"Like ever?"

Nick's forehead formed a tight ridge, a real warning sign. Colt ignored it. "No dating? None?"

"The girls need me. They come first." Nick jerked his head to the upper post. "Come on, Brock."

As Nick and Brock moved on, Colt and Hobbs leapfrogged them with the four-wheeler, and by the time Nick and Brock reached them again, Colt decided to let the subject slide. Nick had always been more cautious, and he'd done an impressive job with their father of bringing the Double S to incredible standards. Colt respected that. And with Cheyenne's current school issues, Nick didn't need his older brother's teasing. Right now, Nick needed his support.

"We've got to call it, guys," he told the group about two hours later. The uphill activity warmed him, but the lengthening shadows had grown cold. He was plenty hungry, and it was almost meeting time. If they headed down immediately, he might be able to slap a quick bologna sandwich together. "Brock, can you take care of the horses while we head into town?"

"Glad to."

They arrived barnside with no time to spare. Colt made sure his plans and notes were in the back of the ranch SUV, then headed into the kitchen, where a dear, familiar smell greeted him. "Is that rhubarb I smell? Isabo, I think I love you."

Isabo didn't give him her customary smile of appreciation. In fact, she barely looked up. "With strawberries, yes. It's cooling now. It should be ready after the meeting."

"Try this, Colt. It might look funny, but I think you'll like it."

He saw himself sitting in their old kitchen, a kitchen trimmed in apple this and apple that. Funny, he hadn't thought of that old apple décor in a long time.

"What is it?" He'd eyed the fork full of pie filling and made a face. "I don't think I like it."

"It's one of my favorites." His father's voice rang through, hearty and happy. He turned and saw his father's face, a smile so wide and true that Colt felt happier seeing it. "And no one makes it better than your mother, Colt."

He didn't want to make his mother sad. She worked so hard to make things nice for him. To take care of them all—him, his dad, all the workers. And Grandma Mule when she came to visit. He took the fork and tested the tiniest bit.

Sweetness burst on his tongue. He hesitated, surprised, and tried a little more. The sweetness hit again, followed by a tangy taste, like those candies he liked so well, the ones that mixed up sweet and sour until his mouth wasn't sure which he liked better. "It's so good, Mom!"

"You like it?" She'd leaned back and smiled at him . . .

This time he could see her face. Her bright blue eyes, her blond-brown hair pulled back in a western-style ponytail. He couldn't see what she was wearing, but he could see her, his mother, in his mind's eye, and that was the first time he'd been able to remember her clearly in decades. And all because of a pie.

"I'll look forward to a piece when we get back, Isabo. My mother used to make strawberry rhubarb pie. It was one of our favorites."

"Your father said the same. Angelina made sure the freezer was full of rhubarb last spring. It is a nice treat to have something out of season."

"It really is." Was he that overhungry, or was it the glow of a good memory that made his stomach gurgle in anticipation? "I'll look forward to it. Has Angelina already left?"

She looked at him then. Something in her eyes put him on alert, but she only nodded. "She and your father have gone. Sam said he didn't like being slow, and he likes it less when everyone's watching."

Nick came through with a fresh jacket on and keys in his hand. Cheyenne grabbed hold of his sleeve before he got to the door. "How come you never let me do anything I want to do?"

"Because I'm the father and it's my job to keep you safe." Nick sighed. "I don't have time to talk about this now, Cheyenne."

"You never do!"

"You're being overdramatic, Cheyenne."

She made a noise and stomped her foot as though proving his point.

But Colt thought the kid was pretty much on the money. She'd brought things up to her father repeatedly, and he either pleaded for more time or just said no. Colt might not be a father, but he'd been a kid. Back then he eventually refused to listen to his father and did his own thing. After knowing Cheyenne these past weeks, he was pretty sure she was cut from similar cloth.

"We'll discuss this later," Nick told her. Her expression said later wasn't good enough, but Nick ignored it. "You're busy enough, your schoolwork needs more time, and I'm the decision maker." Nick leaned down and kissed Dakota, then Cheyenne. "Gotta go. Be good for Isabo, okay?"

"It's not fair." Cheyenne looked mad enough to cry. "I'm almost nine years old. I should be able to make my own choices!" She crossed her arms, her jaw set. "You never listen to me, you never have time to listen to me, and I don't care what you say. I'll do what I want!"

"Your little tirade has earned you nothing. No treats and no screen time for you tonight," Nick informed her as he moved to the door. He faced Isabo. "Sorry to leave you in a lurch."

Isabo waved them off. "We are fine. We have much to do here. Go to your meeting, and there will be pie waiting for your return. The town must be fixed, yes?"

"Yes," Colt agreed. "Maybe together we can really make a difference." His words drew her gaze up, but she didn't smile in agreement. Instead, she gave him a cool, questioning look before shifting her attention to the kids at the table.

"Will I like the pie, Isabo?" Dakota asked.

"If not, there are cookies. But first, let us finish our reading in the other room. Talk of pie will be for later."

"Mr. Colt?" Noah raced out of the front room and threw himself into Colt's arms. "Do you *have* to go away again?"

Colt hugged him and kissed his smooth, soft cheek. "Just for a little bit."

"But why?" He leaned back and locked eyes with Colt. "Can't you just stay here? Pwease?"

He'd like nothing more than to grab food, eat, and play with Noah, but he shook his head, regretful. "Can't do it, bud. I've got to get to town, and I'm already late."

"I don't want you to go." Noah buried his face into Colt's neck. "Pwease don't go away."

Colt breathed in the scent of him. Maple syrup, something fruity, and a hint of chocolate from the plate of cookies. "Kid, you smell good enough to eat."

Noah laughed as if eating little boys was an actual possibility.

Colt noogied his head and set him down. "I'll be back soon, okay? With Mommy."

Noah looked confused. "I th-thought you were going away."

"To the meeting, same as Mommy. I'll see you in the morning." He bent low and looked into Noah's eyes. "You can tell me all about the story you read with Abuela tonight, okay? Uncle Nick wants me working the cows mighty early these days, so don't sleep in."

Noah gripped his hand, suddenly happy. "Okay!"

The boy's smile made him feel good—the way he thought a father would feel. The way he wished his father had felt for him when he was little. He'd like the chance to show Noah the kindness he'd missed. Teach him the ways of the ranch, how to clean a barn, tend a saddle, and care for folks around him. That was the big difference between Gray's Glen and New York. Here, he actually cared for the people. What happened in Gray's Glen took on a personal feel because it *was* personal.

He let Nick drive and thought about ranch things he'd brushed off long ago. A well-run ranch should spawn family unity—although the occasional squabble couldn't be avoided. They'd gotten it backward. They had the squabble part perfected, but they'd completely messed up the part about family unity.

And yet that same enterprise encompassed land husbandry, animal appreciation, respect for life, and attentiveness to food production. His father was brilliant at all of them. If Christine Stafford hadn't died, how different would all this be?

There would be no Nick. No Cheyenne or Dakota. There would have been no need for Angelina's services in the cool, shady glens beneath the Cascades. He might have never worked on Wall Street. Did it all happen for a reason? Or did it just happen, and as humans they needed to apply reason? Either way, he was determined to make the best of what lay before him. A second chance, a new bend in the road, not just for him and Angelina but for all the Staffords.

The school lot was full. Cars, trucks, and SUVs lined both sides of the square. Nick parked close to Hammerstein's, and they hurried across the scramble of construction zones. Nick pulled the middle school door open. Colt stepped in just as the crowd voted to approve the minutes from the previous meeting.

He moved to a nearby seat. Nick followed. Angelina and his father were diagonal from him, close to the opposite exit. He tried to catch Angelina's eye, but she and Sam were focused on Hi Baxter, Johnny's older brother, as he moved to the podium. Hi swept the room with a look, then paused long enough to get the crowd antsy before he began. "Most of you know why we're here tonight. And it's not to rubber-stamp the same old, same old way of doing things." He settled his gaze on Colt's father, a silent call-out. "It's to look at all our options." He stressed the word *all* with pretty fierce intent for a small-town councilman. "All the choices we can make now as a community. Not a monarchy." A murmur of assent crossed the room.

Colt expected Sam to react.

He didn't. Instead he sat there, letting Hi spew as though it wasn't directed to him at all. Colt bided his time, the tube of plans firm in his hand, but kept an eye on his father.

Lucy stepped into the meeting room from the door nearest Angelina. She moved to her side, bent, and said something in Ange's ear. Angelina whispered something to Sam, stood, and quietly followed Lucy out the door.

Where were they going? Why now? And why hadn't she even glanced around looking for him? She hadn't texted him back, hadn't answered his calls. Generally, when a woman set her hat to ignoring a man, she had a reason, but Colt had actually been on good behavior for days. For him, that was some kind of record.

"And like the phoenix rising from the ashes—"

Colt bit back a snort and texted Angelina again.

"—the tragedy of our fire can be turned to good if we rezone the acreage at the end of West Chelan Pass and Martin Street from farmland to commercial as we reinvent our master plan."

Nick jabbed his midsection. "Hey. Einstein. Pay attention. He holds the right of first refusal to buy that land from old Mrs. Porter," Nick whispered. "She sold part of the farm to the developer who built the houses near mine, but she held on to the rest. Hi's been after her to sell for years. He wants to put a strip mall in there."

"A strip mall? In Gray's Glen?" Colt couldn't imagine it. "There couldn't be a worse idea."

"Well, the mayor's up for reelection next fall. Due to the declining population and lack of jobs, there's more than a few people clamoring for change. No one's quite sure what they want. This whole underinsured situation has everybody thinking hard about what to do."

Jobs. Security. Homes. All things he'd ignored as a financial powerhouse in New York, but here in his hometown, they were crucial elements of well-being.

Colt approached the podium once Hi moved back to his seat. Would they like his ideas? He'd been so sure they would that he hadn't considered someone else might be looking to turn the situation to an advantage. Was Hi's solution best for the town? Or best for Hi Baxter?

Colt breathed deeply, braced his hands on both sides of the podium, and faced the filled-to-capacity room. "I want to thank Hi for his suggestion of rezoning tonight, without the bother of studies or approvals or plans. He's got a real git-'r-done attitude." He faced the audience and made eye contact with multiple people. "He's right. Unfortunate circumstances can lead to progress, but it's crucial for us to choose what kind of progress we want."

An old-timer in the back shouted, "We mostly want jobs so our kids stop runnin' off soon as they graduate high school and never come back. I ain't seen no one figure that out since you was a pup, Colt, and if Hi's line of stores can bring some jobs along with it, I'm inclined to favor 'em."

"I hear you," Colt said. He drew the roll of plans out of the shipping tube at his side. As he did, Josh Washington set up a drafting easel on Colt's left. "And I agree, jobs are the basis for stability. Well . . ." He looked at his father and thought of how the town had rallied around the thought of rebuilding the church. "Jobs and faith, it seems." He smiled, then shifted his attention to the layout Josh posted. "Let me show you what Josh and I have been discussing."

He anchored the paper while Josh pinned the plans to the board. "I agree with Hi that we could benefit the town and our families with some change, so this is what Stafford Enterprises is ready to propose." He accepted a pointer from Josh and motioned to the attractive layout. "What you're seeing looks like a street of shops, probably more suited for New England, and I apologize that we couldn't have them redrawn with a more western facade for this evening's meeting. However, that adjustment is already in the works."

He indicated the upper sections. "Above the businesses, we've got two levels of senior living apartments with affordable rent that stretch for two-thirds of the available space. The apartments will share a common party/gathering area here"—he moved the pointer down—"with a full kitchen, three meeting rooms, two bathrooms, and plenty of room for folks to come together for family events or town functions." He pointed to the next section. "This gives us room for shops and small businesses at the street level— clean, fresh, and new but designed with old-style western warmth. And over here"—he moved the pointer north—"we propose an assisted living house with a small memory care unit, a place where folks like Coach Irvine can live out whatever time God gives them, close to friends and family."

"Don't know how it can be affordable when it's that fancy," said an old woman. "Why do we need fancy? Plain's good enough for most folks around here."

"Jemma Myering, who put a burr under your saddle?" Wandy demanded from behind Nick. "If you're going to do something, I've always thought do it right, not half baked. Don't we all love the way Hammerstein's keeps its old-fashioned appearance?"

Most of the room seemed to agree. "Then why not use an Old West theme on this idea, if folks like it?" She turned more toward Colt. "Where exactly would we be building this, Colt, because it's a mighty big piece you've got there."

"We'd like to put this along the stretch where the fire did the most damage, the section of Chelan Pass overlooking the town. There would also be the future possibility of building patio-style homes up here." He used the pointer to display the location, but part of his attention was on the far door. Where had Angelina gone, and why hadn't she come back? He'd really wanted her to see this. "We're hoping that future plans will include a health clinic just north of the complex," he explained, continuing to make eye contact with as many people as he could. "We'd still need to drive to Ellensburg for major medical care, but a clinic would give us good solid services right in our own backyard."

"What about them homes that burned? And the folks that rented 'em?" called a man from the far back.

"Well, that's where Josh comes in. You all know my father owns this parcel down below." He pointed to the east end of town. "We'd like to raze that old machining building and build six small homes in its place. That way the families would be closer to schools, the park, and the playground."

"I'd be happy not to look at that old building anymore, that's for certain," Jemma Myering said.

"And neither one of these proposals is dependent on zoning changes or acquiring land," he reminded them. "The Staffords already own the land, and my father is investing his own money to fund both projects. I'll be here to oversee them."

Sam had been sitting quietly, listening, but now his head came up. He stared at Colt as if confused.

Josh stepped to the microphone. "I've talked to Colt and signed on to do the construction for the new homes on Jasper Road. I've already ordered the demolition of the old building. We intend to leave as many native trees standing as we can. I've also recommended Slater Commercial Construction to bid on the larger residential/business complex Colt has presented." He ran a hand over his short, nubby hair, then gave the plans an admiring look. "I don't know if you can envision this like I am, but here's what I see. When the church is rebuilt with logs and a western-styled entrance, and just uphill these western-style storefronts are facing the square along with the church, the whole thing feels right and good, like it fits us and our town.

"Now Colt here's told me that I've got the job for the houses no matter what folks decide about the big project, so it's not like I have a horse in that race."

Folks around the room nodded their understanding.

"But I love this idea. And what my old basketball buddy won't tell you is that he got the idea when he found out Coach Irvine had to move nearly forty miles away to be cared for. Most of you know the coach. You know he's a man who gave life and love to this town and community. When Colt found out about that, he went right out, used some of his fancy New York connections—"

Colt rolled his eyes and the crowd laughed.

"—and got these plans sent in overnight. Now that's action. And that's all I'm going to say about that, but action wins my vote every time."

The mayor started to stand, but Nick leaped to his feet in the audience. "Colt, gotta go! There's been an accident at the ranch."

"Go." Josh motioned to the plans. "I've got this."

Sam might have been worried about walking slow getting to the meeting, but there was nothing slow in his gait as he rushed to the nearest door. Colt followed.

As soon as they were outside, Nick pulled up alongside them with the SUV. Colt opened the front door for his father, waited until Sam was in, then closed the door and jumped into the backseat. "What's happened?"

"Cheyenne."

Colt's mouth dried out and his chest went tight. "How bad?"

"Don't know. They called an ambulance." The shrill sound of an oncoming siren punctuated his words. "She's unconscious."

"Unconscious?" Colt leaned forward. "How does a kid go from being just fine an hour ago and now she's unconscious?"

"She was trying to ride a horse."

Cheyenne . . .

A tough, angry little girl, abandoned by her mother and thwarted by her well-meaning father. A totally stubborn, in-your-face Stafford who wanted exactly what her father loved—a chance to be part of the Double S. If only Nick had given her some leeway. Some hope.

The lights of the ambulance and the accompanying sheriff's car flashed ahead of them, lighting their way back to the ranch. As they made the turn just beyond the cedar-sided Catholic church, a glint of light flashed off the bronze cross.

Colt bit back recrimination. If the kid knew how to ride properly, she would have been a whole lot safer on the ranch. But right now he needed to shut up, pray, and get ahold of Angelina.

His call went straight to voice mail. He tried again. Same thing.

Calm down. Take a breath. Your brother needs you. Remember that whole thing about how often you should forgive your brother? Put him first now. Him and his beautiful, naughty little girl.

He refocused his attention on his father and brother but couldn't shake the feeling that something was wrong—really wrong—with Angelina.

"Trust in the Lord with all your heart and lean not on your own understanding" . . .

The next verse talked about straight paths. Colt had never taken a more convoluted route to get to a straight path in his life, but maybe that's how it was supposed to be.

They pulled into the ranch drive right behind the ambulance. The sight of Cheyenne on the cold, hard ground broke his heart but not his resolve. No matter what else happened, once Cheyenne was well enough to mount up again, he'd be teaching that girl to ride, no matter what his stupid brother said.

THIRTEEN

*A*ngelina decided it was better to help Lucy get Brendan Bennett out of whatever trouble the kid found himself in than listen to Colt spew pretty promises he didn't mean. She slung her purse over her shoulder and followed Lucy into the upper wooded area north of the middle school.

Tears were streaming down Brendan's face when they reached him. "I didn't know. Honest, I didn't. I thought it wasn't any big deal, I swear!"

"Turn off the tears. Get ahold of yourself." Angelina pulled out her no-nonsense cop voice as though she used it every day. Hysterics and apologies wasted precious time.

He sucked a deep breath and regained some control.

"What's happened? Who needs help?"

"Mark."

"The Battaglia boy," Lucy offered. "His older brother trimmed trees for me last year."

"Where is he?"

"I don't know exactly." Brendan looked about to lose it again, but a sharp look from Angelina had the boy squaring his shoulders. "We were on top of the ridge, and one of the guys from the canyon offered us ten-dollar hits."

"And you took it?" Angelina made sure her tone said that was about the stupidest thing she'd ever heard. "*¿Cuál es su problema? ¿Por qué haría algo tan estúpido?*"

"Huh?"

She paused, remembering that she wasn't dealing with Latino street kids in Seattle. "We'll discuss your lack of intelligence and gratitude later. Where's Mark?"

"He was up there." He pointed up the hill. "He can't breathe right, and he sounds funny. He looks funny too. I ran for help, but when I got back, I couldn't find him."

She raced up the hill, followed by Lucy and Brendan.

No Mark.

She turned toward Brendan. "Where is he?"

He shook his head, scared. "He was right here. I swear. He—"

A sound came from the woods to their left. Angelina darted toward the noise, pushing through needle clutter and thin broken weeds. While the town was still bathed from the westward-angled sun, the forest was dark and chilled. "Mark! Where are you?"

No answer came. She held up a hand to pause their progress but heard nothing further. She pulled out her cell phone, hit 911, and then choked back angry words when the phone refused to connect. "Lucy, do you have a cell phone?"

She shook her head. "Can't afford one."

Brendan held up empty hands. "My brother said I don't get one until I can pay for it myself."

"Lucy, go back and tell Colt we need an ambulance up here now.

Suspected heroin overdose, possibly fentanyl laced. You." She motioned to Brendan. "Stay with me. I'll kill you later."

He gave her one quick nod, fear and remorse covering him like a shroud.

Lucy turned and pushed through the forest toward the road while Angelina prayed they would find the boy alive and get him to Ellensburg before it was too late.

———— ⬥ ————

"What do you mean they're gone?" Lucy looked around, but Wandy was right. There wasn't a Stafford in sight.

"Nick got a call that someone was hurt up at the ranch," Wandy Schirtz explained. "He and Colt raced out with Sam."

"We need an ambulance," Lucy announced from the back of the room, interrupting the speaker. Mr. Hammerstein was seated in front of her, and Mark Battaglia's mother was just beyond. "Mr. H., call 911. Mark took some sort of drug, and he needs help. Mrs. Battaglia, you better come with me."

"My Mark?" Fear and shock widened the woman's eyes. "Mark would never do something like that. He—"

As Mr. Hammerstein stepped out of the way to make the call, Wandy reached out a hand to Mrs. Battaglia. "We won't fret about the whys and whats now, Catherine. If Mark needs help, he gets help, no matter what. You go with Lucy."

Two volunteer fire department medics stepped up to go with the ladies. They hurried up the hill, and when they crested the top, Lucy

pointed. "In there. Brendan Bennett and Angelina Morales are trying to find him."

<hr>

"We're here!" Angelina called the words as soon as she heard footsteps pushing their way. "Follow my voice. We're—"

The men crashed into view just as the fire siren sounded a
second time.

"I hope that ambulance is quick," she told them. "We also need
to alert the local police, sheriff, and the state police to the possibility
of fentanyl-laced heroin being sold to local teens."

She relaxed a little when she heard the shrill of an approaching
ambulance siren. But when it shrieked by, she stared, dumbfounded.

"Not our ambulance," said the first volunteer. "That's a different
call. We'll have a backup from Moore's Ambulance here soon."

The slow response was unacceptable. "He could have been dead
before anyone got here."

The EMT eyed Mark and shook his head. "He's coming around,
so I think he's going to do all right. Maybe not an overdose after all."

Mark was doing better because Angelina carried an overdose
kit and an EpiPen in the zippered compartment of her purse—
cop leftovers from her former life. But what if she hadn't been
equipped to help? What if she hadn't been there? Mark would be
dead, another young life snuffed out by one stupid, foolish teenage decision.

The mingled sirens of a police car and the commercial ambulance raced toward their location. Within minutes a gurney had

been brought into the woods, the boy locked and loaded into the back of the rescue wagon, and his distraught mother tucked inside.

Rye Bennett, who had arrived as the cop on duty, looked shocked, tired, and overwrought as the ambulance pulled away. He turned toward his younger brother, and instead of beating sense into him, Rye crossed the narrow space between them and took his fourteen-year-old brother into his arms.

And then he cried.

Brendan cried right along with him. Long minutes later Rye loosened his hold, stepped back, and finally noticed Angelina. "Why are you here?"

His question made no sense. "Lucy came to find me when Brendan told her something was wrong."

"No, I mean—" His expression darkened, and he jerked a thumb to the police car. "You need to come with me. There's been an accident, Angelina. Cheyenne Stafford came off a horse, and they took her to the hospital, unconscious. I—"

Her heart froze. Her fingertips buzzed. *Dear God, no. Not Cheyenne. Not Nick's beautiful, headstrong, animal-loving daughter. While I was in the woods fighting for one child's life, one of my sweet babies was waging a battle of her own.*

She hurried to the police car, praying. Brendan hopped into the back. Rye got behind the wheel and broke every speed limit to get her to the hospital emergency room. Turn by turn, all she could think was how they couldn't lose Cheyenne. How this family had lost too many of their own by death or abandonment. She thought of how badly Sam wanted to become the God-fearing parent of a normal family. Losing Cheyenne would destroy that too—which meant they couldn't lose her. She prayed. She prayed loud and long and didn't pause until Rye pulled up to the ER door. "Go. I'll park."

She raced into the hospital, looking left, then right.

No Staffords.

She charged the desk. The admitting nurse drew back and looked a little nervous. Angelina didn't much care, and she wasn't about to be put off. "Cheyenne Stafford."

The nurse stayed calm but sent a "stay close" look to the security guard just inside the door. "Are you family?"

"Yes."

"Mother?"

"Aunt."

The nurse scanned her computer screen, which, of course, had no aunt listed. Angelina could tell she was about to refuse to give her information when Rye came in behind her. "Colt says she's in the PICU, third floor. And he's going to talk to you about keeping your cell phone on and charged as soon as Cheyenne is out of the woods. He said he kept trying to get you but got no answer."

"Thank you, Rye."

"No, thank *you*." Gratitude and respect deepened his expression. "I don't know what you gave Mark, but Brendan said he was near death until you did it. Whatever you did, Angelina, God bless you." He squeezed her shoulders, and she didn't miss the emotion in his eyes. "Take the red elevator up. I'll be up once they've got Mark settled."

She hurried off, found the red elevator, and hit the button.

Two kids, nearly dead. Two beautiful souls, almost extinguished because of stupid human choices. If Cheyenne was all right—

No, *when* Cheyenne was all right, she was going to make sure the girl learned everything she needed to know about riding, ranching, roping, as Murt had suggested. On a busy ranch, staffed with cowboys, there were plenty of teachers on hand if Nick wasn't willing to do it himself. And if she had to stay longer to make sure it got done, she'd do it.

Nick might hate it, he might hate her, but right now Nick's anger was way better than a child's funeral, and she had every intention of telling him that.

Once they knew Cheyenne was going to be okay.

Colt was pretty sure his heart ceased beating when he couldn't contact Angelina.

It started again when she walked through the third-floor elevator doors. He wanted to yell at her for not picking up her phone, for not texting him back. But first he needed to hug her, so he did.

He held her close, glad she was there, and when his heart calmed, he stepped back, keeping his hands on her shoulders.

"How is she?" She pointed to the double doors of the pediatric intensive care unit where Nick was just visible. "How bad is it?"

"The fall knocked her for a loop. She was unconscious, then woke for a little while, then out again."

"Concussion, I expect." Sam had appeared from the coffee cart around the corner and handed them each a cup. "I've had a few of

those. Nick and Trey both had one growing up. Not you, though."
He met Colt's eyes, and though it wasn't an expression Colt had seen
all that often, he knew it was a shimmer of pride that brightened
Sam's eyes. "Best seat in the saddle, then and now—except for Murt.
That's a gift from your mother. Lots of folks ride horse. But there's
only a handful that ride with the horse."

He reached around and withdrew his wallet from his back
pocket. There, in a dingy plastic old-style photo holder was a picture
of Colt and Christine, sitting horseback, just before her death. "This
is how it was." He pulled the picture out of the sleeve and handed it
over. "And how I'd like it to be again."

He wasn't talking about the horse or the pose or the fact that
Colt and his mother sat saddle the same way. He meant the loving
look in Colt's eyes as he smiled down at his father, who was taking
the picture. A little-boy look so pure and sweet that Colt's heart
ached to see it.

"You look so happy." Angelina touched his face. "And cute."

Regret deepened the lines in Sam's face. "We were happy. And
then . . ." He paused. Sighed. "We weren't."

The thin picture felt heavy in Colt's hands, weighted with responsibility. His father was asking for another chance. Not a second
chance; he'd had plenty of those over the years. But another chance.
Maybe his last one. ". . . *as we forgive those who trespass against
us . . .*"

Old words. Wise words. Simple and spot on. He looked down at
the picture, then up at his father. "I'm willing."

A slight smile eased the lines on his father's face. "Me too."

Nick burst through the double doors. "She's awake! She knows me, she talked to me, and she's awake!"

"Thank God." Sam Stafford reached out and grabbed Nick into a hug, awkward and rusty from disuse. "Can we see her?"

"For a few minutes, two at a time." A young woman moved their way and extended her hand. "I'm Dr. Fuller. Yes, she's awake, and I expect that what we had was a mild to moderate concussion."

"Mild? Moderate? We almost lost her, for heaven's sake!" Indignation hiked Sam's voice beyond hospital-friendly levels.

The look she gave Sam shushed him right quick. "My rodeo, my rules, Mr. Stafford. Those are medical gradients, not insults. And if you want to see your granddaughter—"

Sam held up his hands in apology. "Sorry, sorry. Old habits die hard. I'm fine, Doctor. Really."

Angelina frowned at him. "You need more practice on this whole calm and patient thing."

"I aim to see he gets it," Colt whispered, just loud enough for Sam to hear.

"And the next time she gets on a horse," the doctor continued, "make sure the helmet is securely fastened."

"There won't be a next time," Nick declared. "There shouldn't have been a *this* time."

"Oh yes there will." Angelina parked herself in front of Nick. "I'll make sure she learns from the best of the best, right there on the family ranch. That will be my goal before I move back to Seattle."

Move back to Seattle? Over Colt's dead body. He didn't want her in Seattle. He wanted her with him, on the Double S. He'd made the decision to stay here, to be part of Gray's Glen. Could she seriously still be thinking of going back to the city?

But no way was he about to interrupt her speech, because his brother looked pretty sheepish, and the woman was on a roll.

"We'll teach her to ride, curry, pick hooves, rake straw, and pitch manure because there's nothing more dangerous on a farm or a ranch than a person who knows nothing about a farm or a ranch." She leaned closer, and Colt was pretty sure his brother quaked a little. It made him feel kind of good to see it. "And don't for one minute think you can stop us. I rode herd on the toughest streets of Seattle for years, and I can go a round or two with a grudge-holding cowboy."

Nick stared at her, then looked at the stark hospital corridor stretching to his precious child's room. He gripped his hat tighter. "You're right."

Humble pie.

His brother Nick was eating a big slice of humble pie, and Colt didn't even dare call him out on it because he was so stinkin' happy that Cheyenne was going to be all right.

"Dad, come on back," Nick said. "Then Colt and Ange can say hello to her."

"Five minutes." The doctor wasn't all that big, but she talked big, and Sam and Nick both nodded.

"Yes, ma'am."

Colt started to turn toward Angelina as Rye Bennett came through the elevator doors. "How's she doing?"

"She's going to be fine," Angelina told him. "What about Mark?"

"He'll do all right too, if his parents don't kill him first. I want to tell you again that you saved that boy's life. I'm making sure everyone knows it." He glanced at Colt. "If this cowpoke can talk you into staying, Angelina, I think the entire town would extend our budget to put you on the force. And I'm talking sooner rather than later. Clear-thinking, fast-acting deputies are a wonderful asset to any community, and I'd like nothing better than to have you working with me once things are settled with Sam."

Rye's words offered a choice she would have loved to accept. He had just paid her the highest of compliments. In police work, to be recruited went beyond winning a job the regular way. Being recruited meant you'd already passed the rookie regimen and had some muscle of respect welcoming you aboard. But Colt was leaving and her mother needed a chance to live her life, the life of her choosing, finally. "I'm honored, Rye. Truly," she insisted when his face looked skeptical. "But I can't stay here once we've got things settled at the Double S."

"Of course you can. You love it here," Colt argued.

She did, but— "We've had this conversation. My mother's needs come first. And—"

"What if Isabo wants to stay?" Colt interrupted, as if trying to convince her. But that made no sense because he was leaving.

The big jerk.

"Because I think she does," he continued. "I think she loves being part of the ranch, taking care of folks. And running the show."

What did he know about her mother? About anything? Why

tease her to stay when he was on the verge of going back to New York? She turned cool eyes his way. "I don't think that's the case, which makes it irrelevant."

"But if it *is* the case," Colt insisted, "then why would you consider leaving? Because I thought we might enjoy"—he moved closer and tucked one lock of her hair back behind her ear with surprising tenderness—"time together. To get to know each other. Pick out china and silverware and towels nobody's allowed to use. All those schmaltzy things folks do when they realize they don't ever want to live apart again."

Smooth, so smooth. Her heart broke a little more inside, but she wasn't about to fall for his sweet-talking ways. "Easy talk coming from a guy who's leaving," she said softly.

"Leaving?" He glanced at Rye, then Angelina. "Who's leaving?"

"Don't mess with me, Colt. Your little friend stopped by today to deliver your very lucrative contract. She was hoping you'd follow her back to New York like a good puppy, but Sam assured her you weren't available until later."

"Someone came to the house today?"

He seemed genuinely surprised, but she'd been fooled before and no way was it going to happen again. "I put the information on your desk. You must have noticed it."

He indicated his ranch clothes with a glance. "I climbed off a horse, took time to thank your mother for making my favorite pie, and kissed Noah." He paused, then made a face. "This explains the cold shoulder from your mother. And Noah wondering where I was going. And kind of begging me to stay."

"Well, he's young and unaccustomed to the ways of men."
Angelina started to take a step back.

Colt didn't let her. "So someone shows up out of the blue, says I'm
leaving, and you all believed her? What kind of detective does that?"
He shot a look of question to Rye, but Rye looked more amused than
dismayed. "Let me just clear this up, once and for all. I'm staying here.
Yes, I was contacted by several New York firms because the market
correction has stabilized and a bunch of my personal investments are
starting to roll in big, but I refused every"—he kissed Angelina's right
cheek—"single"—he kissed her left cheek, gently, sweetly—"one of
them. I'm here and I can handle my own funds from the ranch. I'm
not going anywhere, Angelina." He slipped both hands behind her
and held her gaze. "Which means I need to convince your mother to
stay right here in Gray's Glen so I can court her daughter properly."

"Court me?" Was she hearing him right?

Rye slipped away, leaving them alone in the hospital corridor.

"What do you mean?"

Colt's face, his dear, beloved face, said his meaning should be
obvious. "It's what a fellow does when he wants to marry a girl and
she needs some convincing," he explained.

Marry her? She swallowed hard.

"Do you need convincing, Ange? Because I was thinking we
could wait until the church is done and get married in the same
church my parents did. Well, the same, but different," he added,
smiling. "But if you don't need convincing, I'd be happy to call the
reverend right now and see when he's got time."

"Is this really a proposal?"

He kissed her, long and sweet, the kind of kiss that could last forever and still not be enough. Not ever enough. "Let's call it a proposed proposal," he whispered when he was done kissing her. "I think you deserve the real deal, Angelina. Wine, dinner, dancing, romance. And a ring would be nice. But from this moment forward, I want you to know—and trust—my intentions. But as I said, if you'd like to hurry things along, well . . ." He sent her a lopsided grin. "I'd be all right with that too."

He meant it.

She read the sincerity in his face, in his eyes. And then he did it, just as his father and Nick were coming through the electronically locked double doors. He went down on one knee and took her hand. "Mary Angela Castiglione, a.k.a. Angelina Morales . . ."

She burst out laughing because there really wasn't any other choice.

"I have managed to fall crazy in love with you."

She flushed at the words. Tears pricked her eyes again, but for a very different reason.

"And I'm pretty sure you've got a little something going for me too."

She gave a single nod, and he looked downright delighted.

"Will you do me the honor of becoming my wife? Letting me adopt your son and make him ours? Grow old with me and them?" He pointed his thumb back toward his father and brother. "And live with me on the ranch my father built? Forever and ever until death do us part?"

She couldn't believe this was happening. Hours ago she'd been distraught, dismayed, and disillusioned because she'd believed a stranger. Colt was right. Good detectives make sure of their facts before they come to conclusions. She put one hand to his cheek. "It would be an honor, Colt."

Nick and his father cheered, which brought a nurse scurrying their way, scolding them. Angelina was too busy being kissed to notice. "We'll wait until the church is done," she told him when he stopped kissing her. "Because I like the tradition of Staffords being married in a house of God."

"That just gives me all the more reason to work fast, darlin'." Colt grinned and wrapped an arm around her shoulders. "Let's go kiss Cheyenne good night and head home to that pie. And as soon as things settle down and Dad gives us an hour off, we're going ring shopping."

"Or . . ." Sam said.

Colt paused. "Or?"

Sam withdrew his wallet once more, and from a tiny zippered compartment, he withdrew a lovely set of rings. "These were your mother's, Colt. I mean, it's all right if you don't want to use them." He glanced from Colt to Angelina to make sure they both got his message. "We didn't have all that much back then, so they aren't real big and grand, but they were hers." In his hand lay a plain gold band and a simple three-stone engagement ring—a diamond flanked by two small sapphires. "I got the blue stones because they matched your mother's eyes. Your eyes, Colt. It was about as sentimental as I ever got," he admitted. "Anyway, she loved them, and they're yours if you want them."

"Ange?" Colt turned her way.

"I can't imagine anything nicer or more sacred. Yes, Colt. I would be honored to wear your mother's ring and marry you."

He slipped the engagement ring on her finger, smiled, then turned back to his father. "You carried it with you always."

"I couldn't have her, so . . ." Sam swallowed hard and turned away. Angelina's heart broke over what he couldn't put into words— that he'd wanted to always have a token of his beloved wife close to him.

"Thank you, Sam." Angelina crossed the narrow space between them and kissed his cheek. "But I'm going to wait to wear this until I have a chance to talk to my mother."

Colt groaned, and she shot a sharp look his way. "I don't want her to feel tied down. I want her decisions to be made by her."

"Works for me."

Sam's yawn reminded them that he still had a long road to recovery.

"We'll say good night and get you home," Angelina said.

"Don't worry about me," Sam told them, but he did take a seat in a nearby chair. He looked up at Colt and smiled. "I'm doing all right. I think I might have just had the best day of my life in a long time."

"Me too." She reached out and squeezed Colt's hand gently. "Me too, Sam."

*C*olt watched Angelina make her way toward him and mentally captured the moment. Beautiful . . . so beautiful. He reached out an arm, drew her in for a kiss, then tucked her in front of him while Murt worked Dakota around the nearest paddock. The aged wrangler had wasted no time getting Nick's younger daughter in the saddle, and Dakota was loving it. "Is Nick on his way back with Cheyenne yet?" Colt asked.

"They just left the hospital," Angelina said.

"Good. Did you call Tony and tell him you're staying put?"

She leaned back and looked up at him, surprised. "How do you know about Tony?"

"Heard you talking on the phone awhile back. Figured it was good to know about the competition."

She laughed and elbowed him in the gut, and not too gently either. "Tony is married with two kids. We worked the narcotics squad together. But yes, I called him and told him I had a change in plans. Now we just need to tell my mother."

"Your mother will be thrilled for you," Colt told her. He nuzzled her cheek until she sighed. "For us."

"But Seattle is hours away, and we'll be here." She sent a worried look toward the front porch where her mother sat sewing.

"You're cute when you whine."

"I don't whine."

"Prove it. Let's go tell your mother the good news." Walking backward and tugging her along, he led her back toward the house.

"Mami." Angelina took the porch rocker alongside her mother while Colt perched on the rail nearby. "We need to talk."

"Like we don't talk every day?" Isabo said but set the sewing down. "Are you all right? Is Cheyenne all right, or is there more to tell? I still cannot believe she slipped out that back window to show her father what she could do! I should have checked on her again."

"Cheyenne is fine. Nick's bringing her home. But there is more news to share," Colt said.

Angelina took her mother's hand. "I know how you want to go back to Seattle."

"I do?" Isabo looked up with interest.

"I will keep my promise to get you back to Seattle, but I won't be moving there with you."

Isabo looked from one to the other as if this was no big surprise. "So. You think this is news?"

"Told you so." Colt aimed a smug look toward his future wife.

"You're not helping." She turned back toward her mother. "I'll help you get back there and get settled. *We'll* help you," she added, and this time she smiled up at Colt. "Mami, Colt has asked me to marry him, and I've said yes."

"Without asking her mother in lieu of her father?" Isabo redirected her attention to Colt in a no-nonsense manner. "Perhaps you thought my permission was not needed because I am a woman?"

Colt squirmed. "Well, she thought I was leaving. And you thought I was leaving. And—"

Isabo's laugh cut him short. "So now that we have this love thing settled, why must I leave?" She got up, crossed the porch, and gave Colt a nice big hug, then turned back to Angelina. "Do you not want your mother around?"

"Of course I do!"

"Then why wish me back to Seattle when we could all live here, Mary Angela?"

"You want to stay here?"

Colt snickered out loud on purpose.

His beautiful fiancée ignored him.

"Why would I not want to stay where it is the most wonderful place in the world? I love being here, being part of such a marvelous endeavor. I am busy here."

"Yes, exactly," Angelina agreed. "But you weren't supposed to be working all the time, taking care of a house and kids. You were supposed to be able to relax and enjoy life a little. With Dad."

"Well, that part cannot be changed, can it?" Isabo reached out and took Angelina's hands. "But the wish for all that was not mine. That was Martín's. I like being busy. I like doing, not being done for, so for me, this is wonderful! Working here, helping you, helping Sam and the children. Oh, this is when I am most happy!"

"Then you want to stay?"

"Yes! I would not leave if you asked me to." Isabo hugged her. "We get to plan a wedding, my little bird. How very special is that? A thing I have waited for as any mother would." She hugged

Angelina one more time. "I must go. I must call your Aunt Rose and see if she can find us the old lace used on your grandmother's gown. It will be your something old and so beautiful!"

She dashed off as Noah raced up from the pond with Rye, Jenna, and Brendan following at a distance. "I found a fwog, Mom!"

"Fr-r-rog," she reminded him as she bent low.

"Fw-w-w-og!" he announced, triumphant. "Mr. Rye said I hafta put him back, but I wanted to show you and Mr. Colt first."

"I love him, bud." Colt lifted the boy high in his arms. "And I love you."

Noah looked up at him with an expression so sweet and good Colt wasn't sure if his heart broke or healed to see it. "I l-l-love you too, Mr. Colt."

Healed, most definitely.

Holding the boy, seeing Angelina's look of love, hearing the sounds of ranch life around him, he realized he'd come full circle— back to the faith, hope, and love he'd lost so many years before.

And it felt real good.

FROM THE KITCHEN OF THE DOUBLE S RANCH

Detective Mary Angela Castiglione is now living on the sprawling cattle ranch owned by beef tycoon Sam Stafford and his three sons . . . and working with the sheriff's department. She's got the best of both worlds, at long last. But on the ranch, she hasn't been known as Mary or "detective." She's been Angelina, the strong-willed, capable, pious house manager who isn't afraid to pull a gun or wield a rolling pin as needed. Angelina is a wonderful blend of her law-and-order father and her take-charge mother. She's great on the force and in the kitchen, and she understands the importance of sacrificial love. And she makes a killer cherry cake! Everyone on the ranch loves it, and we hope you will too! I wanted it easy, so we've got six simple ingredients and whipped cream frosting. A perfect blend for a crowd-pleasing dessert!

ANGELINA'S CHERRY CAKE

1 white cake mix

1 1/4 cups maraschino cherry juice

25 drops of red food coloring, if desired

6 eggs, separated (a temporary separation! We'll get them back together for the happy ending soon!)

1 tablespoon almond flavoring

24 maraschino cherries, chopped (more or less is fine)

Whip egg whites. Set aside.

Mix cake mix, cherry juice, egg yolks, almond flavoring, and red food coloring (if desired for the deeper color). Blend well on medium speed. Mix in chopped cherries. Fold in egg whites using a spatula. Don't overmix; we want those fun little air bubbles in the cake!

Line two 9-inch cake pans with parchment paper. Divide batter gently between the pans. Bake at 350 degrees until toothpick inserted in center comes back clean, or until cake springs back when lightly touched with finger. Depending on pan size, this cherry "sponge-type" cake takes about 25 to 35 minutes.

Remove from oven. Cool about ten minutes and then tip out of pans onto cooling rack. When cool, frost with Whipped Cream Frosting below.

WHIPPED CREAM FROSTING

3 cups heavy whipping cream
2/3 cup sugar

Pour whipping cream into big mixing bowl. Add sugar. Beat on medium, and then on high until cream is thickened and holds a peak. Don't overbeat or you'll have sweet butter, and then you have to go to the store, buy more whipping cream, and start again!

Spread whipped cream frosting on first layer. Top with second layer. Frost sides and top with remaining frosting. Garnish with slivered almonds and maraschino cherries, if desired. Keep refrigerated.

A fabulous, easy, and praise-catching cake from the Double S kitchens!

READERS GUIDE

1. The last thing a proud man like Colt Stafford wants is to come home in disgrace. Broke but not broken, he comes back to the Double S to help his ailing father, but he's coming home after a stunning financial collapse. Have you ever had to eat humble pie of the highest order?

2. Angelina Morales is at a crossroads. Her hard-sought anonymity must come to an end for the good of her son, but how can she balance her split alliance to her widowed mother, her son, and the employer who offered quiet shelter to all three of them? When you're caught in a tough situation, how do you examine your choices? Does faith and God's timing help make your decision, or is it sorely tested?

3. Sibling rivalry goes back to the earliest times. Colt has to face his younger brother's smug attitude and deal with it, because Colt's not in charge at the Double S. Nick is, and that's a bitter pill to swallow. How do you handle difficult family relationships?

4. Angelina is one tough cookie, but there are so many more layers to her psyche. What strikes you the most about her character?

5. How do you see Hobbs's and Murt's roles in this story? What is it about this pair of old-time cowboys that glues the Stafford family together?

6. Colt can't remember his mother's face when the story begins. Her pictures were put away after her death, and he can hear her voice, but can't see her face. And then, the aroma of Isabo's rhubarb pie brings back her image. Had Colt blocked the image because it was too painful to remember? Or is it simply a little boy without enough time to make a permanent memory?

7. Sam Stafford is his own enigma. Struck with bad health in the midst of change, he's unable to fix things himself. He's frustrated and angry. How does having to step aside and let his sons handle things help Sam? Do you find yourself able to hand over the reins as needed? Or do you struggle to maintain control?

8. Colt's decision to intervene and bring Isabo and Noah to the main house is a turning point in many ways. When you see something that needs to happen, where do you get the courage to see it through?

9. Angelina's torn by her love of family, her jobs, her position, and her career. Guilt has steered her for years, but the town fire holds up a looking glass. She sees the woman she needs to be, a trained officer, a defender. When faced with opposing choices, how do we decide what's best, and in a very "me-first" society, should we always put our own needs first?

10. Colt's introspect and intuition are fed by Hobbs's and Murt's wisdom. He trusts them where he's never been able to trust family. What makes a trusted outsider so important to a dysfunctional family?

11. Colt doesn't have just one wake-up call. God tweaks him with a series of nudges, but those nudges culminate in a decision when he meets Coach Irvine's wife at the burned-out church. When you're finally ready to take a stand or make a decision, where do you find the courage to stick to it? Colt was offered a golden opportunity by Wall Street standards, to come back into a position of power and watch his former boss squirm. And yet, he shrugs it off. Why is he able to turn his back on Lower Manhattan then?

12. Angelina was waiting to be hurt. She predicted it. She steeled herself against it. And when it happened, she knew she'd been foolish all along. But she was wrong, and how easy is it for us silly humans to prepare ourselves for a downfall instead of clinging to the joy of optimism? Do you guard your emotions so you don't get overly invested? Or do you jump in with both feet and sometimes become unpleasantly surprised?

13. This story pits two strong families against each other. The Castigliones have lived two generations of sacrificial love, and Angelina carries on that tradition. The Staffords have lived for self-gratification and bear the weight of that now. How do two such diverse families blend to strengthen one another? And could that happen in real life? If so, how?

COMING OCTOBER 2016

BOOK TWO
of the

SS DOUBLE S RANCH SERIES

Home on the Range

The Stafford Family saga continues with Nick, the son who stayed. Nick is determined to succeed in all the areas his father failed: in marriage, parenting and managing the ranch. However, in spite of his best efforts, his life has fallen apart. Can Nick find the courage to change, face his past, and find a second chance at love and life?

MULTNOMAH
BOOKS